Widowmaker Outpost

Widowmaker Outpost

I.O. Adler

Lucas Ross Publishing

Contents

Widowmaker Outpost
A Cyberpunk Mystery Novel
by
I.O. Adler
Dawn Moriti Book One

Chapter One

Dawn Moriti's prey rose early.

Hub foot traffic brushed past her as she collected her drone. The bug-sized mechanical crawler snapped magnetically into place on the back of her glove. Its feed waited for her, kept unsent in case any overzealous Commonwealth security might be sniffing about.

With a hard blink, she saw in fast forward frames what the bug had seen. The woman she was after was not only out and about, but hadn't moved from her spot on the other side of the canal for the past twenty minutes.

Her dark eyes darted back and forth, absorbing the information. She applied lip balm before doing a touch up with purple lipstick.

The target had been smart. She hadn't used her ID in a month, avoided authorized credit stations, and even evaded face recognition checkpoints. Her rap sheet file listed her as missing and presumed fled from the city.

Dawn had guessed otherwise when she accepted the contract.

Kaja Stepnova, age twenty-three, parents alive, with two younger brothers and no savings worth mentioning and zero clearance with any of the New Pacific corporations. No specialized training, no out-of-city contacts. A target with few prospects for survival without her support structure.

Unless Kaja was intent on starving in the wilds or slaving in a land commune, she had no choice but to remain within the city, and Dawn was closing in on her. And the bounty would wipe out the last of Dawn's debt and she could get out of town.

Kaja's sister-in-law ran Hippolyta's Tea Shop on Pearl Street, right on the canal. And the sister-in-law was willing to employ a fugitive from the law.

Dawn joined the flow of pedestrians moving along the sidewalk. Most had their head down as they marched to work, some already blathering on their devices or headsets. A mother tugged at her son, who wore a backpack and heavy coat. Other children accompanied their parents.

A school day, Dawn realized.

Everything normal in Earth's "Last Free City." No one looked up as they went about their morning routine, not really. Just like in Meridian Corporation-dominated River City. And just like Seraph with its heavy-handed militia rule and veneer of enfranchisement for its desert-dwelling citizens.

To blend in, she was dressed in cargo pants and her long lavender jacket, but felt underdressed that morning among the corporate types who walked around her. Dungarees were back in, as were buzzed hair-cuts, spacer style, perfect teeth set in perfect smiles, with high heels and platforms for men and women, and aggressive painted cheek pips. These last were solely for the young hunter-killer attorneys on the prowl for Wei-Howard Surety.

Buying a breakfast scone has never been so warrior-like.

Meanwhile, her jacket had a few tricks. Electronic countermeasures, for one. Target modification would make her shorter, taller, wider, thinner, and would confuse gait-trackers. Any unknown bug placed on her would be disabled. Laser targeting wouldn't work; a shooter would need to be aimed manually.

Shouldn't work, she reminded herself.

The jacket's maker had been vague on specific permutations of laser technology, and she wouldn't be around to collect on a warranty if the countermeasure failed.

Gleaming towers on either side of the avenue. Brackish water in the center canal, the morning light spackled white on the gray.

The moon was still out, about to set low on the horizon. As if it were a giant lazy eye staring down. Was anyone up there watching? Were the Caretakers even alive in their crater cities, monitoring the Earth via satellites among the cloud of debris from the shattered orbital ring? A bitter remnant making sure no one took to the sky with a plane, a shuttle, a rocket, or helicopter on anything but an overcast day. The threat of a nuke or kinetic strike persisted decades after the hostilities ended.

Even Dawn kept her head down, if only to fit in.

As she crossed the canal bridge, the familiar itch ran down her neck.

The Hub was not the place to be when you're hoping to avoid scans. Everyone watches everyone. While the corporations had to live by Commonwealth rules and kept their private security teams out of the beige zones, they had their own operatives and hired contractors like Dawn to carry out their every whim.

As of a month ago, Dawn had a sizeable bounty on her own head. Canceled, according to the dark net, but were any of the faces in the crowd hunting her for a private reward she didn't know about?

Focus.

Do the job, get paid, get out.

Kaja Stepnova, as far as Dawn knew, was wanted by Commonwealth security. Her charge? Assault and battery. Her husband, Hillar Stepnova, had been hospitalized with a fractured skull.

Dawn braced herself for what kind of genetically enhanced beast she would be facing down, but the young woman behind the counter of the tea shop was of slight build. Blond, young, with hard lines on her mouth but a bright smile as she handed a customer a four-pack of hot beverages.

Hippolyta's had a small line. Dawn queued up and studied the price board on the wall.

"What can I get you?" Kaja asked. Her name tag read Wendy.

"Vanilla Chai, hot." Dawn waited for her drink and made a show of examining the baked goods behind the glass. "How are the lemon bars?"

"They're from yesterday, but they're good. The raspberry oat squares are from this morning if you want fresh."

Kaja set the hot paper cup on the counter. Chewed fingernails worked the screen of the order tablet. Her left pinkie and ring finger had swollen knuckles. Arthritis or an injury? Weary eyes, a fading bruise on her chin, the smile tentative as she waited for Dawn.

Dawn tapped her device to pay and did a hard blink, capturing Kaja's face on her implant. She took the tea and found a small table outside where she could watch the counter.

The line inside Hippolyta's Tea Shop only grew.

The tea took the chill from her fingers as she read up on her quarry. Kaja's warrant had no more information, the bounty set by an Evergreen Corp security officer. New Pacific Commonwealth approved the warrant, meaning the charges were substantiated. But Dawn could find no filed report detailing the incident with Kaja and her husband. Hillar Stepnova was a mid-level exec in Evergreen's quality assurance division.

When she double blinked again to clear her eye screen, Kaja was gone.

With a stifled curse, Dawn left her cup and jogged to the corner of the tea shop. Kaja was pushing a scooter out onto a rear walkway.

"Wendy!" Dawn called. Kaja ignored her. "Kaja! Wait!"

Kaja thumbed the ignition switch, but the scooter engine only clicked. When she spammed the button, the electric engine finally caught. Dawn ran, almost catching the back of the scooter, when Kaja straddled it and zipped off.

The scooter shot past a few pedestrians, but Kaja braked hard as a group of school children appeared on the sidewalk ahead. When Kaja hit the brakes, Dawn caught up with her and knocked her off the bike. The bike engine quit. Dawn got her quarry down and pinned her. With precise moves, Dawn placed a wrist tie on Kaja before hauling her to her feet. The children were watching.

Dawn got Kaja marching the opposite direction. "Why'd you run?"

"I saw you scan me. I'm not on any dating app."

Sloppy. Dawn filed away the need to be more careful. Even an untrained observer could spot someone using an eye implant's image processor. She brought up her device, scanned Kaja's face, and hit send.

"Look, Kaja. The cops are coming. But you have options. Commonwealth police will be recording as soon as they arrive. Tell them you are opting out of all corporate contracts. This will throw you solely into the jurisdiction of the Commonwealth. They won't hand you over.

Evergreen will have to fight to bring about their own charges, and from what I see, they want you to come quiet."

"You really think they'll keep me safe?"

"I'm tagging your case to a cop I know. Detective Satoko won't let you get scooped up, assuming you're not hiding anything that's not in the warrant."

Kaja's face had grown pale. She had her head down and stared at the ground. Besides the bruise on her chin, the light revealed faded yellow marks on her neck.

"Your husband do that?" Dawn asked.

"Yeah. He was also my boss."

"He's the one you put in the hospital?"

Kaja nodded stiffly.

"It sucks, I know. State your case once you get to processing. No doubt Evergreen will want it to go away. They might even dismiss the whole thing."

"Right. Wishful thinking never got me anywhere but into trouble."

They waited. Dawn couldn't help but read the Commonwealth finder's contract as it popped into her inbox. Disbursement pending. Dawn needed to still hand over the suspect. A third of what Evergreen would pay. Which meant a sliver of debt remained. One more job. Always one more...

She summoned the cancel button. With a thought, she could message Evergreen security and earn the full bounty. But she closed all screens and kept an arm on Kaja's shoulder.

The notion she'd ride out of New Pacific to Seraph, back to River City, or to some brain-dead number-crunching gig in a private community faded. She'd need to pay for a hotel, for her gear, for pending implant updates, for food, all while avoiding her own hunters.

The itch on her neck grew worse.

The group of kids was gone. Others walking along the footpath stared but no one slowed down or made eye contact. No doubt some were recording, using AR glasses or handheld devices. Few with visible implants. Even the cheap stuff was expensive and getting them replaced, as Dawn had done after being assaulted by tech thieves, could put a sizeable dent in the wallet.

A woman in a cream pant suit with matching sharkskin purse whispered into a watch.

Where was Commonwealth security?

"Problem?" Kaja asked.

"We're moving."

Dawn took her jacket off and threw it over Kaja's bound hands before marching her away from the crashed scooter. Cutting through the alley, they crossed the main drag and approached the canal bridge.

Pedestrian traffic was more congested than before. Her software made a quick sweep, but it was impossible to scan for face IDs without being distracted. She quit the program and directed Kaja over the canal and towards a wine shop. Wrought-iron tables and chairs stood outside in a square of potted mandevilla growing on delicate trellises.

The shop was closed.

Dawn got Kaja seated and joined her, with her back to the wine store windows. From her seat, she could watch for any approaching security vehicle. As the seconds ticked by, she wondered if her message to the police hadn't gone through. What would delay a pickup this early in the morning?

She breathed. Counted. Practiced her mind-calming exercise. Reapplied her lipstick and tried not to fidget.

The fading adrenaline rush almost made her forget only a few minutes had passed.

The prickling...

Someone following her? No. The woman in the cream suit was nowhere in sight. To anyone passing by, Dawn and Kaja were sitting and waiting and unobtrusive. This early, people had places to be.

The flash of a targeting laser. Dawn got Kaja down as something ricocheted off the metal table. Who was shooting? No time to look. She hurried the woman between a row of plants as a second projectile whizzed past.

No report of a weapon.

She was about to get them running in the same direction as most of the foot traffic, but up ahead, a large man almost as wide as he was tall ambled towards them with a furrowed brow. His hands were thrust into the pockets of his duster. Visible modifications marked his skin, turning one side of his mouth into a steel-stitched sneer.

"You missed," the gorilla murmured. "Target's still up."

A soldier or fellow hunter. With someone else sniping from on high, it meant a team was after them.

All Dawn had was a pocket dart gun, and she had no intention of getting into a shootout in the Hub.

The glass door to the wine shop was locked. Still in a crouch, she grabbed a flowerpot and swung it against the glass. It exploded into a thousand white pebbles that cascaded down as Dawn shoved Kaja inside.

Smack!

A dart struck the doorframe. Whoever was out there wasn't trying to kill. The big ape vaulted the waist-high gate to the shop's eating area. He had a big chrome pistol in each hand.

Kaja slipped away, sprinting past a Please Wait to be Seated sign and vanishing through a swinging door.

Dawn slipped her dart gun from its thigh holster and fired into the floor. The *phump-SPAK* caused the hunter outside to dive for cover. She raced for the swinging door. Kaja was on the far side of a cozy kitchen, fighting to open a rear exit.

"Wait!"

Too late.

The door pushed open, partially blocked by a food waste bin. Kaja slipped through before Dawn could catch her. A sharp cry and a thud. Dawn pushed the door open wide enough to see Kaja on the ground with a dart in her chest.

She spun in time to see the giant knock the swinging door wide. Before Dawn could shoot him, a little person in a tac suit appeared beneath the giant's tree branch arm and fired a burst of tiny flechettes. The projectiles stitched up Dawn's arm and shoulder and cheek.

An electric tingle was followed by an instant jolt that sent Dawn to the floor and the world spinning.

Chapter Two

Dawn had been inside worse jail cells.

The toilet worked, no cell mates, the bunk had a pad, albeit lumpy, and only one person shared the jail, which meant it was quiet. The paint on the walls and ceiling, a mint green semi-gloss, appeared fresh.

She rubbed the burn marks where the needler had struck her. The projectiles had been removed or dissolved, but the skin remained puffy. A knot had formed on the back of her head. Had she fallen? Couldn't remember.

A faint recollection of four, no five, soldiers or bounty hunters or cops peeling her off the wine shop's kitchen floor and throwing her into the back of a van. Short drive, then dragged down the steps into her cell. Her implant had no signal. A quick inspection confirmed her lock picks, drones, and device, along with her sidearm, were gone.

An antiseptic bleach smell stung her nose. The floor was damp, as if it had been recently mopped.

The woman in the neighboring cell leaned against the bars. Kaja Stepnova. "I guess I'm not the only one with people after me."

Dawn rubbed the bump on her scalp. "I wasn't asking to be caught."

"I covered my tracks. How'd you find me?"

"You were smart sticking to the beige zones. But Commonwealth cameras can be tapped." She left out the role her suite of drones had played. "And getting a job at your sister-in-law's shop was dumb. Our captors say anything?"

"When I asked questions, the big guy told me to shut up in Estonian. So how much am I worth?"

How much, indeed? Dawn paced the cell and pushed on the door for good measure. The real question? How much was someone willing to pay for both of them?

A corporate team willing to seize targets in broad daylight? Risky.

No logos in the cell, no screens piping in zone-specific programming, no monogram on the towel. No clues to the identity of who was holding them.

She knew she should rest, but she counted out the paces to either side of her cage.

An electric buzz preceded the sound of a door opening. Soft boots descending steps.

"Hello, Dawn."

Tall, with a thick neck and muscular build, Dawn's sister Eve was everything Evergreen Corporation could hope for in one of its genetically modified goons. Unlike the big guy Dawn had first encountered, Eve had no visible mods and had never gone under the knife. She had once criticized Dawn for allowing her employer to insert a state-of-the-art eye after she had returned from a coast vacation with a wasting bacteria that almost cost Dawn her vision. Back before Dawn had gone freelance.

Eve's hair was buzzed except below the ears where a rich mane of shoulder-length braids dangled. She wore a vest of soft armor and a burner on her hip. Black swirling tattoos covered the dark skin of her arms.

Dawn placed a hand on the metal barrier. "Evergreen hired you to arrest me?"

"I'll get to that. Pascal is missing. I need you to help find him."

"Pascal? He's with mom. What does this have to do with me?"

Eve gave a joyless laugh. "I tell you our brother's gone and you want to make it about you?"

"You're the one who sent a team after me in the middle of the Hub. What are you thinking? Even Evergreen isn't that dumb."

"Well, maybe I am. When a profile matching you got tagged by a traffic cam this morning and then went blurry, I knew it was you. If I didn't grab you, you'd slip away. Still wearing that dumb jacket. So who's the girl?"

Kaja had been listening and watching. She nodded at Dawn. "I don't have anything to do with her. You can let me go."

"No one's going anywhere until I say so. This doesn't involve you. Sit down."

Kaja did as she was told.

Eve leaned centimeters away from Dawn. "You roll into town and jump into work with both feet and don't call home?"

"Next time I'll synch my schedule with your secretary. What happened to Pascal? Mom was supposed to be watching him."

"Mom's in jail. Mom's been in jail for a couple months, as it turns out. Pascal has been on his own."

"What do you mean? What happened to her?"

"Don't know. We don't talk much. You know that. I got flagged by Commonwealth Sec in a message after the apartment was forfeited. When I called the manager and threatened him, he told me."

"I don't believe this. Where were you?"

"On assignment. I've been back a week."

"Their rent should have been paid out until the end of the year. I sent money."

Eve's voice grew louder. "To who? To mom? And what do you think she did with it?"

"Hey?" Kaja said. "Can I get out of here so you two can have your reunion in private?"

"Shut up, or I'll come in there and clock you."

"Kaja's got nothing to do with this or with us," Dawn said. "She's a low-end bounty. I was going to hand her over to the Commonwealth where she'll get a slap on the wrist."

Kaja folded her arms and kicked the bars. "Stop doing me favors."

The com on Eve's neck warbled. She tapped it off. "Money's not going to solve this, Dawn. I need you to untangle this."

"Why? You have a team of goons—"

"Don't call us that."

"What do you want me to call you? Professional soldiers? Peacekeepers?

Evergreen runs assassins and thugs, and you're one of them. You have the resources and the muscle."

"It's more complicated than that. Pascal joined Commonwealth Services. From what I've learned, he did his initial training while mom was around. Then he got his call date right after she got busted. My status as Evergreen keeps me from learning anything, except all my messages to him go unanswered. It's like he vanished. I can't talk to mom for the same reason."

"Ask your bosses to help you."

It was the first time Eve lowered her gaze. "They said they'll work on it. Which means wait."

"So you found me and grabbed me so I'll make the inquiries. I've got my own problems. I need to get this woman to Commonwealth security. I have a bounty to collect."

"Not as long as I have you both here, you don't. You want to run after what I told you? Head back to River City and that joyboy junior exec you were banging? More adventures in Seraph pretending to be Herron-Cauley? My boss may not care about me or Pascal, but they're interested in you. I don't even have to call anyone. I'll leave you here for the day shift to find you and they'll get a nice payday out of it."

Dawn felt her face grow hot and her mouth dry. "You'd hand me over?"

"In a heartbeat. Pascal is your brother, too. Tell me you don't care. All those credits you sent weren't so you could put a roof over mom's head."

She hated when her sister was right.

"I'll look into it. Commonwealth Service wouldn't take someone like Pascal. It's probably some New Pacific computer glitch. I do this, you give me Kaya back."

The cell door clicked open and Eve swung it wide. "Deal."

Dawn straightened her jacket and wiped a smudge from an elbow. "I'll need my gear back. I'll find Pascal. You know how he is."

"That's what has me worried. You know who you'll need to see once you set foot outside that cell."

Chapter Three

Dawn had all her equipment save her dart gun.

"For safekeeping," the soldier keeping watch told her.

The rest of Eve's team appeared bored or distracted, a six-pack of enhanced and well-armed psychopaths who looked like they'd all been on a seventy-two hour stim bender and weren't about to crash any time soon.

Dawn hurried out the door into daylight and got her bearings. Whatever the facility was, it had no signs or gate, but this was Evergreen Corp territory. Not a place for the run-of-the-mill drunk drivers and credit cheats. A private jail for special guests, and Eve had the keys.

She was on the outskirts of Evergreen District near the manufacturing sites. Evergreen was in the power business. Dwarf reactors, solar panels, batteries—everything that kept New Pacific juices flowing.

Pedestrian traffic was light. Electric cars, trucks, and buses coasted past, along with automated delivery vans and a few robot dogs. Pedal bikes remained popular. Late morning, so most of the productive citizens in the zone were at work.

A limo drifted by, using the center emergency lane to cut past the traffic.

Work was a subjective term.

She pulled her jacket hood up and opened an app on her implant to summon a ride. Eve had made no promises that any of her Evergreen connections would stop the local sensors from flagging Dawn.

"Need a lift?"

The little soldier who had shot her followed her outside. He had changed out of his tactical suit and now wore a blue blazer, shorts, and a bright backpack. His weapons were left behind or concealed. He pushed a mop of blond hair from his eyes and clicked a fob. A nearby compact car lit up and its gull doors swung up.

"I left my bike parked in the Hub."

"Climb in. I'll take you where you need to go."

"No, thanks. I'll get a cab."

"Eve wants me with you. Let's make it easy on both of us."

Dawn got in the passenger seat. The soldier settled in next to her and tapped the steering column. The car closed and started up, its navigation system prompt waiting.

"I don't need a babysitter," Dawn said. "I told Eve I'd do as she asked. You'll only get in the way."

"The sooner you tell me where we're going, the sooner we're out of each other's hair."

"Central lockup. You know the way?"

He tapped the destination on a virtual keyboard. The display vanished as the car got into gear. The driver's name flashed on the UI. Linus Spalding.

"This your ride or did you steal it?"

"It's mine. No smoking or eating, please."

As they drove, Dawn checked the side mirror. No one was obviously tailing them and no drones. "Why doesn't Eve just send you?"

"Ask her. But I've got the same restrictions as she does."

"Then why are you with me?"

Linus offered a wicked grin. "Most cops don't scan children."

She gave him a fresh appraisal. The haircut, the suit, the backpack—dressed like a schoolboy on his way to the local prep academy.

"So you're the little sister," he said.

"Is this the get-to-know-me phase? You're coming along; it doesn't mean we need to talk."

He made an amicable gesture before turning on the radio. The hard, driving beat and Thai lyrics hurt Dawn's ears. She stared out the window and tried to tune it out, preparing herself for what was to come.

***

As she walked alone through the dirt yard, the last security door closed behind her. The New Pacific Commonwealth's lockup was a large concrete building with a wall and crenelated towers, every bit the castle out of a dystopian fantasy serial save for the dragon and the evil overlord's henchman riding about on horseback.

The jail had an indoor reception area, a barebones chamber with tables and chairs where families were meeting their incarcerated loved ones. All the inmates wore red.

Dawn's mother was the only one outside, waiting beneath a sycamore with wilted leaves. The rest of the yard had a few picnic tables, along with several sun-bleached plastic chairs. The sun shone bright through the white overcast.

Jenelle Moriti stood as tall as Eve, but not muscled or augmented. Her cornrow hair was tied back in a ponytail. When Dawn emerged from the shadow of the interior gate, she perked up and headed straight for her, drawing her younger daughter into a hug.

"You're tense," Jenelle said.

"My being here is risky. They can see my face on a dozen cameras and it will take just one bored tech looking to make a few credits to run a simple tracking program to know they can turn me in."

"So dramatic. You always knew how to draw a frowny face on such a beautiful day."

"I'm not here for you. What happened to Pascal?"

The warm smile on her mother's face remained unchanged. "He's a bright boy. So bright. Like both of my girls, he has gifts."

"Eve said he joined Commonwealth Services."

"I know. He's an adult. He's old enough to make his choices, and I never held you or Evie back."

"He can't handle a job outside. You know that. We agreed on this last time we talked. I sent you money—"

"For which I'm grateful. But the last time we talked was almost two years ago. He's matured. He's come so far in every way imaginable."

Dawn laughed. "I don't know how they even took him. They'll give him corrective surgery, an implant, or, I don't know, try to fix him. We both agreed we didn't want that."

"Maybe that's not what Pascal wants."

"None of it matters right now. What matters is that he's missing."

Jenelle's smile vanished. "What do you mean?"

"Eve looked for him. It's like he doesn't exist. I haven't started digging yet, but he signed up and then poof, gone. I need you to tell me anything about what he told you before he signed up. What service sector did he request? Did he have a sponsor or duty officer?"

"Slow down. You're talking too fast."

"What's wrong, mom? Got a headache? A few weeks in jail didn't clean you up enough, or are you finding your 'medicine' here too?"

"I need to sit."

Dawn felt her hands tremble as she followed her mom to a table.

Jenelle toyed with a necklace. A golden circle on a petite chain. "I'm clean. That's what you're wondering, isn't it?"

"How long are you in?"

"Another few weeks, depending on my psych eval. What did you learn about Pascal?"

"Nothing. I came straight here when I heard."

She was clutching the circle tight. "It was a civil service job. That's what he said he wanted. He's been doing better. Focused. And he needed to get out and not be a burden. Those were his words. How could I say no?"

"By being a responsible mother, that's how, mom. You don't get to pick what job CS gives you unless you have a friend up the food chain."

"Pascal said he spoke with the recruitment officer. He said they promised a parks department job. Pruning flowers at the conservatory, mowing, pulling weeds. He said he enjoyed seeing the birds in the park and the pay would help offset what you were sending."

Dawn fought to keep her voice calm. "I was sending enough. You both knew that."

"Try convincing Pascal of anything when he sets his mind to it. He's not a child anymore."

"You don't get off that easily. Where were you? Why are you here?"

Jenelle scowled. "A monthly deposit into my account doesn't mean you get to show up and talk to me like this. I messed up. If you had been around, it might have been different. I can't do anything about it now."

An announcement over a loudspeaker and the family groups inside were hugging and saying their goodbyes.

A corrections officer emerged into the sun. "Moriti? It's time."

"Who was Pascal talking to about service, mom?"

"I don't know his name. But the office is on Jewel Street. Pascal had the bus schedule marked on the kitchen white board and planned his trip for a month. Like so many of his endeavors, I didn't think he'd actually do it."

"He did. You weren't around to stop him."

Jenelle rose. "You find him, honey. Bring him back to me. We'll all be together. I'll be out soon enough, and it'll be better than before. I promise."

She vanished through the open double doors where the other prisoners flowed.

Chapter Four

The Commonwealth Services recruitment office stood wedged between a game arcade and a frozen yogurt shop. Dawn's street app confirmed three schools in the vicinity, with the enlistment station smack in the center of them.

Service and Responsibility!

Build Together!

Adventure Awaits!

Each recruitment poster boasted young, smiling people with tools at the ready and a can-do expression on their acne-free faces.

Restore Her to Her Former Splendor!

This last poster on an A-frame sign on the sidewalk boasted two images, before and after, of a scarred, ashen hellscape juxtaposed by a lush forest and waterfall. The pool was blue and a butterfly swept out towards the viewer.

A hologram.

It fought for attention against the blur of sounds from the arcade and a tinny guitar cantata in a pentatonic scale blaring from the yogurt place.

Dawn scoffed at the notion that the Commonwealth could get anyone to sign on with so many distractions, yet here she was. Pascal had fallen for it. As if he understood service. Her older brother needed a guiding hand to make sure his shoes were on before heading outside.

Linus drummed fingers on the car door. "You going to tell me what we're doing here?"

He had driven them to the suburban neighborhood without comment, but Dawn wasn't in the mood for questions. The Hub was too far away to walk to get her bike, so she'd need him for the moment. She got out of the car and slammed the door before marching across the street to the office.

The door was propped open. The narrow suite had two desks and one clerk stooped over a terminal and busily clicking away. A younger man with a brush cut and a buttoned shirt open at the collar. The *zip-pew-pew-ping!* of a game played from the flatscreen monitor's speakers. A name card on the desk claimed Ranveer is Serving You.

Dawn sat in one of the stiff chairs across from him and cleared her throat.

Ranveer sat straight and double tapped, closing his game. "Oh, hello. Welcome to Commonwealth Services. How can I help?"

"I'm looking for a recent inductee. Pascal Moriti. He signed up with CS at this office a couple of months ago."

"One of our junior volunteers? It's a popular program. Is your child enjoying his service?"

"I'm not here for a child. Look him up. Someone here signed him on, and it was a mistake. He's not able to look out for himself, and I need to find out where CS placed him."

Ranveer clicked, typed, and squinted. "Pascal Moriti? Not a minor. I'm afraid I can't share any of my information."

"My mother, Jenelle Moriti, is his conservator. She's unable to come and sent me. I'm his sister."

"If you have proof of legal guardianship, then I can talk to you. Unfortunately, without such proof, I'm prohibited from divulging information about our volunteers. Have your mother call our office."

"She can't. I'm here now. Is there a form I can fill out or a manager I can talk to?"

Ranveer's smile grew more profound. A subscript under his name plate read Director.

She nodded demurely and put on her best professional voice. "So you're in charge. What can you do for me? We haven't heard from Pascal in weeks, and we're worried. My mother is in no condition to talk to you. His assignment, his current supervisor, anything would put us both at ease."

"Let me scan your ID and I'll submit the request and have our legal department get back to you. But at this time, I can neither confirm nor deny Pascal Moriti's presence in our system. Privacy is one of CS's hallmarks. Surely, you understand."

Dawn forced a smile. "If you could be a dear and print out the information request forms so I can bring them to my mother."

"Certainly." He got busy clicking.

The suite had a back room, but the other desk had no teacups, personal belongings, or knick-knacks, and the terminal was powered down. But forcing access to the CS terminal would bring her the wrong attention. Maybe worth it. If she could discover Pascal's whereabouts and solve this here and now, she could pass the information on to Eve and get out of New Pacific. But something in her gut told her Pascal's situation wasn't anything as simple as a clerical error on his whereabouts.

She casually brushed a drone onto his desk without him appearing to notice. She blinked and activated the remote bug's macros. It would hide, watch, and listen until prompted to do otherwise. Dawn doubted the office had counter-espionage measures. Once Pascal went on break or visited the restroom, she could use it to access what she needed.

The outside door swung shut when Linus entered and kicked away the doorstop. "This guy giving you trouble?"

"I've got this under control," Dawn said.

Ranveer half-rose from his chair. "I'm sorry, are you also here for the same request? We were just in the process of filling out the information request forms—hey!"

Linus marched around the desk and hauled the clerk down to the floor. A thirty-centimeter blade was in the soldier's hand, drawn from a concealed sheath behind his neck. He pressed the knife to Ranveer's throat as he kneeled on him.

Dawn pulled Linus off the man. "What are you doing?"

"Cutting through the red tape."

"Were you listening?"

"I was right outside as lookout. Of course, I was listening."

Ranveer fumbled with a device on his hip. Linus tore free from Dawn and smashed the butt of the knife down into the man's face. A sharp pop, and blood spilled from Ranveer's nostrils.

Linus snatched the device away and crushed it under his heel. "Get what you came for."

Dawn crouched at the computer. The simple interface had personnel files and other records. She sorted inductees by name and scanned for Pascal Moriti. Didn't find it. She used the search and likewise came up with no results. How was that possible unless her brother didn't actually sign up for CS?

"You people can't do this!" Ranveer mewled. "I only have a few credits. Take...take what you want."

Linus flicked the knife's edge with a thumb. "Here's where you stop talking. Any luck there? Clock's ticking."

Distracted, Dawn navigated back to scan the icons. "The clock wouldn't be ticking if you didn't decide to turn this into a smash and grab."

Browser. Games. Personnel, Office Finance, Scheduler. She barely noticed her drone finding her glove and reattaching itself. Had someone erased Pascal from the CS files? She had no picture of her brother on a device, so she couldn't use it to question the office manager.

"Does this place have a security system?"

"Answer the lady," Linus prompted.

Ranveer shook his head. "No alarm. No cameras. It's a safe neighborhood. I won't tell the cops about this. Please don't hurt me."

A slap across the back of the head. "Of course we won't, buddy."

Dawn scrolled through pages of ID pictures in the Personnel folder. All taken by the office's camera against a white pull down backdrop. Plenty of smiling children from the past year eager to enter the youth volunteer program. A few adults, too.

No Pascal.

What had her mother said about Linus signing up for Commonwealth

Service? Planned it ahead for a month. Linus had plotted out the bus route, and probably which path he would walk and who he would talk to once he arrived.

She opened the scheduling app. Years of records, with very few meetings with anyone besides a circuit manager who showed up every few weeks and took Ranveer to lunch. But there, on a date several weeks back, was an 11am appointment on a Monday.

Pas Maroni.

Had the misspelling saved the entry from getting wiped?

Dawn turned the screen so Ranveer could see. "You met with Pas Maroni. Pascal Moriti. You must have seen his real ID when you signed him up."

"I've signed up a lot of people."

"Not that many. This was for a salary position. Tell me about him."

Linus was glaring at the man as if waiting for the word to break something.

"All right!" Ranveer blurted. "He was a perfect candidate, like everything we could ever expect to come through that door. He confirmed how much we'd pay and wanted to start right away. High marks in school, heavy science. He was a little funny, you know? Barely asked questions. Quoted the commercial and said he 'wanted to restore her to her former splendor.' Just like the sign outside, right?"

"Get to the point."

"When I asked if he was willing to accept a full-time assignment that would require a posting outside the city, he agreed. Thumbed the pad, and he was in."

"And then what?"

"I filed the application and he got processed. I got the report he entered induction the next day, which was fast, but sometimes the planets align, right? I'm sure he's fine. Let me contact my regional manager and he'll see to it you can reconnect with your brother."

"What's your manager's name?"

"Barry Salado."

To Linus, Dawn said, "Come on, we're leaving."

Linus stared at Ranveer before tapping himself on the temple with the tip of the blade. "I've got your face and name and everything there is to know about you. Any cops, and you'll find me at your bedside and it won't be for cuddles. You call this Barry fellow, and I take out your family and their pets."

When they were outside, Dawn asked, "Was that necessary?"

"You want the cops after you?"

"Intimidation rarely works."

"Huh. And here I was doing it wrong all this time. Works for me. What's next?"

"You and I parting ways. Drop me off at my bike. It's time to take this inquiry up the food chain."

Chapter Five

Dawn had a tail.

Her motorcycle was where she had left it, parked in a Hub lot with zero surveillance. A helpful dark website posted maps of each zone of New Pacific. She had taken the time to confirm that the weed-infested property just off the canal had no cameras.

But two vehicles were taking turns keeping her in sight as she navigated the city's midday traffic.

One was Linus in his compact car, the second another motorcycle with sparkling orange fenders. Eve drove the bike, her build and hair below the line of her yellow helmet impossible to miss.

She decided not to lose them yet. The last thing she needed was to be involved in a cross-town chase and get tagged with a traffic citation.

So Eve didn't trust her.

A minor irritation compared to the run-in with her mother at the jail and then having to deal with Eve's psychopath snack-sized teammate. Dawn would find Pascal happily working in a Commonwealth farm district property measuring microbes and contamination and shoveling dirt. His missing records were a clerical mistake. Eve would get confirmation their brother was fine, Dawn would get her prisoner back, claim her credits, pay off her debt, and leave New Pacific in the rearview mirror.

Her thoughts grew sour as she reminded herself of one of her mother's silly bromides. Don't count your chickens. Like any of them had ever been around a farm animal.

But the simplest jobs could go pear-shaped. Stay focused. Instead of speeding, she slowed down. Eve Moriti and Linus pulled up behind her as she stopped early at a yellow light. When it turned green, she puttered forward, barely fast enough to keep her bike upright. Car horns honked as traffic passed her by.

Eve pulled aside next to her and matched speed. "What are you doing?"

"If you wanted to come with me, you could just ask."

"Figured you'd try to give us the slip."

"I'm going to the CS Central building. You sure you want to follow me there?"

"Lead the way."

Ten minutes later, they pulled into a parking lot. No avoiding surveillance there. Dawn locked her helmet to the bike and activated the alarm. Eve parked next to her and kept her helmet on.

Dawn perused a collection of IDs before selecting one. "They'll have you take it off inside. Full body sweeps here."

"And what do you have there?"

"Golden ticket for most Commonwealth buildings."

She didn't explain more. Eve caught up with her, the helmet left behind. She didn't let Dawn out of arm's reach.

The white concrete building had a ramp to one side and wide steps to a series of brass-edged doors. Executives, employees, and regular citizens were coming and going, along with a few Commonwealth cops. Everyone needed to go in person to the Central building from time to time. Licenses, permits, court—if not the heart or lungs of the city, it was the nostrils.

Dawn paused at the front door. "Even if you want to hold my hand, we go through scanners one at a time. Don't make this weird."

Eve gave a non-committal grunt as they entered the spacious lobby. Visitors had a line and a metal detector where a couple of guards stood looking bored. The executives and cops used a turnstile and swiped their badges.

Card in hand, Dawn slipped away from her sister and joined them.

For the moment, she was Jill Foster, Office of the Chief Accountant. The department called a small basement a block away home, but their clerks had access to almost everything.

The turnstile light went from red to green. She was through the checkpoint. Her implant found the building's virtual directory. A faint yellow line popped up on her artificial eye, showing which elevator to take.

She chose the stairs.

Two flights up and she was in a spacious hallway with shiny doors leading to the various departments comprising CS services.

Barry Salado, Circuit Manager, had a window office and his door open, but a secretary named Keiko at a desk blocked the way.

"Welcome to CS services. How can I help?"

Without missing a beat, Dawn pulled her device out and squinted. "I have a few service record requests I need to notarize."

"I'd be happy to assist. Did your client send in the forms?"

Dawn grimaced. "No, they're having server problems, apparently. If you didn't get the information, I have it here. It's for confirmation of future benefits packages." She put Jill Foster's card away and slipped out Deborah Mills, attorney with Herron-Cauley. The corporation had offices everywhere, while operating chiefly out of River City. "It's for three of your recent inductees, and we're offering a matching pay package once they complete their agree-upon service."

"Poaching our best and brightest," Keiko the Secretary said without a hint of sarcasm. She handed over a tablet. "Enter the names and service numbers, along with your authorization credentials."

A hard blink, and Dawn filled out the form three times using two of the inductees' data from the recruitment office.

She bit her lip. A touch of self-conscious guilt before handing back the tablet. "This third one is missing its service number. I'm sure you can fill it out from your end."

"Let me see. Hmm. These first two are fine. But I'm not seeing a Pascal Moriti on my end. Perhaps they've been discharged? No, no record there. Is there an alternate spelling?"

"His name is spelled correctly."

"I'm afraid I can't help without a service number."

"I'm going to need this confirmation today. Is there an alternate data sorting record you could access? Perhaps he used a corporate identifier."

"If you had his other numbers, the system would have tagged him."

More lip chewing. "This is strange. On my end, I see he signed up for service only a few weeks ago. Promising young man, very bright, and my boss was eager to present him with a solid offer. Can you double check? Or is your manager Mr. Salado available?"

Keiko the Secretary looked eager enough to hand off her Deborah Mills problem. She leaned back in her chair and looked at the open door to Barry Salado's office.

"Barry, can you come up front?"

Dawn considered dropping off a drone, but sensed no duplicity in the secretary's tone or body language. Keiko was a receptionist doing her job.

The elevator outside dinged. A moment later, Eve ducked in through the doorway.

Keiko the Secretary's mouth was open as she turned to face the latest visitor.

Eve put a casual hand on Dawn's shoulder. "I'm with her."

Dawn fought to keep a neutral expression. "We were just finishing up here. The Circuit Manager is going to be helping with one last detail, and I'll be right out."

"Car AC wasn't working. I'm happy to step in and help with any heavy lifting."

Barry Salado straightened a thin tie over his wrinkled shirt as he rushed out of his office. He double-grasped Dawn's hand and pumped it in a clammy grasp before likewise greeting Eve. Eve wiped her hands on her trousers before they all joined him in his office.

He pulled out chairs for them. "Keiko shared her screen. I'm sorry we're unable to help." He closed the door and dropped his voice. "You should have told me you were coming. I'm sorry I didn't meet you at the elevator."

Dawn straightened in her chair and kept her face neutral. "That's...fine. You have no record of Pascal Moriti."

"As promised, the records have been cleaned. I didn't think you'd need to come by in person to confirm this."

"No backups, either?"

"None, I assure you. My IT man is the best at what he does."

She ignored the itch running down her neck. "Interesting. I found his appointment was still in the recruitment office's scheduler. Seems your IT man wasn't as thorough as we might have liked. We'll need to talk to him. But later. Let's first go over everything you remember about what you were told."

"I...I don't know what else there is to add. You wanted his induction records deleted. I did it."

"What else was cleaned?"

Eve's chair creaked. She reached over to a crystal bowl with tiny mints and grabbed a handful. "Be specific." She began crunching and settled into a laconic glower.

Barry scurried to his side of the desk, his hands fumbling with a pair of AR glasses. "Oh, dear. A misspelling. Let me see. Ah, yes. The recruitment office scheduler was a mistake. My man there is an imbecile. I just corrected it. But the rest of the team was on payroll and had records. Pay history with their credit unions and so forth. So they couldn't just be erased. Their discharge had to be listed somewhere. I dated it all as you asked."

"Let me hear you say the dates and their names."

"I assure you, I made no mistake—"

"You heard her," Eve growled.

He related a date from a month before, three days after Pascal had met with the recruitment officer. "The names. I don't even have the spellings. Let me see. No, they aren't there. Verna Cho, Nathan Greer, Timothy McGuinn, Rebecca Wong, and Race Saputo. I got them all. I haven't thought of them and wouldn't have, but for this visit."

Dawn's implant committed the names to memory. An initial search produced nothing, but the Commonwealth net rarely synched well with any of the corporate splinters.

Crunch, crunch, crunch.

Dawn tuned her sister out and leaned forward. "You seem pretty nervous."

"Of course, I'm nervous. You're in my office with your bodyguard.

I thought this was supposed to happen with no questions. You could have called."

"Then we wouldn't have the pleasure of seeing you in person. Can't look you in the eye over a text message. What about induction training for Pascal?"

"He was in and out after a week before his assignment. The record wipe is thorough. I'll make sure the trace program goes through every department's scheduler again, if you want, but that might trigger a flag. Erasing medical history isn't easy, you know, and your boy had his physical. This...is a rather thorough inquiry. May I ask why? Besides the scheduler, was there a flag?"

"You may not ask why," Eve said.

Dawn held up a hand. "You can ask. We're worried about any available public document requests. CS is a sieve when it comes to its data. Pascal and his fellow recruits...what about their assignment sheets? Their supervisor?"

Barry made a face. "You should know that. Verna is the team manager."

"And any correspondence they made during their assignment?"

"Redacted. They were isolated, so anything sent went into a queue until they exchanged data capsules. This review is necessary? There's nothing about this anyone will see. Let Evelyn know I followed through. The one mistake at the recruitment office will be corrected."

"I'll let her know."

He blinked twice. What had she said? A mistake? His eyes darted up and to the left. The quickest motion, but her own implant caught it and translated it. Commonwealth central used a standard Evergreen Corp office suite for its software. Barry Salado's AR glasses were high end, but the default com settings meant a hard glance up and left and a hard blink was a panic button.

The circuit manager had just called security.

Dawn rose and exited into the main office. Stairs and elevators in the main hallway. But if security was coming, she wanted to avoid them.

"Excuse me, miss?" Barry called.

Eve was right behind her as Dawn hurried past a handful of office workers going about their business. Window suites, a break room, a washroom. Her implant shared an emergency exit if she took a door straight ahead. It led to a back hallway and rear stairs. She took them three at a time, smashing open the door at the bottom.

A group of maintenance workers vaping on the outside landing stared as she and Eve stormed past them. Eve stopped her.

"We need to leave," Dawn said.

"Linus is coming. I pinged him for a pickup."

The compact car pulled up near a row of air units. They piled in. She hated to abandon her bike, but getting away fast was better than being stopped by overzealous security forces.

Linus punched it, driving manually and rolling over a bed of flowers to bypass a yard arm blocking access to the back lot. They were out on the main boulevard and speeding as Dawn kept watch.

"Evelyn isn't a woman," Eve said. "You'd know that if you checked the corporate directory."

Dawn's jaw tightened. Eve was right. Evelyn B, Director of Security, Commonwealth Services. How high did this go? It wasn't just Pascal, but the entire team. Vanished.

"I was made. They got a good look at my face after I blew two IDs. I need you to drop me off down at the Hub depot."

"Why?" Eve asked.

I'm running.

"I'm grabbing a tram to throw off anyone chasing us. Show up at a few stops, get seen, and then I'll use my spoofing mask and find myself a new ride. You need to ditch this car and go back to your squad. This is too hot right now for either of us."

"Ooooh, it's too hot," Linus mocked as he weaved through traffic. "Thought you said your sister was tough, Evie."

Dawn ignored him. "They're willing to bury Pascal and his team, as if they never existed. Think they'll stop and let us off with a warning?"

"Nah," Eve said. "They'll come at us hard. And they have my face, too. I just got word from my CO to report in. They're looking for both of us. But if you think you can turn your back on Pascal and give me the slip, you're wrong. We finish this."

"I've seen this kind of thing before. Been paid to help do it. When you delete files like this, you're covering up a crime. We need to face the fact he's probably dead."

"If Pascal's dead, then we bring home his body. And then we track down the people who killed him."

Chapter Six

"Linus, go to the garage," Eve ordered.

The soldier didn't hesitate as he took a corner and sped up an on-ramp to an elevated thoroughfare. After ten minutes, they exited and were caught in traffic and a series of stop lights and checkpoints.

Linus had driven them out of the beige zone and away from any Commonwealth eyes. An overhead sign read Evergreen Corporation Welcomes You!

Dawn considered getting out of the car at each stop. But if she ditched Eve, what then? She was still in debt and hated to lose her bounty. Could she forget Pascal and leave the city? Was he actually dead? What had happened to him, and why?

A series of turns and they were in a commercial district. Manufacturing, mostly. Every business there operated under Evergreen law, with its blessing and its supervision. The corporation proved one of the largest in New Pacific and boasted about it at every turn. AR tags identifying each business were everywhere, and an ad would play for anyone who glanced at a sign or storefront for more than a fraction of a second.

They pulled down a driveway shared by a dozen workshops and garages. A large rolling door opened as they approached. Linus drove the car inside. The door clanked shut behind them. The large interior space was barebones, housing a van, another compact hatchback, and a scooter.

Dawn felt her back twinge as she climbed out of the cramped seat. "What is this place?"

Linus had his device out and was holding it up in the air. "Safe house. Looks clean. No one's been here, Evie."

"Double check," Eve said. "I'll touch base with the rest of the crew. Dawn, you stay in my sights."

Dawn ignored her as she walked through the garage. One wall had tools and a workbench, and a row of bunks were placed haphazardly around a barrier of flimsy partitions. A shower and bathroom were in the back. A set of plastic body armor hung on a dress dummy. A small compressor sat nearby with an airbrush and cartridges of paint. The space reeked of solvent.

Eve's voice echoed as she spoke loud on her phone. Something about duping her and Linus' tags so they'd appear to be back in the barracks with their squad. Linus appeared to be texting.

The garage had a side door. Alarmed, Dawn confirmed. All she had to do was run, and running was something Dawn Moriti was good at. She felt her breath come up short as her hand hovered over the doorknob. A tremor ran from her fingertips to her wrist. The room swam. She braced herself against a wall and closed her eyes.

Pascal, refusing to eat anything yellow. Pascal, in his throwing and slapping phase, where cups went flying and he would hit his sisters and mother and himself. Pascal, refusing to sleep until every knick-knack in Dawn's room had been repositioned to the way they had been a year prior in their old apartment, despite the fact many pieces in Dawn's button and figurine collection were new.

Her last words to her brother. "Why can't you be better?"

This she had said before leaving the apartment for the last time and abandoning her promising new job at Evergreen Corp. She had created a network back door and sold it to the highest bidder on the dark web, and had made enough to cover a year of expenses. Most of this she spent on upgrades, including a better eye and brain implant. More jobs came, which took her to River City, spying on and for Meridian and finding enough freelance work to pave a future away from New Pacific and her family.

Her implant opened a virtual space that looked like her old bedroom. She moved to the shelf with the buttons and took her favorite and rolled it in her hand. Imagined the soft printed aluminum, the shine, the tree pattern with the branches that reminded her of fingers reaching heavenward.

Counting, she squeezed the button. Clenched her jaw until it hurt. Finally, her breathing calmed. She dispelled her bedroom. Back in the garage, with Eve still talking and Linus distracted. A tap with a circuit disrupter in her glove, and she could switch off the alarm. Could slip away.

A quick scan via the local splinternet and the Evergreen law enforcement channel. Commonwealth Security had flagged three individuals with a break in at their central offices. The alert had been sent out wide. Cooperation with neighboring corporate agencies expected and appreciated. Dawn could drop a tip and have Evergreen cops visiting the building. Eve would be arrested while Dawn made good her escape.

Yet she paused.

Why can't you be better?

Eve had been out of the house and their mother was rarely home unless stoned stupid or recovering from a bender. Dawn had been the parent for that last year, and she had abandoned them. The credits she had sent hadn't been the care Pascal needed.

By then, the throwing, the tantrums, the self-harm were in the past. Her brother had learned to cope, and wanted to do more. A new ambition every week. Painting printed figures of people in space suits for a tabletop game he refused to play, modeling birds from recycled and found items, memorizing science papers and facts, and getting into arguments in online forums. He showed a knack for the tactile arts, learning slide guitar, drawing sand table fractal patterns, and hand stitching books. He sewed. All harmless, all things he could do inside where he would stay out of trouble. With enough credits, he should have been content.

What had prompted his interest in public service?

It could be anything, Dawn realized.

Community PSA looking for recruits, a billboard, a flyer, a comment on a forum. Commonwealth Services had become his new fixation, and neither his sisters nor mother had been around to stop him from signing up.

A BOLO flashed. Her browser was still open, with the Evergreen law enforcement tab now red. The suspects from the CS Central building had pictures along with biosignatures. Two of them, Eve Moriti and Linus Spalding, were flagged as Evergreen soldiers. Their accomplice was a known felon with a lengthy rap sheet. Espionage, falsifying corporate identity, theft, information fraud, trading in corporate secrets, credit counterfeiting, assault, trafficking in passwords, extortion, damaging Evergreen corporate property, arson, and multiple counts of defrauding a corporate officer.

Dawn's face and biometrics popped on the screen.

They didn't appear to have Linus's vehicle. Yet.

She returned to the center of the garage. "Is your car registered in your name?"

He didn't look up from his screen. "Relax. I have the shadow app running. No one will trace it."

"That app is garbage and easily bypassed."

"I helped write that app. I'm sorry you're not a fan."

"It only broadcasts a blur filter over any recorded images. If the camera is too far away, it doesn't work. Traffic AI will flag the car and they'll unscramble it. Looks like all three of us got tagged by Evergreen. Your bosses will be calling if they haven't already."

Eve looked up from her phone. "Nice of you to care. You looked like you were about to leave."

Dawn reminded herself that Eve's enhanced eyes and ears missed little. "We don't get Pascal back if you get us caught."

"No one's caught. We've been on the outs with Evergreen before. Fortunately, our bosses in security are the forgiving types as long as we come back. But you're on a few people's lists. We swap vehicles. Linus, the garage is burned. Pack what you want to keep. We leave in five."

"Come on," he whined. "We're safe. I was careful. You can't believe her."

"I don't. But I have confirmation. We were made. Take the scooter and go back to base. There's no reason for you to get in any deeper."

"All these cars are mine. I'd rather not have you scratch them up. I'm with you, sarge."

"All right. Four minutes and change. Hurry up."

Linus busied himself at the workbench, filling a duffel bag with gear.

"Go after Evelyn B?" Eve asked.

Dawn had considered it. "Too risky. I can't believe he hasn't been looped in on the security breach."

"You wanted to go up the food chain."

"The direct approach will only get us caught. We know Pascal signed up, trained, and received an assignment. Someone knows something, but getting anyone at central to spill the beans now is going to be tricky. I have another idea."

Eve was listening.

Chapter Seven

Verna Cho's address was the first on Dawn's list.

Reilly-Bigg Corp zone, with most of the signage in Chinese. The neat rows of townhouses made finding her home easy. The place was in the middle of a long avenue. Dawn dreaded the thought of getting boxed in if they had to run.

Light traffic and few people about. A light mist fell. Not much overt security either, until Dawn realized every home had a door camera. No doubt the Reilly-Bigg shard of the splinternet had someone watching and recording.

Verna was the supervisor of Pascal's missing team. Dawn decided showing up in person would be better than calling or reaching out with a message. She told Eve and Linus to wait in the car, their new ride only slightly more spacious than Linus' compact now parked in their garage.

"Why does she get to tell us what to do?" Linus said before Dawn closed the car door.

The townhouse was a deep rich red with white trim and roof, with a gravel and desert plant garden in the small patch of dirt out front. Loud music blared from inside.

A quick check confirmed Verna lived with her mother and two children.

Dawn flipped through her IDs. Only two she considered triple-A grade that could make it past extensive scrutiny. No Evergreen Corp left, which was unfortunate. Those worked the best throughout New Pacific. Everyone played nice with Evergreen. But Dawn had burned the last of those fake credentials following her acquisition of the Caretaker IFF device, a misadventure that should have earned enough credits that she wouldn't have had to pick up another bounty ever again.

Her Riley Jackson ID would do. Not top notch, but Riley had a profile listed with Graphene Financial and would be perfect here. She rang the bell. Couldn't hear anything above the din of bugle calls and rock jams shaking the window. Pounded on the door until a small girl in footie jammies opened it.

"Is your grandmother home?" Dawn asked.

The girl ran off, leaving the door wide. "Gramma!"

Hands crossed before her, Dawn maintained a pleasant smile. The music paused. An older woman in lavender sweats appeared. Her frizzy hair was a mess as if she had just woken up, but she wore haptic gloves used in VR sims.

"Yes?"

Dawn showed her Riley Jackson ID. "I'm with Graphene Financials about a payout on a claim for Verna Cho. Are you Wei Cho?"

"That's me. There was more insurance?"

"I'm happy to go over the details. Commonwealth services says you're the recipient and I'm here to confirm some specifics first. May I come in?"

Gramma Cho led her to the living room. A double wall screen had a paused game. A fantasy world with purple trees, pink clouds in a silver sky, and a dragon in mid-flight strapped with a saddle and a lance. Gramma Cho peeled off her gloves and set them on a shiny black recliner next to a VR headset.

"Moon County Adventures?" Dawn asked. "That's my brother's favorite. He played the early ones, but didn't have the VR experience."

"The latest game is killer. So you're with...?"

"Graphene Financials. We handle some of the Commonwealth's life insurance claims. But our integration with their network is undergoing a review. I need to confirm a few details."

"I was told there'd be no one asking questions, and I wasn't supposed to talk to anyone."

Dawn nodded gravely. "That's exactly right. It's a serious situation and from what I've heard, it's best we keep the details of our meeting private. Do you have any recording devices in operation? A voice- acti-vated assistant? Children who can overhear us have this discussion?"

"Everything's muted. The kids are upstairs playing their own sims."

"Verna was your daughter?"

"My youngest girl. Thirty-five years old. Worked CS since she was in her twenties until...what happened. You should have all that in your records."

"Of course. But these virtual forms ask everything. Thank you for your patience. What did you hear about the accident?"

Gramma Cho's face hardened. "I didn't hear anything. Is this some test of the NDA? Like I told the CS lawyer, I heard nothing, I've told no one, and I'm surprised at this visit. Graphene Financials, you say?"

"I signed the same NDA. There was a second policy. It will pay out like the first once we get through this and I can file the forms. Where was Verna serving?"

"Somewhere up north. It's not like she called often. The little ones liked to hear from their mother. Poor reception, she'd always say. I told her—I *told* her—to get an assignment back in the city. She wanted the remote posting because it paid extra."

Dawn couldn't help but glance at the gaming rig. The chair was part of the set-up, with force feedback and body position response. Want to feel the dragon under your butt or the rocket racer between your legs? This was the chair for you.

"Money tight?"

"We managed. We're still grieving. If there's another policy, why didn't the CS lawyer mention it? They told me there'd be no other inquiries."

"They were wrong, to your benefit. Did Verna ever share anything about her crew? She had five employees working under her."

"The number kept changing. Whatever new posting she was last on, she wasn't supposed to talk about it. She'd only call from some bar when she had a night off, and the reception wasn't good."

"Did she talk about the nature of her team's assignment?"

"I knew well enough not to ask. But you know how the little ones get. Verna told the kids a few things. Talked about measuring wind, air samples, geology, soil. It was Verna's specialty. Geology. Could have been a teacher if she hadn't quit school early. Kids these days will do that, and Verna was one of them. I supported her through three years of secondary school before she dropped out."

Dawn caught the bitter tone and hoped Gramma Cho's other daughters and grandchildren learned to navigate her toxic gravity well.

The pause screen continued to animate around them. Moon County Adventures kept prompting Do You Wish to Continue? The wall screens didn't have a dead pixel on them, and the headgear, chair, and gloves were shiny and new.

"What bar did she usually call from?" Dawn asked.

"Place called Black Bird was the last one. Sometimes she only sent a message because the lines would be down. Verna said it had the best food when she couldn't stand to eat any more of the rations in her research station. But she could only make it there once a week."

"Last time you heard from her?"

"A month ago. Then, a couple of weeks later, I got the call and a visit from the lawyers. You recording this conversation with that fancy eye of yours? I noticed you didn't set up a privacy spike. Can I see your ID again?"

Dawn maintained her smile as she searched for Wei Cho. Felt her stomach sink when one of the seven results matched Gramma Cho's height, face, and eye color. Wei Cho, information technology advisor with Evergreen urban planning, retired.

Gramma scowled as she pulled a phone from her belt. "You're not with Graphene Financials, are you? My answering any of your questions puts my payout at risk. I'm calling the cops."

"Wait. I can't tell you who I am. I'm not here to jeopardize your situation. My brother was with Verna's team."

With her thumb poised to activate her device, Gramma Cho narrowed her eyes. "Don't suppose you'll tell me his name. Verna didn't mention much, but she did complain about her workmates."

"As much as I'm tempted, the less you know, the better. But Verna's entire team disappears and no one knows anything."

"What do you mean, disappeared? There was a car accident. They shipped Verna's body back. I was there to view it before disposal."

"You saw her body?"

"I didn't *want* to see it. They told me I wouldn't recognize her."

"Did they have the rest of the team brought back?"

"There were four other sets of remains. The coroner service didn't say why there weren't six but said they needed to remain sealed because of contamination. By then I had signed my NDA and I didn't ask. Look, Riley Jackson, or whatever your name is—we're out of debt for the first time in like ever. The kids are going to an excellent school and will be on track to do something more than work as a city janitor or a research station caretaker. I'm done with your questions. I'm sorry for whatever pain you're going through, but you need to leave."

Dawn rose from her seat. "One more thing. Did you hear from any of the other families? Or see them when you went to receive Verna at the morgue?"

"Yeah. They had us all there at the same time. No one wanted to talk, but I saw them. Everyone has someone to say goodbye, right?"

Chapter Eight

"That's it?" Eve asked.

They were once again driving, with Linus at the wheel. Eve had turned around as best she could in the tight cab so she could face Dawn in the backseat.

"Four bodies came back. One of them was Verna Cho. If her mother is right, the team had six people. According to her, the report called their deaths a result of a car accident."

"And you believe her?"

"She's an old woman caring for her grandchildren. She caught on that I wasn't supposed to be there."

Linus glanced at her in the rearview mirror. "You left her capable of calling this in? I thought your sister was a pro, Evie."

"Shut up and drive, soldier," Eve said. "Are we safe, Dawn?"

Dawn scanned the local security net for any calls. "We're clear so far. She has a lot to lose if the Commonwealth finds out she let anything slip."

Linus was once again focused on the road. "We can go back and squeeze her harder."

"We're not going to hurt anyone," Dawn said.

"So that's it, then. Your brother is gone. My condolences. Not the first time there was a coverup. So some exec was drunk and slammed into them. Let me find the name, Evie drops a bullet on him from a klick out, we drink away the tears."

"Not many executives cruising around near a northern research out-post. I have the name of a bar from where Verna called her family. Can't be too hard to find the name of the town. The Commonwealth listing for its stations will fill in the nearest facility."

Eve turned to face forward, a fist absently thudding against the dash. "There's the lawyers who talked to Verna's mom. There's the coroner. Still rocks we can overturn here."

"Not with the amount of heat on us."

Dawn checked the splinternet. It took longer than expected. A place called Black Bird not listed with any corporate directory had a visible delivery record for food and alcohol.

"Salina Crossroads has a bar with that name."

Eve made her own check on her device. "That's a ways north. Lots of hills and marsh and not a quick drive."

"There could be a dozen little drinking holes called Black Bird," Linus said. "The kind of place not receiving any deliveries from a legit supplier. That's a thin lead."

Review sites, travel planners, public records of incidents requiring a police report using the filter "bar" and "Black Bird." Dawn found no others. "I see just the one. Commonwealth has a weather station eighteen klicks north of there." She shared her findings.

"And the sarge is right. It's a long way to go for a bar. If Pascal was one of the sealed bodies, the coroner could tell us."

"Verna's mom said there was family present for the other lost team members."

"And I didn't get an invitation," Eve said. "So he's out there, or at least his body didn't come home."

"Yeah."

"So there's a chance."

Dawn didn't want to say, as if confirming Eve's statement would jinx it. One more dead from something as common as a vehicle accident. He might have arrived late to the coroner, or his remains hadn't been recovered. A paperwork glitch could explain Eve not receiving a notification.

But who had found the wreck? If it was only an accident, why the NDAs and lawyers and the coverup?

As much as she wanted to speak with the coroner and the other family members, the questions she needed to ask couldn't be answered by any of them.

"I'm going to make the trip to Salina Crossroads," Dawn said. "Check with the law up there and go visit the research station."

"If the lawyers got to the families, you think the cops up there will talk?"

"Maybe, maybe not. Let me do this, Eve. You have your unit to get back to. If my time in Seraph taught me anything, there's fewer places to hide outside of New Pacific."

"I'm already in trouble. And if this is our best lead, I want to be there."

Linus turned on the radio and scanned through the stations, finally settling on a crooning duet set to a country guitar melody.

"Turn that down," Eve said.

He chuckled. "Sorry, sarge. Not going to happen. We can't have a road trip without music. Can we make a teensy-weensy stop before we hit the road? Snacks and more ammo would be nice."

***

"I hate the countryside," Linus pouted.

Eve had her chair fully reclined and an arm on her forehead, while Dawn fought to prop herself against the car door comfortably while making the best use of every square centimeter of the back seat.

"No signal," he continued. "No messages, crappy reception, and the road is terrible."

Holes pockmarked the pavement. The music was a pipe organ piece, the classical-religious sermon channel the only thing that came in clearly, and they were out of range of the splinternets.

They flowed with the moderate traffic along the two-lane road through a dozen smaller communities, mostly farms and small industrial centers. Some flew the Commonwealth flag, some appeared to be affiliated with smaller corporations, and a few were independent and boasting no affiliation. These last hinted at it by their names: Freetown, None-of-the-Above, and Profit.

The communities were comprised of single-level businesses and clusters of houses. All had trading posts with signs that they took Commonwealth credits, so they weren't as autonomous as they might believe.

Fabricated homes stood next to ramshackle cinderblock dwellings with scrap metal roofs. Some stretches of road had people living in tents. A few communities appeared to be doing better, especially around the larger farms. Here, the residences were as solid as anything in New Pacific. But supplies and machinery were no doubt more expensive and scarcer. Folks were free to strike out on their own, but with no corporate support, their independence came at a cost.

Children played around a rusted-out excavator near a roadside dirt pit. Even the smallest shanties with plastic tarp walls had gardens and greenhouses. Dogs on leashes, birds in fields, even a few horses grazing at pasture—life went on beyond New Pacific.

Tune to 600 for Environmental Updates, a sign read.

While a few of the communities they drove through had meshnets, most required a login, even as a guest, and Dawn wanted to avoid any trace of her passing through. An update on the weather might prove wise, though.

Eve had her device out. "Storms blowing from the north."

"They can track you even out here," Dawn said.

"It's a burner. Plus, until they start running fiber optics, there's few places out here who want to maintain a link to any of the big corporate nets and have them hog their antenna bandwidth."

Linus had the autodrive on but a hand on the steering wheel. "I love it when you talk dirty."

They stopped at a farm stand where they could buy apples, grapes, strawberries, cantaloupe, mushroom jerky, and artichokes. Rice and some printable goods, too. Locals with no obvious corporate affiliation, judging by their dress, were buying and selling. Using NP credits and chip readers, from the looks of it. A sign out front boasted Seraph and Meridian Credits Accepted, along with another bragging about Clean Restrooms.

Linus stretched before trotting off around the back of the building. Eve sat on the hood.

Dawn felt knots in her back reluctantly ease as she paced in front of the car. "Why don't you buy us some cherries? I didn't think any orchards were growing anything edible."

"Look at you, up on your horticulture. I'm not leaving you alone with the car."

"Suit yourself."

Dawn went inside and marveled at the assortment of produce. Along with the fruit mentioned in the sign, she found corn, plums, figs, walnuts, and lettuce. They were selling baked goods and trinkets, too. A row of material printers chugged on one side of the large market. Locals waited as household goods or machine parts were fabricated.

She was picking out a package of lemon bars when she saw two uniformed NP cops walk in. They surveyed the place before heading past Dawn towards the back counter. She avoided eye contact. They appeared to be talking to one employee.

She set the bars down and headed outside. A six-wheel runner with a light rack and the Commonwealth logo waited at the curb. Eve waited inside their car.

Dawn climbed in. "Saw them?"

"Yeah. Just relax. This area gets patrolled."

"Those cops weren't here for the pastries. They were asking questions. We should leave."

"Linus isn't done with his bathroom break. Just calm down. I saw you doing your breathing exercises back in the warehouse. I thought your implant took care of you."

"You remember. Sometimes the implant doesn't help. Why do you think I never wanted it for Pascal?"

Eve shook her head slowly. "And mom listened to you. He could have been living a normal life, and we wouldn't be dealing with this right now."

Before Dawn could respond, Linus slapped the window. Waved before climbing into the car.

"You two okay?"

Eve pointed towards the police runner.

"Huh. How sneaky of them. Does that mean we don't have time to pick up some fresh walnuts?"

"Drive."

Dawn kept watch out the back as they got on the road, but the cruiser didn't appear. No drones above, either. In the clear, for the moment. But she didn't stop looking as she counted virtual buttons in her head.

Chapter Nine

Linus took them down a secondary road for an hour before finding another route that led north. Rougher than before, hill country, with long patches of dirt and plenty of deep ruts. Farms to either side, with many open-air fields where workers toiled in the gray afternoon. Long swaths of murky marshlands and groves of eucalyptus trees divided the properties.

He had given up trying to find a radio signal. "No way we'll get close to Salina Crossroads today. Hate to drive this at night."

Eve was having a hard time holding her device steady as the car bounced through a rough patch of road. "Nearest town?"

Dawn had saved her map. The farms and settlements were many, but most appeared private. "Here's something. Dunlop. Has a bright local meshnet. Be good to have a signal."

"I had something quieter in mind. Linus?"

"Kettle Park. Saw the sign at the last turn. Be there in thirty."

Dawn had missed the sign and didn't know what Kettle Park was. She found out soon enough.

They were near a crossroads when Linus pulled into a broad driveway. They paid a woman at a booth a few credits before pulling around several long trucks and a row of motorcycles and smaller vehicles. People had tents erected around a central clubhouse. Beyond stood a series of rough-hewn rectangular stone blocks standing in a circle. Some were placed on top of others, looking like the beginnings of a card house constructed by a giant.

The park's guests were out and about, leaning, socializing, and watching the new arrival.

Dawn studied the faces. "This can't be better than Dunlop."

Linus found their assigned lot. "It's private. No law's coming in here unless something's on fire."

"You expect us to sleep in the car or on the ground?"

Eve tapped the dashboard before climbing out. "I'll take care of you, baby sister."

She had an extra bedroll in the small hatch space. Dawn searched for a signal, but only found private users with no content to share she was interested in. Linus laid out his bedroll on the soft grass next to a picnic table. Eve set the other two out beside to the car. She produced a few meal packs and, with the pull of a tab, all three heated up and belched steam.

"Stir fry, faux chicken cordon bleu, or spring medley?"

Linus pulled the cordon bleu across the table.

"I'm going to take a walk," Dawn said.

The sun was setting. Some neighbors had a party going on around the stone blocks. They drank beer from a keg. A swirling light display shifted between red, purple, and green, playing shapes across the slabs. But otherwise, their corner of the campground was dark. Families, travelers, gangs, and solo truckers all settling in for the night. They smoked, cooked, sang, brooded.

A group of five children raced past, almost knocking her off her feet.

From one of the camp lots, an older woman in a hoodie called out and hurried towards her. "Trance? Nummers? Lift?" When Dawn ignored her, she hurried to catch up. "Joy boy? Joy girl? I also do palm readings."

"No."

"Purity prayers that really work, then? Written on handmade paper. Good luck charm? Have your aura read?"

When the woman put a hand on Dawn, Dawn shoved her off and walked faster. The woman was cursing as Dawn hurried towards the stone blocks.

A group danced about in the center to the beat of a drummer. Others were clapping and stomping. Dawn didn't see any religious meaning to the display, just people enjoying themselves. She watched and nodded along and kept an eye out for the pushy peddler.

At a nearby lot, an RV stood parked with a side canopy open. A banner read New Pacific Clinic and Health Screening. A couple of Commonwealth nurses or doctors appeared to be giving campsite residents checkups.

Service and Responsibility.

Was this what Pascal wanted? Had he gained some newfound sense of community obligation or compassion?

She applied lip balm and watched.

A smack and a thud. The peddler was scurrying away from Eve.

Eve approached Dawn while brushing her arm. "The lady touched me."

"Check your pockets. Were you following me?"

"Supper's too hot. Wanted to see what the commotion is all about."

"People letting off steam, as much as I can figure."

"It's called normal behavior. Why don't you join them? You look stressed."

"I want to know what happened to Pascal. You picked a place off the grid, so there's no chance of contacting any local agencies to ask questions."

"It's safer here. I've stayed in a hundred places like this. These are the kind of people who mind their business."

"If you say so."

Even as she considered questioning the clinic volunteers, Dawn headed back towards the rented lot and whatever lukewarm insta-meal remained.

Eve followed her. "Eat your supper, Dawn. Get your sleep. More driving tomorrow and we'll all need to be fresh. And D? Either Linus or I will be up keeping watch. In case you decide you need to go for another stroll."

Chapter Ten

Her drone skittered across the ground, a single-minded bug obediently heading over the gravel and dirt towards the New Pacific medical team. Their presence meant the Commonwealth felt comfortable sending trained personnel and expensive equipment into the untamed north. Like they had done with Pascal.

Dawn had questions and her drone would look for answers.

What kind of security did they have on hand? Did they have radio signal? If not, how were they keeping in contact with home base, and how would they call for help?

As her drone made its run, Dawn got comfortable, lying on her side in her sleeping bag near their compact car. Linus was on his back nearby, singing to music he had piping into his earphones, while Eve sat on their picnic table, her face lit in blue as she read on her device.

Neither appeared to notice the drone's departure. Dawn kept her eyes closed as she directed her tiny machine along.

The party at the stone blocks was winding down, the musicians packing up and the revelers dispersing like moths with no flame.

At the pop-up clinic, the last of the patients were gone. The two-person medical team was a man and a woman, and they were locking up cases of gear and stowing them into the side of the RV. Dawn piloted the bug through the vehicle door, hopping up the three steps to the vehicle's interior. A tablet sat on a table in the kitchen area. The drone checked for a network and found a private hotspot. Its source was the RV itself. No outbound signals. So they were storing data. The vehicle dashboard had a shortwave radio. The bug scanned a frequency cheat sheet pasted underneath.

Roadside assistance, supervisor, emergency.

They weren't relying on any network. Would they risk sending digitized information over the airwaves?

No doubt things would be the same further north.

The medics were washing up. One put water on the stove and pulled out ramen noodle packs and freeze-dried vegetables from a cupboard. The other closed the door.

Dawn took the drone to a cracked window and sliced open the screen. Once outside, it dropped to the ground. Dawn ordered its recall.

Not much had changed since she had last been this far north. The region's independent streak meant Commonwealth data lines were still being cut and radio towers were suffering from vandalism. Free scrap for someone. It would be some time before the Commonwealth or any other corporation gained a meaningful foothold.

Dawn tried to get comfortable on the hard ground as the drone approached her. But she had it pause. A hard blink, and it was now creeping towards the picnic table.

Eve's brow was furled as she studied her device. The drone crawled up the table. Couldn't quite see the screen. The glow vanished as Eve put her tablet away.

"I'll squash it, Dawn."

Pretenses of stealth cast aside, the drone leaped to the gravel and returned to Dawn. Linus continued to croon.

Dawn took her gloves off and rolled onto her side. "Don't suppose you'll tell me what you're reading?"

"Just getting ready for what's coming."

"You never read before and your lips aren't moving. Did someone help you learn?"

Eve ignored the jab. "This is mission prep. Why don't you do something useful instead of screwing around and trying to goad me?"

"I wasn't trying—"

"Go to sleep."

Dawn stopped herself from responding. Could hear Eve wasn't in the mood and had taken her question as an insult. Her sister had never been a proficient reader and hated books. Their mother had never gotten her the tutoring she needed for what was probably dyslexia. No doubt somewhere in her training, the condition was flagged and addressed.

Had their mother held back needed care for all her children?

These were the questions she pondered as she drifted.

***

"You really pissed her off."

Linus kept the car on manual driving as they exited the campground. He appeared bright and his grin wide as he squinted into the sun. Dawn sat in the front passenger seat while Eve sprawled out in the back, already asleep.

Dawn's best guess? Her sister had sat up all night keeping watch.

"What did you say?" Linus probed. "I missed it while meditating."

"You were blasting music. It's not like we were whispering."

"That's my wind-down routine after a humdinger of a day. If you don't want to talk, that's fine. Teeth brushed? Bladder drained? Because we're off, everybody!"

He flipped on his music and sped out onto the road. They fell in behind a van heading northwest. He didn't pass it.

Dawn counted trees, drummed her fingers on the door, and fidgeted. On her bike, she'd have cut lanes and made time. A robot delivery dog bounded past them along the shoulder.

A thought occurred to her. "Your team...when it was out on a mission, how did you keep in contact with home base?"

"I thought you were in the service. Evergreen can't be much different from Meridian."

"I didn't work for them directly. In New Pacific, I started out with CS, and rarely with a team once they trained me. I was usually on my own with orders to not contact my handler unless it was an emergency. I used burner phones. Then I went independent."

He turned the music down. "Coded messages when necessary over the radio. Digitized and encrypted, of course. Why?"

"Pascal's team in their outpost. I was wondering how they checked in."

"Radio relays, since no one here gets fiber optic data. It's easier to talk to River City or Seraph from New Pacific than it is our own communities out in the sticks."

The delivery dog ran off ahead and out of sight. Linus turned the radio back up.

The weather asserted itself by midmorning. A dusty brown cloud enveloped the road. Linus activated the climate filters. The car grew stuffy and visibility was minimal. Traffic crept along, the van in front of them replaced by a row of smaller vehicles. Sand peppered the windshield.

The road condition only got worse, with plenty of jarring bumps and potholes. Linus flipped an AR lens down.

"You have signal?" Dawn asked.

"Nah. Just the car reminding me of how much I still owe. Continuing down this road will void the warranty."

They were passing between a row of businesses and homes. Shutters were closed over windows and traffic lights blinked amber in the haze.

"First time?" Linus asked.

"I've been in bad weather."

"By the time this blow makes it to New Pacific, it'll be a light breeze with lemon scent. Hey, boss?"

Eve unfolded herself and leaned between the seats. "What town are we in?"

"Best guess? Spooner Knoll," Linus said. "Population: too small to be interesting. Elevation: too close to the edge of nothing for anyone to care."

They pulled around the back of a diner with a white sign boasting The Best Apple Pie on Planet Earth. A dozen other cars were already parked, with more pulling in. Their passengers braced themselves against the storm as they ran for shelter.

Linus killed the engine. "You sure about this, boss? Not that I mind getting a fresh cup of tea, but I thought we were keeping a low profile."

"Doubt word is out for us this far north."

Dawn didn't want to wait. The sand stung her eyes as she got out and ran for the diner. The air reeked of sulfur. By the time she made it through the establishment's first set of doors, her throat felt raw and her sinuses ached.

Fans blasted clean air down on top of her as the doors sealed. A second set of doors swung wide. The place was packed.

A harried server with orange hair and a pink apron hurried past. "Seats at the counter only. Be with you in a minute, hon."

Dawn surveyed a case filled with pies, baclava, tarts, and donuts before finding a seat at the center of the counter.

The booths and tables had families and groups of workers. Unlike New Pacific, everyone here was dressed in work clothes. Filter masks either around their necks or clipped to their clothes. Most faces wore a film of dust.

Dawn guessed she fit right in as she studied a menu under the plexiglass countertop.

The server passed behind her and brushed her shoulder with her hand. "Menu's current, dear. Tea's hot. Get you a cup?"

"That's fine." She took a napkin and dabbed her lips clean before applying lip balm. The place felt more crowded than before. Sweat on her brow.

Linus slid into the chair next to her. "What's the matter? You look nervous."

"Places like this aren't my favorite."

"What's wrong with it? Family dining not your bag? Or maybe it's the homey offerings? Still not sure what rhubarb is or why anyone would put a vegetable in a pie, but maybe I'll order us both a slice and we can have an adventure together."

"Tea's enough for me."

Eve hadn't followed them inside.

Dawn casually surveyed the diner. She tried not to show it as the server brought her the tea, but there was something about the place that made her skin itch. She normally wasn't bothered by people. And she had almost jumped when the server had touched her.

Not many people on their devices. Could that be it? And why would they be? With only a local meshnet, there wasn't countless streams from the media platforms.

A young mother was wiping the nose of a toddler in a booster seat. Another child next to her was making a mess with his oatmeal. Her hair hung bedraggled around her face and she appeared ready to hyperventilate. But she continued to speak in a low, calm voice to both children as they fussed.

It's how Dawn felt but without the children.

Find Pascal, ditch Eve, get out of Commonwealth territory.

She had barely noticed the man taking the seat one down from her. The star patch on his shoulder marked him as a local peace officer. A Commonwealth employee. The server brought him a plate without him giving her an order. Eggs and toasted flatbread and a glass of cola.

He waved for the server as she hurried off. "Hey, Anne? Hot sauce?"

But Anne the Server was out of sight.

Linus reached across Dawn with a bottle from his collection of condiments on the counter before him. "Here you go, officer."

The cop took the hot sauce. "Thanks, bud."

"No problem. How's business out here?"

"Busy, with the weather. Spring harvest has extra traffic on the road."

Dawn shrank in her chair and sipped her tea.

"You two driving through to somewhere?"

"We're not together," Dawn said too quickly, hating that she sounded exactly like someone trying not to be noticed.

Linus grinned wide. "What my employer is saying is that we wouldn't normally stop in a place this provincial. But like you said: the weather. Right?"

The cop barely glanced at her as he shook green hot sauce on his eggs. "Welcome to the country."

"How long until this blows through?" Dawn asked.

"Hard to predict. Meteorologists can only guess. Usually a couple of hours and the worst of it passes by. The good roads have reflectors and lights. Stick to those, and if your driver is any good, you should be able to manage. You folks are driving that little car, aren't you?"

The cop had seen them?

"That's us," Linus said.

"You should have thought about that before hitting the road. Can't tell you the number of cars like yours that we have to pull out of a ditch with a tow rig. Best wait until you can see the sky before you hit the road."

Dawn took a last sip before setting her cup down and placing a credit chip on the counter. She rose to leave.

Linus had just received his rhubarb and strawberry pie. "Hey, wait!"

"Come on."

He picked up the pie and was jamming it into his mouth as he followed.

Anne the Server hurried after them. "Don't you want your change?"

"Keep it," Dawn said. "You're on a local net, aren't you? How do you log your credit transactions, assuming you do?"

"Melanie, the owner, usually handles that. It's encrypted and done safely, if you're worried. At least once a day we have signal for an information burst to a relay."

"Is the reception good enough for that? I hear it's spotty up here."

"It is. But between independent antennae sharing their signal and the dogs with their data services, we manage. Thanks for the nice tip."

Dawn filed it away. The wind braced them with grit as soon as they stepped outside. But it felt like it was easing.

"Why couldn't we have finished pie?" Linus asked through a full mouth.

"Because you like talking to cops."

He was on her heels as she headed through the parking lot. "I was being sociable. You acting all funny is what's going to draw attention."

"If you and Eve would have left me on my own, I'd be on my bike and would have made it to Salina Crossroads. Or we could have gotten a four-wheel-drive runner made for this kind of weather."

"Nah. First, we wanted to make sure you weren't trying to slip away. Second, a runner would have let the cop know we know what we're doing. And then the real questions would have flown."

"That doesn't even make sense."

She tried the door to the compact. Slammed her fist on the window. The taste of sand would never be out of her mouth. The door unlocked and she piled in, slamming it shut behind her.

Eve was on her device as Dawn and Linus brushed themselves off.

Linus took a drink from a water bottle. "Evie, you missed pie. Rhubarb. Not bad. Not bad at all."

"I'm sure I did."

Dawn turned to look at her sister. "How is it you have signal?"

Eve put her device away. "No one has signal."

"So what top secret document are you reading that had you out here packed in the car alone during a storm?"

"One that requires privacy. Enough with the questions. Let's roll."

Chapter Eleven

"So this is where Pascal died."

After tasting the clean air, Dawn surveyed the scene and tried to imagine what might have happened.

Early afternoon, and they were at a three-way crossroad, the intersection of two muddy tracks with deep ruts in the hills miles away from the last of the farms.

Eve snapped a picture with her device and studied the screen.

Dawn crossed the street to a knocked-over sign. One arrow with Salina Crossroads written on it pointed to the ground. The other arrow was bleached and weathered, the paint illegible. It pointed skyward.

"You sure this is the right place?" Eve asked.

"Skyline and Road 442 meet here. Road 442 then runs north. This is it."

The dull thump-thump-thump of deep bass and percussion reverberated from their car. Linus had reclined his seat back and appeared to be napping.

Besides the sign, there wasn't any suggestion anything amiss had happened. The air remained heavy, as if it might rain again at any moment. Their vehicle was covered in speckled dirt and the windows streaked.

No wreckage, no plastic or metal debris, no spilled hydraulics or coolant. But with the wind and storms, it all could have washed away or been cleaned by a road crew.

Dawn clenched her jaw as she examined the sign. A creeper vine circled it. The sign must have been down for weeks, well before the accident. And the road? Unless either driver had been literally hovering, even the most robust four-wheel drive couldn't have been traveling fast enough for a lethal impact that killed all passengers, could they?

She walked back towards the car. "This can't be where it happened. Unless the signs are all wrong, or there's more than one of both roads."

"Unlikely. You said it's the right place."

"It's what was on the report. But the report was slim on real details."

Eve stared at her blankly. "What are you trying to say?"

"We need to talk to the Salina Crossroads cops. Hear why there were only four bodies."

"And tell them what? We're secretly investigating the crash because we suspect a cover-up?"

"Unless you have a better plan, yes. We have that and the Black Bird bar. You twisted my arm to come with you, Eve; we do this my way."

"We're not talking to them. Something weird is going on. Pascal didn't come home. The cops are in on it."

"Might be. We don't know."

Eve nodded towards the north road. "I want to see their base."

"We don't know who's there. That's riskier than going to visit some underpaid community deputy and letting him know we're checking on insurance information."

"Dipping into the same playbook twice?"

"I doubt anyone's warned them," Dawn said. "My credentials are solid."

"It's...harder for me to hide. Unlike you, I can't just whip up a new identity and have people believe who I am."

"I'll make the inquiry and do the talking. Plus, we can decide how we want to approach the base if it comes to that. Our little car might not be up for the drive, especially if we want to avoid being noticed."

"Huh. What are you thinking?"

Dawn explained her plan as they drove towards Salina Crossroads.

Pop-up domed insta-habs stood next to cinderblock-walled homes with sheet metal roofs. Most lots had greenhouses, with several attempts at open-air gardens that were barely distinguishable from the weeds.

A steady drizzle cut down on visibility. The roads were better, with enough stretches of asphalt or concrete to make their ride relatively smooth. A sign pointed them towards Lodging, Food, and Services. The south side of town had larger stretches of land dominated by industrial-sized hothouses.

Behind a row of chain fence, workers trudged about in the weather, loading trucks.

Linus switched the stereo off and tapped his AR lens. "Reilly-Bigg property. Employees: three hundred. Grows strawberries, tomatoes, rice. They offer a health, room and board, and pension package that competes with Commonwealth Services."

Dawn studied the ag compound using her own suite of software. Blinked a few times as she processed what she saw. "Static cameras, electrified fence, motion sensors. Looks like it's more of a prison than a farm."

"But they're hiring. No experience necessary."

The front gate had a guard house. A lone security officer sat inside, oblivious to the passing traffic.

"Something to aspire to, truly."

At a nearby traffic circle, Linus took the first right. Another diner, an inn, a hardware store, a bakery, and a grocery shop with a row of food vending machines. Past a small park with elm trees, a white pavilion, and benches, were three bars. One was the Black Bird.

Eve pointed down a side street. "Cop."

The six-wheel runner, according to Dawn's memorized wiki, held seven passengers besides the driver and cupula gunner. The cupula was down, with no mounted topside weapon. Light ballistic steel armor, puncture proof tires, and a backup power plant and battery suite allowing for thirty hours of operation even with its engine off-line or destroyed. A current model usually seen in service to the Commonwealth or the larger corporations' security forces.

The Salina Crossroads city logo emblazoned on the front hood looked like a hand grabbing either an onion from the ground or the topknot of a perp. No cops in sight, and the window tint made it impossible to see inside the vehicle.

"Pull over," Dawn said.

In the back seat, Eve unfolded herself. "I thought we're doing recon. This isn't the time to be flagged by the local law."

"I doubt they've been updated on Commonwealth BOLOs. Put us in that alley."

Linus found a place near a recycling dumpster. They were out of sight of the police runner.

"Time to eyeball the local color?" Linus asked.

Eve grabbed her coat. "Stay put in case we need to leave."

She joined Dawn under an overhang. The rain pelted down harder than before, but the air smelled earthy and crisp. Tiny pellets of hail bounced on the street.

"Plan?"

Dawn found the local net and read for a moment before leafing through the ID cards she kept hidden in her belt. "See who's here. According to the city's directory, the department is two blocks down. And see those buggies?"

She pointed across the street at a small lot near the edge of the park. Three black luxury off-road vehicles were parked next to each other. All three bore the Reilly-Bigg corporate crest.

Eve put her collar up. "We're not the only out-of-town visitors."

Dawn led her to the closest bar.

Shije

Libations + Wine + Tapas

While the Black Bird and a place called Walter's Pub appeared to be watering holes, judging by the neon in the windows, the front glass of Shije had faux white drapes pulled to either side and cursive scrolling on the window lettering. Tasting room open.

"What's the play?"

The door offered a reflection. Dawn adjusted her hair and touched up her lavender lipstick before pushing on the door. "Let me do the talking."

Three men in suits occupied a polished ebony bar. Five bottles stood before them, along with an array of oversized wineglasses and platters of dainty appetizers. A young woman in a white tuxedo shirt, bowtie, and rolled-up red sleeve bands stood attentively behind the bar with another bottle in hand.

A deputy in a tan police uniform sagged on a stool between the men.

Dawn led Eve to a nearby high table and took the tall menu standing in its center. Eve put her elbows down but raised them when the table tilted.

The bartender hurried over. "Food menu is current, as are our wines. Specials include gambas al ajillo. Real prawn and not artificial, of course, and Manchego and figs, a personal favorite."

After a brief consideration of the menu, Dawn set it down. "Both specials. And two glasses of whatever those gentlemen appear to be enjoying most."

"Excellent choices."

The server left them.

Eve didn't appear to know what to do with her hands. She kept wanting to look over her shoulder at the bar.

"You're doing fine," Dawn said.

At least one of the well-dressed men had a visible implant, an odd fashion trend of showing a colored stripe of silver or gold on the skin. In this case, along his neck and beneath his right ear. He was bald, and the only one wearing a tie.

She touched her own ear and pointed. Eve nodded. Anything they say might be overheard. But silence could likewise draw attention.

Dawn crossed her legs and rested her chin on her hands. "When did you last talk to mom?"

The strained grin that crossed Eve's face would frighten most mortals. It was the threat of murder behind her eyes. "Just last weekend," she lied pleasantly. "We chat every day normally, you know me. We go on and on about hair, makeup, recipes. But I don't want to bore you with the details. How about you tell me what *you've* been doing these past months?"

"Corporate keeps me busy. Glad to be on my last site inspections and happy you could come so we could catch up."

As she continued to banter about deadlines, her fictitious supervisor breathing down her neck, and the endless forms she needed to file following each inspection, Dawn shook loose one of her drones onto the table. It dropped to the floor and scurried. It was underneath the first barstool when Eve gave her the slightest shake of her head.

With a blink, she stopped the drone. The tiny bug paused in place as the server came by and brought wine, the prawns, and a cheese and fig plate. When the server left, Dawn set her bug in motion again.

"Don't," Eve mouthed before continuing in a normal tone. "I'm sure it isn't all work. You get to see the country, don't you? And this is nice for a small-town lunch."

Was there something besides the server making her rounds that Eve was trying to warn her about?

The deputy and the corporate men at the bar continued to laugh. Scratch that. All except the one with the implant. He sat forward, his head down, as if reading or studying something. But his hands were empty.

She recalled the drone. "You're right. There's a surprising number of beautiful places to see, even up here. We should make a tour through the canyons to the east. I hear they're spectacular. I've banked quite a few vacation credits."

The drone crept up her legs and reconnected to her glove. But something else scurried beneath their table. Too fast to see. She used her eye to summon a still image. Another drone. Ice fingers gripped her spine. A tiny graphene spider similar to hers. No knock-off gear for these guys.

Where had the thing gone?

Eve sipped her wine. "Catch the latest Moon County Adventures spin-off?"

Dawn nearly knocked down her wineglass. Steadied it. "I...must have missed that one."

"You get to play through one of the seven families trying to win the Orchard King's prize golden apple. It's silly fun."

If the drone was like hers, all it had to do was touch her to map her out, and the exec at the bar would see what kind of advanced cybernetics she was packing. If it managed a good look or, even worse, a skin sample, they'd soon know she was there using an alias. Of course, she could fry the drone with her jacket, but the gig would still be up.

Eve was poised to get up. Eyes glanced at the exit. "Why don't we powder our noses?"

Dawn gave the smallest gesture. A raised index finger. *Wait.*

They were there for what the cop might know. If they left now and showed up again later, it might raise more questions. The executives might be interested in Salina Crossroads for a hundred reasons that had nothing to do with Pascal or the alleged car accident.

But the bald man with the high-end drones gave Dawn pause. This was a counter-espionage agent. Eve was right.

They needed to get out of there.

Run.

But the cop was here, drunk, and pliable, and Dawn realized she had an asset she didn't normally enjoy while working.

She hopped off her seat far enough from the table so the drone would miss her. Then she went to the bar and put a hand on the cop's shoulder.

A quick check of the town's website confirmed seven deputies. Even before the deputy turned to face her, she had a name.

"Eric, we were just leaving but I just noticed you here. I wanted to say hello."

The bleary-eyed young man gave her a nonplussed look. "Eh?"

"Jillian. Jillian Franks, Jandro Labs. Your boss introduced us a couple of months back and you gave me the grand tour. Do you have a moment?"

The tall exec next to him with the ice-blue eyes said, "This is a private meeting. You can hook up with Deputy Sanjay when we're finished."

"I missed your name. Reilly-Bigg boys, aren't you? I'm sure your bloated compensation packages will allow a brief interruption of your power lunch."

She scooped up the deputy's arm and led him from the bar.

Blue Eyes grabbed her wrist. Eve appeared next to her and seized his arm. Squeezed. He grunted in pain as he let go. None of the other

Reilly-Bigg execs moved. The bald, enhanced spook studied her, his jaw clenching.

Dawn got the deputy walking. "I'll have him back to you in a sec, boys."

Her motion tracker spotted the spider skittering towards her. She tried to swerve out of the way, but the deputy stumbled over his own feet and threatened to go down. Eve was at his other arm and kept him moving.

Dawn stomped and felt a crunch.

The bald man started and his eyes widened as if he had received an electric shock. He glared at them and down at the floor where his crushed drone lay.

Bottle in hand, the server was hurrying after them as they made it to the door. "Is there a problem?"

"Yeah," Eve said. "You've got bugs."

Chapter Twelve

"They'll call for backup," Eve breathed as Dawn brought the woozy cop out to the corner by the tapas bar. "Hell, they might come after us. At least one of them was packing."

Dawn glanced about in search of their car. It wasn't where they had left it. "Where's Linus?"

Eve fumbled for her phone.

"Uh, excuse me?" Deputy Sanjay said. "Who are you again?"

Feigning a smile, Dawn fought to keep the man standing. "I'm sorry you don't remember me. We need to have a conversation. Those boys in there your friends?"

"I have papers to sign. I should go back in and finish up. I don't...what's your name again?"

"Jillian. Jill's fine. You have an office we can walk to? Or even better, let's take your runner there out so we can have some privacy."

"No autodrive. And I shouldn't be driving."

Eve held out a hand. "Keys? We'll get you to your office."

It was a card key on a clip but at the last moment, he wouldn't hand it over. She yanked it away from him and they got the deputy moving to the sheriff department runner and into the back seat. Eve shoved him all the way in and joined him.

The bald executive appeared on the sidewalk. The sheen over his eyes told Dawn they were being recorded and he was no doubt summoning help. She slid the card into the dash. Hit the start button. The engine wouldn't budge.

A dash light blinked. Biosignature required.

"Want him in the front seat for a thumb scan?" Eve asked.

"Deputy, is there an impairment sensor in this rig?"

Deputy Sanjay leaned forward. "Yeah. We can't leave. My work's here with those gentlemen." Slack face, glazed eyes, and he had a hard time keeping his head up.

"How much did you have to drink?" Dawn asked.

"Jus' one. Strong wine. Boss is going to be pissed."

"I think those 'gentlemen' gave you a little something to help you relax. We have a couple of questions for you. Is anyone else on your force around?"

Sanjay slurred, "Boss is down south dealing with a property dis-dis-dispute. Wanda's in the office. But I'm senior deputy."

Eve got him sitting back and had to hold him up. "What did we just interrupt?"

Dawn reached back and shook his knee. "Sanjay? What were those men having you sign?"

"Ennn."

She waited for more. Shook him again. "En? I don't know what that is. Eve, look for a trauma kit in back."

Her implant confirmed the vehicle model had storage for all manner of policing and emergency equipment, including a pop-up surgical suite. Would Salina Crossroads spring for the deluxe first responder package?

Eve was reaching in back and rummaging through the gear. "Basic first aid. No Clear Head shot, if that's what you were hoping for. We have company."

The execs were hurrying their way. Blue Eyes motioned for them to come out.

"We don't have time for this." Dawn leaned over her seat and pinched both of Sanjay's earlobes. He screamed. She didn't let go. "There was a car accident a few weeks back. A runner from the Commonwealth weather station. You remember?"

"Yeah, yeah! Ow! Let go!"

"Focus, Sanjay. Where did it happen?"

"R-road 442 out west. Intersection with Skyline. Please. I'm going to be sick."

"What happened?"

"They all died. All of them. We found the scene a few hours later. No one called. It was just one of our patrols. They must have been drinking, they weren't wearing their safety belts. It was a dumb accident. Why is everyone so interested in this?"

She felt a twist form inside her guts even before she asked the question. "Who else?"

"Reilly-Bigg. That's why they want me to sign the non-disclosure." He wasn't having problems pronouncing the word this time.

"In exchange for what?"

"What else? A lump of credits. Let go of me!"

She released him. He sagged back, but Eve clamped down on his neck. Her large hand held him fast. "How many bodies did you find?"

"Four. We turned them over."

"To who?"

"RB Corp has the best medical facility here, better than the local meat locker at the clinic. Their doc runs the morgue. Is this part of a test? Boss told me he'd handle the paperwork."

The bald exec had a device out. The runner's door lock popped open. Dawn tried to relock them, but the button on the armrest did nothing.

"I'm in here!" Sanjay shouted.

A car horn preceded Linus pulling up street side next to the runner. One of the Reilly-Bigg execs ducked and tumbled out of the way like a skilled acrobat. Blue Eyes was pulling a weapon. Linus was leaning out of his car and lobbed something in their direction.

A bright flash and a throaty POP erupted from behind the armored runner. Eve piled out the side door and Dawn hurried to keep up. Linus was driving off even as the sisters scrambled to climb in.

"You threw a *grenade*?" Dawn asked incredulously.

The corner of Eve's mouth turned up ever so slightly. "I didn't pack them for nothing."

They made a sharp turn and were soon back on the main drag, heading east. Dawn looked out the back. No one was following yet, but the underpowered vehicle would never evade the executive's buggies or the runner, if they used it to pursue them. She could only hope the deputy was too loopy. And the execs had their man back.

Eve and Linus fist bumped.

"Why are you celebrating?"

Her sister chucked her shoulder. "Because we got out alive. Those guys weren't run-of-the-mill pencil pushers."

"I noticed. Combat reflexes. High-tech surveillance drone like mine. And they wanted that deputy to keep quiet about the things we were asking about."

"We asked our questions. We're alive. Why are you pouting?"

Dawn's jaw tightened. "I'm not pouting. We didn't learn much we didn't know."

"But we confirmed some information. R and B is willing to drop coin on Deputy Sanjay's silence. Probably visited his boss first. And we know something else. There's another team in town running defense, and they know we're here."

Chapter Thirteen

It was going all wrong. Theirs was supposed to be a quiet inquiry. Eyeball the Black Bird Bar and go from there.

Dawn didn't do loud.

It was why she worked alone, went in quietly, observed, gathered information, and got out. Leave no trace, if possible. Light a fire to cover your tracks only in emergencies.

They had fought with corporate muscle men, assaulted a Salina Crossroads deputy, and exploded a grenade in the street, and they had just started their investigation.

The price of working with Eve.

Linus hadn't let off the accelerator. "I need to know where I'm going."

They were leaving town, heading through rows of properties with weed-choked yards and a few smaller greenhouses. The homes were older, weathered, and some appeared abandoned.

Dawn reapplied fresh lip balm. It took a minute of scanning to find a specific private network. The signal was weak. Exactly what she was looking for. "Slow down. Take the next right."

Trading Post, the sign read. It turned out to be a giant barn at the end of the lane, with a large dirt lot filled with vehicles. None were military, and no law enforcement.

"Spotted their advertising on the town network. Buy, sell, trade anything."

"You brought us to a flea market?" Eve asked.

They left a complaining Linus in the car as they entered the barn. The large space had some twenty booths and tables set with wares. Clothes, printed consumer products, baked goods, produce, machine parts, tools, and even a few weapons. A vendor was placing a fresh tray of miniature pumpkin pies out on a decorative stand, the aroma of nutmeg and cloves heady.

Dawn's mouth watered as she surveyed what else was on offer.

At the back, a metalsmith was hammering out a bent piece of steel on an anvil. A woman with wooly eyebrows scowled as Dawn approach.

A white sheet lay on the ground with boxes of engine parts.

"All prices firm."

"Is that a way to speak to a customer with credits?"

"Sheila near the front sells finger pies and chai lattes, sweetie."

"I'm looking to trade. We're in the market for some off-road bikes, three of them, in good condition. You look like you have the parts and I'm guessing you might have a lead on some complete machines."

The seller looked Dawn over. "Huh. I've got bikes. You ladies want to join me out back? Mind your step; it's muddy."

They had two functioning motorcycles and a quad bike with a cargo trailer. The quad bike's engine sputtered when Dawn started it up.

"This isn't an electric engine," Dawn said. "None of them are."

"Nah. Biofuel. It has an adapter for hydrogen, but the unit's corroded. Spent a little too much time in the wet, I'm afraid."

Eve loomed behind them, arms crossed. "It's a piece of junk. They're all junk."

The seller wasn't fazed. "They'll all get you where you want to go. We talking price?"

"No, we're leaving. Come on, Dawn."

Dawn raised a hand for her sister to wait. "Yes, we're talking price."

When Dawn heard how much all three vehicles would cost, she checked the credit chips in her belt.

"Give us a moment." She took Eve aside. "How much do you and Linus have on you?"

"You don't want those bikes. Riding isn't my strong suit. We can get this done another way."

"How much?"

"Pocket change," Eve said.

"That's what I figured. Have Linus bring the car back here." To the seller, Dawn asked, "How do you feel about trade ins?"

Eve was stowing their equipment in the quad bike's cargo trailer. Dawn checked each bike's fuel gauge. Enough for a couple of day's riding, if each vehicle were tuned properly. Both motorcycles were well-used, but clean besides superficial rust. She adjusted the mirrors on one and got comfortable.

"Uh-uh," Eve said. "You're on the quad."

"I'm a better rider than you, remember?"

"And I'm not having you leave us behind. Off. Now."

Dawn dismounted and stood next to Linus.

He had his arms folded. "You sold my car."

Eve was having trouble closing the trailer's lid. "We needed the cash."

"What if we run into weather? We don't have shelters. We're going to get skinned alive by the next storm."

"So we get sand blasted. Stop whining."

"Not whining. Just pointing out a tactical mistake and a possible oversight."

"Put it in your report. And then you know where to file it."

Linus made a face before looking at the compact that was currently being disassembled by a couple of scrappers employed by the parts seller.

"There's something prophetic about this. So this brother of yours—when we learn he passed on to the great light in the sky—can we go back to civilization?"

Dawn wasn't sure who he was talking to, but Eve appeared to be ignoring him. "We don't know if he's alive or dead."

"So *you're* the idealist between the two of you. So what facts do we need to collect before we reach a conclusion?"

"I don't think we can chance a return to town soon. The Black Bird looked like it was only Verna Cho's watering hole, so that's on the back burner. Five bodies, not six, means we need more information on what we're missing. So we head to the outpost while the heat cools down here. We learn what we can and go from there."

"All right. And when there's nothing to learn? Look, I'm all for a madcap revenge trip with friends, but we need mission parameters. Right, boss?"

Eve finally got the lid shut. She shouldered her duffle bag and went to a bike. "Linus, you take the blue one."

"Blue? Is that what color that front fender used to be? Can't tell from the delaminated fiberglass."

"Get your butt on that seat."

Linus went to the second motorcycle. It was a shorter bike than Eve's, but Linus managed and, after some adjustments, kick started the engine.

Dawn sat on the quad bike. The seat had lost most of its cushioning and the springs and shocks felt soft. She doubted her plan. Rough terrain would still pose a challenge, with two inexperienced riders and three bikes in less-than-stellar condition.

She tapped a spare fuel can attached to the rear. Half-full, and she wouldn't want to trust it wasn't mostly dirty water.

Eve gave her own bike a quick inspection. "You ready?"

Dawn pulled up her hood. "The sooner we go, the better."

While the Reilly-Bigg execs might spot and flag the three of them, Dawn doubted they'd mount a hunt far away from town. It would take time to summon their private security from one of their corporate properties.

And the local police? They were on the lookout for the compact car. It would be in pieces in another hour. Deputy Sanjay and his department would record the incident, but considering the circumstances, would want the situation to go away. The clash at the bar would be chalked up to a hostile encounter with rival corporate operatives and swept under a rug. Anything more might dissuade future payouts.

She wasn't sure where her optimism was coming from, but didn't want to think about Linus' questions.

If Pascal was gone, then what? A knee-jerk revenge quest against whatever Commonwealth Services mid-level manager handled the cover-up?

No, she decided. She'd mourn later after leaving New Pacific. Let Eve handle their mother. Have things go back to how they were, with the Moriti family existing apart, with nothing to bring them back together again.

One scrapper was under the hood of the compact and going to town with a reciprocating saw. A shower of sparks cascaded to the ground. A second man was bringing around a wheeled engine hoist.

"You know where we're going if we're avoiding roads?" Eve asked.

"Yes, I do."

Dawn started the engine and led the way.

Chapter Fourteen

The dark pool of water carried a silver sheen. A metallic glaze clung to the rocky mud. Nothing but the tiniest plants grew within a meter of the placid lake, with the closest poplar trees bare of leaves and long dead.

A sign on a metal post bore a skull and crossbones framed in red.

Linus had pulled up at the edge of a paved outcropping near a dry concrete spillway. "This is the reservoir. Drink in the sight, ladies."

Out of range of the Salina Crossroads networks. Dawn had no way to learn more about the reservoir, but it wasn't the only failed reclamation project inside the Commonwealth's territory. The town directory had omitted it.

They had been riding north along a dirt road for a couple of hours. Dawn's neck and shoulders ached, and the shoddy seat was doing nothing for her backside. Her lavender jacket was spattered with mud.

She pointed at the taller hills to the northwest. "That's where we need to go. Station's up there. Might be good to set up camp somewhere before we get there and we take one bike to go scout it."

"Why not all three of us?" Eve asked.

"My quad's too loud, and I want to make sure we don't trip any sensors. I'm guessing you won't let me go on my own."

"You guessed right."

They found a flat stretch of ground near a grove of yellowing willows. The trees grew around a small stream flowing downhill towards the reservoir. The silvery color was gone from the water here.

Linus was off his bike and rolling his head as he stretched. "Don't suppose we traded for fresh rations while we were surrendering my car to those savages? I'm starving."

Eve remained mounted and motioned for Dawn. "Let's go."

"We'll get there quicker with two bikes."

Her sister's jaw tightened. Dawn switched off the quad bike and got on the seat behind Eve. Eve and Linus exchanged a nod before she gunned it. Dawn clung tight as the tires spat dirt and they raced away from the grove.

Linus waved. "I'll be here, taking in the sights!"

No chit-chat over the next hour as they made their own trail over grassy earth and hard rock. The bike engine was a low rumble as they rolled through the weeds. More than once, they flushed a rabbit or quail from the scrub. A vulture circled overhead. While dark clouds loomed, the air was still and oddly humid.

Dawn patted her sister's shoulder. Pointed to a road marker below them. A clear lane wound up between two hills. Eve stopped and produced a monocular.

"Anything?" Dawn asked.

"We take that ridge to the right, we wind up intersecting the road."

They took it slow as the slope grew steep to either side of them, with crumbling shale threatening to slip out from beneath the bike at several points. After needing to turn around at a few precarious drop offs, they found their way to the top of the ravine above the road.

Eve let the bike idle. "It'll be tricky going forward."

A small tower stood on a rocky face ahead of them. Antennae, an anemometer, and other devices were bolted on the metal structure. A path ran down towards the roadway.

Dawn pointed it out. "Can you manage that, or do we go on foot?"

They rode slowly and skidded down an incline to the stone outcropping before coming to a halt. The station stood at the end of the road some three hundred meters to the north, tucked in between several oak trees. A concrete structure, round on one side and rectangular at the other, with a bastion-like center topped with its own array of sensors.

A fence ran along the station's perimeter. The gate stood open and an armored vehicle was parked out front.

The Salina Crossroads cops were here, Dawn thought, but the vehicle was painted black.

"Can you spot a logo?"

Eve glassed the outpost. "Yeah. That's Reilly-Bigg Corp."

"Stopping by a Commonwealth outpost for a friendly visit, or are they hunting us?"

Her sister kept looking. "Maybe neither. Beast of a machine. Doubt it got word about us, and they couldn't have beaten us here. It's like a Red Banner tank. Even the Commonwealth doesn't bother with armor like that. And unlike the sheriff department runner we saw in Salina, they've got a mini-gun up top. Didn't think anyone was seeing action up here."

"Maybe they're just hoping to scare the locals they can't bribe."

"Hmm."

Dawn watched for motion. Didn't spot anyone out front, so they weren't expecting trouble. "Two choices. We either see if they leave or go in and find out what they're doing. Be good to do that before it gets dark."

"I want to know what they're up to."

"Me too. So we go in. And by we, I mean me."

Dawn ran her suite of software continuously as she closed in on the station. She paused at a slope near the south fence line. Her drones were already on the property and had mapped out the exterior of the building. Every nook, every window, every sensor.

The outpost had no security to speak of save for a camera at the front door. A drone confirmed the camera had no power. The perimeter fence wasn't electrified. The array of sensors was for weather, air particles, and other readings, but nothing to prevent someone from sneaking up on the place.

And why would they?

The base housed a crew of low-level technicians. Pascal had been one member of a team who did what an automated system could do cheaper and better. Dawn doubted the place had much worth stealing.

She sent in the drones to find entry. Minutes later, they pinged their success and were crawling in via a ventilation duct, a plumbing vent pipe, and a loose section of flashing. All three were inside, with her fourth approaching the front door.

The rear hatch to the armored car swung open. A guard dressed in plastic armor and carrying a needle rifle slid out. With the drone's mic, she heard a piercing voice over his helmet speaker.

"If you're not back at your post in five seconds, I'm going to peel the skin from your feet and make you walk home."

The Reilly-Bigg soldier stumbled and nearly squashed Dawn's drone as he ran to the doorway. He turned, adjusted his helmet, and stood at attention. Her bug was a half meter from him. The door to the station stood propped open with a rock.

Dawn kept the drone in place as footsteps approached from inside. A second Reilly-Bigg soldier with no helmet pushed through the door. Taller, lean, with a white buzz cut.

He produced a stim stick and puffed a plume of vapor. "Have a good nap?"

"Wasn't sleeping," the first guard said. "Just lying down. You know my back hurts."

"Stupid, man. You know Cap's in a mood and you're copping Z's."

"Not copping anything. I was reclining but still at my post. There's nothing here. There's nothing happening. No one's going to do anything that requires me to stand at this door with my rifle."

"Don't let Cap catch you again. Otherwise, I'll be the one cutting."

The white-haired soldier snapped closed his stim stick and went back inside.

The guard took a moment to sling his rifle before removing his helmet. Young, plump, with a few days' of fuzz on his chin. He was muttering to himself as he adjusted his helmet strap.

Were these men squatting here?

Dawn sent the drone inside. Two of her other machines were prowling the ceiling while the one that had gone down the sewer vent was listening. Unless someone was hiding or being quiet, she counted five soldiers in total inside, plus the officer who had threatened the sentry.

The station was laid out in two main sections. The round room was a common work area with desks and terminals. The few side rooms appeared to be a large office, storage, and homes to additional signal receiving gear set up as if it were being tested. The second section of the building was a dorm with bedrooms, laundry, a rec room, and a kitchen with a dining area. A central hallway serviced both halves.

She found the officer in the round room. Wiry, of slight built, with captain's pips on the collar of his olive uniform.

He and another soldier had a com array set up that didn't appear to be part of the base's equipment. The soldier typed as the captain paced. The rest of the squad was conducting a search, removing vent panels and tossing the place with no apparent concern for keeping things neat.

Dawn used the drones to check for burner and bullet holes or traces of blood. After ten minutes, the search came up negative. She wanted to do a more thorough investigation and get into the basement, but monitoring the soldiers was her top priority.

"Report," Eve called over the earpiece.

"Seven total, including the door guard. No sign of any foul play."

"Reilly-Bigg here for a cordial wellness check on behalf of the Commonwealth?"

"They're tossing the place. Sit tight. I'm watching and listening. I...hold on."

"What's up?"

"They're leaving."

The soldiers in the residential wing put their screwdrivers in a tool chest and headed towards the front exit. The captain had stopped moving and was with the last soldier at the com array and reading over his shoulder.

"Log out and pack it up," the captain said.

The white-haired soldier barked, "Don't make Captain Fields repeat himself."

They joined the others in the entry hall. Besides the toolbox, they had a couple of caddies of cleaning products, a large hand sprayer, and a shop vac.

"What's happening?" Eve asked.

Dawn shared a screen shot from the closest bug. The outside sentry held the door open as the squad packed their gear into the rear of the armored runner. She propped herself up on the stone ledge to better see.

Muffled breathing on Eve's microphone. "I'll get the bike ready so we can follow."

"Too loud. Wait."

Captain Fields was the first to get into the runner as his troops finished packing. Yawning, the white-haired soldier slammed the back door. The com gear hadn't been loaded. The soldier in the main office was still powering down his setup.

Dawn piloted the nearest bug into one of the cases. A space between the foam and the aluminum siding was a perfect hiding place as the soldier packed the radio.

Outside, a driver started up the vehicle's engine.

"Dawn, if we're going to follow, I need to get the bike off this ridge."

"Let them go. I've got a tracer on them."

"They'll find it."

"It's a risk I'm willing to take. I want to look around the base. That's why we're here."

After exiting the building, the tech with the com gear hid the equipment inside a side cargo hatch. The sentry was the last to leave, closing the door and check it once before joining the others. The engine revved a few times before the vehicle made a three-point turn. It rumbled down the road, away from the outpost.

Her bug's signal strength weakened. A moment later, her software pinged a last message. *Signal lost.*

She checked the other three. A visual and audio scan confirmed no soldiers had been left behind unless someone was hiding. The basement remained a mystery, but Dawn felt confident there was no one home.

An infrared pulse lit up the inside of the facility.

The Reilly-Bigg goons had set the alarm.

Dawn didn't have network access or the tools to disarm it, but she could deactivate the system. If the place was on a network, it would send a signal that someone had tampered with the alarm. The signal tower would surely relay the message. But who was listening?

She slid down the slope and hurried towards the station. "Eve, you still on overwatch?"

"Yeah. They're out of sight. Hope your bug is working. Those are the people we need to talk to."

Dawn tried to keep her voice calm. Her drone was disconnected and lost unless they could find the Reilly-Bigg squad again. If they weren't local, they'd slip away.

"We'll deal with them later. Keep an eye open in case there are any more surprises."

She easily jumped the fence. The front door lock gave way to her pick. A chime sounded from the alarm panel. Her drone zapped it with a pulse. Dawn hurried over, popped the panel off, and connected a spoofing device that would let the system know that the door hadn't been opened and the motion sensors were seeing a rat or mouse instead of a person moving about the outpost.

She listened, breathed, and imagine the station as it had been.

The crew had been placed here to study the weather. No simple task when the wind might contain radioactive microparticles or bacteria that could consume flesh.

Her soft footsteps vanished in the silence as she headed towards the round room. Motion sensors triggered the lights. The air smelled of bleach. The workstations and mainframe had all been gutted, their memory chips gone.

She checked the station's radio. It wouldn't turn on. The front panel hung ajar. The interior was scorched and melted.

Stealing components, she could understand. Radio parts might be salvaged or sold. But this was deliberate destruction.

"Report," Eve called.

"Nothing so far. Let me work; I know what I'm doing."

"Either tell me what you see, or I'm coming in there myself."

"All right, all right. Someone didn't want the radio or computers to ever work again. I'm checking the basement, then the dorms."

The stairs took her to an underground space housing the water cistern, power plant, and sewage treatment. All in working order, from what she could see.

In an alcove behind the water purifier, she found a seat cushion, some food wrappers, and empty bottles of beer. A lone mahjong tile lay under a piece of rubbish. A door led to more storage, another to an incinerator. The storage appeared to be furniture and old equipment, the room appearing untouched. The incinerator hatch was warm.

Inside was ash.

Too small to burn a body? Depended on the size of the pieces. But such butchery would take time and leave a mess. Besides the round room and the wrecked computer and radio, the place didn't appear to have been the site of a massacre.

She headed upstairs. The dorms were messy, with closets open, dresser drawers pulled out, and mattresses upended. No clothes, she realized. No personal effects, no toiletries in the bathrooms, no duffel bags or luggage. Like a corporate training dorm between semesters.

Here the bleach smell was stronger, burning Dawn's sinuses.

Were the Reilly-Bigg soldiers trying to erase the base crew, or had someone come here before them?

More questions than answers.

In a side room were washing machines. A row of shelves held soap, spray bottles with cleaning products, sponges, scrub brushes, an electric lantern, rags, metal polish, and spare light bulbs.

Unlike the rest of the place, it appeared to be in good order and unsearched.

She checked the machines. A cluster of laundry waited in one. An embroidered name on a uniform shirt read Greer. Nathan Greer, one of the base's team members. The clammy wad of clothes yielded nothing else.

Her remaining drones found her and she collected them. She took a step back to consider the laundry room and was about to leave. Paused.

All the cleaning products on the shelf were facing forward, the labels lined up side-to-side. Boxes, the spray bottles, the other containers, all perfectly faced as if waiting for purchase in a New Pacific supermarket. Equally spaced apart, too, with a little finger's breadth to the front of the shelf.

Pascal would do this at home. The kitchen would be immaculate, and woe be it if Dawn put a can or box away crooked, because he would tell her.

"It's not right," he would say before fixing it.

When he was younger, he might throw a tantrum if anyone, even their mother, would enter his room and move any of his tiny model cars or planes out of line where they stood in order of the colors of the rainbow.

Could there be another neat freak like him here, or had a soldier been extra diligent in tidying up after having tossed the place? Possibilities, but she doubted it.

Pascal had been here. He existed.

Whatever had happened to him, they hadn't erased him completely.

Chapter Fifteen

"You're going to get us killed."

Dawn's fingers dug into Eve's shoulders as they rode.

Eve wouldn't let up on the throttle as they barreled down the road that serviced the outpost. "And you didn't say your stupid bug had such a short signal range."

"I told you we'll pick it up again. There are only a few directions they could have gone and they won't be driving fast over this terrain. Slow down!"

If it wasn't for the com set, her words would be lost to the whine of the engine. They hit a switchback and nearly careened into a stone wall. Eve skidded hard, planting a heel down before gunning it. Gravel spat behind them as the bike gained traction and they were once again racing downhill.

"You know we can't confront them," Dawn said. "We need to know what happened first. It means you being patient, not charging at them like a psycho."

"What else is there? They were cleaning up after killing everyone. The rest is just details."

"If they killed everyone, then it didn't happen at the base. Five bodies came home, not six."

"I can do the math. But I'm not new to this. It means there wasn't enough of them to scrape up. He's gone."

"We don't know that. You wanted me to help you. That means you have to listen. We don't reach that conclusion without more facts. Those soldiers know something. Let me work. Committing suicide by assaulting that armored car isn't going to do anyone any good. If that's what you're doing, then drop me off."

Eve slowed the bike. At first, Dawn thought she was going to kick her off, but they continued to ride at a measured pace. The narrow road ahead curve through a stand of bay trees and along a muddy riverbed where a trickle of water flowed between mossy boulders.

Dust rose a few hundred meters ahead of them. The armored runner. They had caught up. Dawn reacquired her bug's signal. Too loud to hear anything without analyzing the sounds, but that would change once the corporate goons made it to where they were going.

Assuming they weren't heading back to New Pacific. Reilly-Bigg headquarters, like most large company nerve centers, were hardened to simple espionage like Dawn's insect drone. If that were the case, they'd need to come up with a new plan.

The runner was taking them back to Salina Crossroads. Eve followed. Neither mentioned going back for Linus. Dawn grudgingly conceded that her sister knew how to shadow. They kept the runner just out of sight, hanging back at any rise or corner to avoid detection. There was no knowing what kind of software the Reilly-Bigg vehicle might have, but any targeting system would spot them if they were careless.

Dawn's drone pinged. They were about to descend into a gully and she realized they were catching up. "They're slowing down."

Eve stopped. They waited until they caught sight of the runner heading off-road. Once it was out of sight, she gunned it.

The track ahead was barely a road, washed out in sections with deep channels. Their quarry was up ahead. Oleander grew tall and scraped at the runner as it drove past. They were driving towards an old farm. A dilapidated windmill marked the corner of a feral pasture thick with grasses and creeper vines. Poison oak and blackberry bushes choked the irrigation channels. A farmhouse with a collapsed roof occupied the center of a wide lot. Beyond it stood a barn.

The armored runner drove around the back of the house. Eve pulled across a field of dandelions and parked beneath an oak tree. They had excellent cover, with a decent view of the front of the farm. No other roads out unless the runner was going to plow through the fields.

"They've stopped," Dawn said.

Eve was off the bike with her monoscope held to her eye. "What is this place?"

"Halfway between Salina and the outpost. Good base of operations."

"Means whatever they're doing, they're not done."

Dawn crouched and studied the farm in search of visible security. The drone's ping placed the armored runner in front of the barn. The structure appeared intact. Adequate shelter.

Her next move? Unless the Reilly-Bigg captain was operating independently, a rogue agent, he must log his activities. Waiting for the goons to discuss their mission near her drone would be a waste of time. She'd need to go in and find the information.

The evening clouds remained thick overhead but it wouldn't be dark for a few more hours. What if the farm was more than just their HQ? Her stomach churned at the thought it might be part of a crime scene. Dismissed the dark thoughts clouding her head. Guessing and worrying would only distract her.

Her software analyzed the scene. No surveillance. Counterintuitively, it might be better to go in while it was still light, as the troopers no doubt had thermal vision in their helmets and would rely on it more once the sun was down.

The drone in the equipment case couldn't get out. She sent in the other three. It took them almost twenty minutes to make it to the farmhouse. She sent one up the brick chimney for a higher vantage point, while the other two went to the nearest corner.

As she had guessed, the runner was parked at the front of the barn alongside a smaller buggy, likewise equipped with large tires and an independent suspension for off-road driving. Two of the goons were outside, one on a crate and the other on a collapsible chair. They had a cooler between them and were eating from ration pouches.

An outside shower was set up around one side of the barn. A teapot simmered on a camp stove. They had a toilet out in the open with a bush offering little in the way of privacy. She sent a drone inside through a knothole to discover cots placed in the stalls.

The white-haired grunt lay on his cot and listened to music on his headphones. A second soldier slept while another pair were playing chess. The captain was at the furthest stall, typing away.

A quick check confirmed no network signals. Whatever report he was composing would be filed and transferred later.

She saw an opportunity. Using one of her bugs, she might download everything from his computer.

Motion from the back of the barn. Through a rear door, a mechanical dog trotted into view. Its head was an array of sensory equipment. Before she could react, it pounced on the drone.

Dawn powered her drone off and watched through the eyes of the other two at the farmhouse.

The dog straddled the bug and stared down at it. Hadn't destroyed it.

The white-haired soldier hopped up from his cot and hurried over. "What have you got there?"

Did he know what he was looking at? To a casual observer, the drone was a small black beetle. He leaned closer as the dog continued to fix its attention on Dawn's little spy.

"Get ready to leave," Dawn whispered to Eve.

"What's wrong?"

Before she could answer, the soldier stepped on the drone. He stared down at its remains for a moment.

"All right," he said to the dog, "back to work."

He returned to his bunk and tapped his headphones before getting comfortable. The dog resumed its patrol and loped outside. Dawn powered down the other two and waited.

"A complication. They have a dog with sensors. They got one of my bugs."

"So we go in and do this in person."

"I'm not ready to take on all of them just yet if we don't have to. We watch and wait from here."

"Doing nothing isn't a solution," Eve grumbled before settling down with her back to a tree.

Fifteen minutes later, the dog appeared at the front of the house and ambled along through the weeds before vanishing near a row of wild sunflowers. Dawn powered on the drone on top of the farmhouse chimney long enough to glimpse what the soldiers were up to.

The captain and two of his flunkies were climbing into the buggy.

She recalled her two drones and got Eve's attention. Signaled it was time to leave. Her tiny bots made it back without the sentry dog noticing.

They kept low as the buggy headed out past their position and down the hill. Eve didn't wait long before following. She had checked her sidearm before getting underway and hadn't said a word, but Dawn worried she might try something.

Dawn tapped her sister's shoulder. "He was typing earlier. He might have his computer and its data with him. If he's dead, there's a chance it's encrypted and we learn nothing. Let's see where he's going."

Eve kept quiet, giving no sign she had heard.

A little after sunset and they were driving through the intersection where the accident allegedly occurred. If Dawn hadn't been paying attention earlier and had a visual map of the spot, it could be one of a hundred junctions in the gray and beige hills.

The buggy had its high beams on and was easy to follow. Eve kept the motorcycle lights off. The dark road ahead of them had unmarked turns. Dawn had to trust her sister's enhanced eyes were seeing enough so they didn't plunge off an embankment.

On the way towards Salina Crossroads, the buggy took a detour. Soon they were driving towards a well-lit pair of open gates. The buggy drove through without pause.

No guards.

Odd.

Dozens of massive greenhouses stood in rows beyond a high chain fence.

Eve slowed the motorcycle as they approached the entrance to the farming compound. Dawn zoomed in with her eye.

Twangy music blared. A plaza with a fountain lay ahead, with dozens of farm vehicles parked haphazardly. Bright colored lights illuminated the evening air, along with paper lanterns and a disco ball twirling inside what appeared to be a warehouse. A small crowd mingled outside, with more visible through the warehouse's rolling doors.

The buggy pulled around the fountain and stopped. Captain Fields was out of his seat, followed closely by his two men. They headed into the barn.

No one challenged Eve and Dawn as they rolled into the plaza. Eve backed the bike up against the base of a porte-cochere support column.

A quad bike with three passengers precariously balanced on the back and handlebars puttered in past them, and a tractor followed. The partygoers were dressed in pressed and collared shirts, long skirts, boots, and hats.

Dawn smoothed down her hair and applied lip gloss. Checked herself in a pocket mirror.

Eve scoffed. "I'm sorry we didn't have time for you to freshen up."

"Give yourself a sniff before we go in."

"None of these clodhoppers mind a rind on a girl."

"We're trying to blend in."

"You're the one who looks like she's had a manicure in the past week. Follow my lead."

Before Dawn could stop her, Eve strode towards the front door to the warehouse. The guitar ditty ended. A heavy bass beat kicked in, joined by an electric violin playing a bouncing melody. The music pulsed from a stack of speakers in front of a DJ's booth. Twirling lights were a kaleidoscope of seizure-inducing colors and shapes beaming from a projector. A three-dimensional orange dragon gyrated above the dancing.

The captain was meeting with two familiar-looking Reilly-Bigg suits at a standing table in the corner near a makeshift bar. His two soldiers had wasted no time in procuring drinks and were surveying the crowd.

Leering, more like it.

One of them was the white-haired soldier who had crushed the drone.

Dawn seized Eve's arm. "Trouble. It's a couple of the guys from earlier. We can't get spotted."

"No one's looking for us. We tried it before your way. Let me try it mine."

Eve cut through the revelers and somehow snatched a mug of beer from someone. She headed for the bar. Dawn hung back and tried to look for cameras, or security, or any sign anyone was watching, recording, or taking notice of them.

Between the blinking lights and the noise, it was hard to concentrate. She wanted to retreat. Give her brain a chance to regroup. Started counting brass buttons, but she dismissed the comforting image. Focused.

A few of the locals (or were they all Reilly-Bigg employees?) gave her an appraising look. She managed a tight smile as she brushed past them.

The DJ wore headphones and dark glasses and appeared to be manipulating the dragon hologram. The beast shimmered and was now red. It breathed flames onto the dancers before shifting to yellow and flying in a circle. It left a contrail of white blossoms in its wake.

She examined the setup. Nothing like the clubs in River City. Makeshift rig, everything manual, and the DJ didn't appear to have implants.

"Got a request?" the DJ shouted.

"Nah. Wouldn't know what to ask for. I'm new here. My family thinks all we do is farm all day and go to bed early. You record the party?"

"Not allowed. Sorry."

He hit a button on his system and the violin medley faded, giving rise to a Mandarin power ballad. The dragon was blue now and coasting slowly in circles. Powdery stars drizzled from its claws. About half the dancers moved off the floor, leaving only a few to slow dance with their partners.

"How often do you have these?" Dawn asked.

"Every Friday, sometimes on the weekends, depending on if the place is available. Manager likes it. It keeps us away from town."

"Yeah, I got the lecture. But the town looks pretty sleepy to me. What's so bad about it?"

"You really are new. Uptight cops, some farmers who don't like us buying out their neighbors. You know."

"Yeah, I guess."

A couple of younger women gathered next to Dawn. One brought the DJ a beer.

"Hey, what's your name?" the DJ called, but Dawn slipped away and headed towards the edge of the dance floor.

At the bar, Eve had joined the two soldiers. They had shots in front of them. As one, they slammed them down. The bartender poured refills. Her sister had a roar of a laugh that set Dawn's teeth on edge.

Eve was always the loudest, laughing at everything while watching sims, and incapable of completing the simplest task without slamming doors, banging pots, or clattering dishes. She even walked loud. Before going out for school, her incessant clomp-clomp-clomps would be jarring if Dawn was home and hoping for a quiet moment of study before facing the day.

Pascal had never minded. Their mother? Oblivious or high. Dawn called Eve the queen of clogs.

A soil smell permeated the warehouse. Dirt, bits of straw, and bits of plant detritus littered the floor near the corners.

Lax security here, and why not? It was a private farm. The Reilly-Bigg cops were there to keep their workers safe, but they entertained outside guests and perhaps employed outside workers. This was no top-secret research facility. They grew food. And while Dawn guessed venturing further into the property would result in a checkpoint or scrutiny, nothing she saw spoke to why the corporation would be involved in whatever had happened at the outpost.

She wasn't the only one away from the dance floor. A few couples had taken to the darker recesses. No one appeared to notice her. Ample opportunity to steal an ID card, but she didn't want to be distracted.

At the corner table, the captain and the two execs all had their screens out and spoke in hushed tones.

Too much noise to eavesdrop. With the music and noise, it would take some time to sift through the audio to understand what was being said. A drone would need to be on them to hear, and she didn't want to risk another getting crushed.

She needed to get closer. As she approached the bar area, a group of partygoers bumped past, nearly knocking her down. No one stopped, not even a mumbled apology.

She clenched her jaw and continued forward. She'd be passing Eve. Her sister was attempting to not make eye contact. Dawn did the same.

Her sister roared. "That's what *I* said! But my lieutenant wanted us there in our greens, clean fingernails, brushed teeth, polished boots. He's never been through a mud storm before. It might have well been raining shit on us the way we looked after ten minutes." Another roar. A double slap on both men's back, more shots. "So much for his dress review. But yeah, if you boys were down south in the last year, it's gotten better. Quiet, even. We might even be doing some good with the Keepers."

A toast, and they drank.

Was this her laconic sibling?

Dawn tuned her out and found a place at the wall near a server's station. The party had a couple of people acting as servers, bringing drinks to the few tables and alcoves set with benches. Most were occupied by men and women in taupe slacks and loosened white shirts and blouses. A few workers, too, but these didn't have much dirt under their nails or scuffs on their knees. They, too, wore loafers or pumps.

Her lavender jacket and pants didn't match either group. Anyone watching would see she wasn't fitting in. She hoped the shadows would protect her. As she feigned distraction and consulted her phone, the dragon swooped towards the bar. It bowed its head in Dawn's direction and blew purple heart rings over her. She shielded her eyes from the sparkling display of laser hologram light.

The DJ waved.

Dawn offered a restrained smile and a toss of her hand.

The dragon swooped away.

While Captain Fields was still occupied with his device, the two execs were staring. One tapped his glasses. It was the bald man with the visible mods. Zoomed in, he'd get a look at her face. A match would follow.

As she pushed past a server, both soldiers next to Eve perked up. They looked in Dawn's direction. Eve was trying to get their attention, but one of them pulled away from her. She caught him. A sharp "oof", and he doubled over. She clamped a meaty hand on the second man and drove his head down onto the bar. He bounced and dropped.

Dawn crouched over them and swiped the com units clipped to their necks. Eve grabbed Dawn and shoved her along as they headed across the dance floor towards the exit.

"Let me guess; time to go," Eve said.

"How'd you know?"

"I heard the call on their coms."

"You didn't have to knock them down. Not subtle."

"They fell. I just helped them along."

They were outside and hurrying towards the bike.

"They'll be after both of us now," Dawn said. "I had it under control. They only spotted *me*."

Eve climbed on and started the engine. "It's all right. I was out of lies and I got what we want."

"What's that?"

"Let me show you."

Chapter Sixteen

The old service station sat on another Reilly-Bigg property neighboring the greenhouse farm where they had found the party.

The local deputies were on the road. Had joined a couple of Reilly-Bigg guards in electric carts in a pursuit. Yet Eve eluded them all during a second retreat from Salina Crossroads. No one was waiting for them on their return an hour later as they rode back to the farm.

They were parked near a row of large plastic water tanks behind a garage.

Dawn stifled a yawn. Late, hungry, and saddle sore. But if the answers to what had happened were here, then they could soon head back to New Pacific and it would be over.

Eve popped a pill.

"How many of those you take a day?"

"Not sure it's your concern."

"It is if you're my overwatch and you're getting shaky."

Eve held up a rock-steady hand. "You're the one yawning."

Dawn tapped her lips. Pointed at the fence across the road. Also Reilly-Bigg property,.

Eve squinted. Whispered, "Sensors? Cameras?"

"Nah. Dog."

"I don't see it."

"Neither do I."

The fence had an external call box near a closed, rolling gate. A single dim light shone from the fence. Beneath it hung two signs.

No Trespassing! Private Property!

Violators will be prosecuted.

and

Beware of Dog!

Eve grunted. "Any bright ideas?"

"This side of their property has a radio signal. It might be where I can tap in and sniff around. So unless you packed dog treats and sleeping pills, I go in and be very quiet."

Her sister patted her sidearm.

"No," Dawn whispered. "Keep your eyes peeled. Be good to know whether the dog is a bot or the real thing. Assuming there's actually a dog in the first place."

She went to the road but ducked into the weeds growing along a ditch when a vehicle approached. It slowed and pulled up to the gate. Captain Field's buggy. Had he been out searching for them, too?

The gate squeaked as it slid on its warped track.

From the shadows and into the headlights, an old hound tottered forward, baying and yowling. The vehicle came to a stop just inside as the gate began to close.

Dawn sprinted across the lane and through the gate, scurrying behind a stripped shell of a sedan with no wheels resting on cinderblocks.

A light in a small trailer popped on. A man in a nightshirt and boots emerged to greet the captain. He called for the dog. The dog continued to bellow, first at the buggy and then in Dawn's direction.

The driver was out of the vehicle. He walked to the back bumper. Squinted as he stared into the darkness where Dawn hid.

Mercifully, the dog changed targets again and was now howling at the driver.

Captain Fields climbed out. "Get this thing on a leash."

The watchman grabbed the hound by the collar. "It's late. Bad enough it's Friday with all the racket on the other side of the compound. Can't this wait until morning?"

The captain went to a panel on a blacked-out metal building and entered a combination. A segmented garage door slid up and the captain went inside.

Dawn's angle wasn't good enough to have seen the number. But she recognized the style of lock. The lock's security system would have a biometric scan. Height, weight, iris, fingerprint—one or all could be enabled and required before entry.

The caretaker brought the dog back to the trailer and chained it to a metal stake.

The driver and the white-haired soldier followed Captain Fields inside. Lights winked on. Dawn kept low and darted for the corner of the door. A glance inside revealed a long truck with a cab for a crew of six. It had rear toolboxes and a heavy-duty trailer hitch.

The tailgate bore the New Pacific Commonwealth logo. It also had small tears in the metal, like claw marks. Or the type of damage a needle rifle might do.

The back window was blown out.

"Cap, do we have to do this now?" the driver asked.

"For the last time, yes. We're not waiting for someone to trip on this. Get the winch."

Dawn retreated behind a forklift. The driver emerged and extended a cable with a hook from a reel on the front of the buggy. He went inside the storehouse. He started the winch and towed the truck out. Then he unhooked the winch, climbed into the truck cab, and started the engine.

She kept low and fought to control her breath even as she tried to see what was happening. The driver maneuvered the truck and made a turn. Then he pulled it further back into the lot towards an open area near piles of gravel and sand. The engine whirred and a metal rattle sounded as if the thing might fall apart at any moment as it lurched forward.

What were they doing?

The driver slid out of the cab and examined the damaged vehicle. A trace of smoke wafted from the front hood.

The white-haired soldier followed with duffel bags. They didn't appear heavy. These he tossed to the ground near the truck while the driver busied himself in the back of the buggy.

The caretaker met Captain Fields. "Could make a few credits on parts. Better than a pile of slag."

"You've been compensated."

Dawn craned her neck. The driver was planting small orbs around the truck. Grenades or explosives? The white-haired soldier brought a second load and threw it down with the first. This received its own orb. They both retreated to the cover of the buggy before the driver produced a remote. He spammed a button with his thumb.

The darkness turned white as phosphorus charges lit up the truck and the pile of belongings.

Reilly-Bigg was covering its tracks and Dawn was helpless to do anything about it.

The captain ordered the two soldiers back into the storehouse. The caretaker shuffled inside the trailer. Chatter as a radio blared.

Dawn blinked away the afterimages of the fire. She hurried past the back of the buggy and tried to make out anything from the supernova glowing in the sandpit. The fire had consumed the duffel bags. The truck was already a glowing shell of steel and melting plastic.

She drew closer. While she wanted to know what Fields might be saying on the radio, the duffel bags looked important. But they were reduced to a puddle of ash.

She merged with the shadows when the driver appeared with another duffel. He was dragging his feet and barely noticed when Dawn pounced.

"What the...?"

Before he could react, she tore the bag from his hand. His eyes went wide and he was about to cry out when she delivered a punch to his throat and snatched his needle rifle off his shoulder. The weapon she flung into the fire.

The dog bayed as she clutched the bag and ran past it towards the gate. It had slid shut.

Thunder boomed from behind her. The captain had emerged and was aiming an oversized pistol. After a tuck and roll behind the rusting sedan, she leaped and swung herself over the fence.

Their motorcycle buzzed. Eve met her on the road. Dawn climbed on and they sped off.

"They burned it," Dawn said.

"I saw. Tell me you found something."

Dawn squeezed the duffel. Soft, yielding. "Clothes, probably."

"The outpost truck could have told us everything. You should have given the word."

"We don't know enough to start murdering people."

"We know plenty. This better have been worth it. Get anything off their radio? No? Now we have nothing but a load of laundry."

Dawn was about to reply when Eve swerved.

Something streaked towards them out of the sky. Three somethings.

Headlights blazed ahead of them. A big runner, and it was driving in the center of the street. Flash and pop as it sent up more projectiles in their direction.

Eve took the bike off-road, bounding across a high berm and driving straight through dense bushes that slapped and scratched at them and nearly brushed Dawn off the seat.

They were buffeted as a missile exploded right in front of them. A wave of pressure smacked Dawn. She gripped her sister.

Eve was yelling, but Dawn couldn't make it out.

A hard brake, and they pivoted, spraying dirt and sand as Eve squeezed the accelerator and took them towards a large shed and a bulldozer. A single light burned above a septic tank.

The runner had stopped at the roadside, no doubt unable to make it past the thick vegetation and broken ground.

Trees lay ahead. Once they got past the shed, they'd have cover. Motion caught Dawn's eye. A third salvo incoming directly above them. The ordnance slammed around them. The shockwave struck like a sledgehammer.

Dawn lost track of what was up or down as she was tossed up and away from the bike and into darkness.

Chapter Seventeen

Dawn fought the numb tingling racing through her limbs. Tasted blood and dust in her mouth. Not enough moisture to spit.

Have to get up. Have to MOVE.

Blinked, but the afterimages of the explosion filled her vision. She couldn't clear her eyes and her ears rang.

Hard earth beneath her. The duffel bag she had taken from the soldier was still in one hand and she pulled it close.

A voice shouting. Eve? No, a man's voice. Hands grabbed her. She pushed at them feebly, but was too weak. She was shoved onto a bike seat.

"Hang on!" Linus shouted in her ear.

"Wh-where's Eve? Linus? Where's my sister?"

He climbed on and punched it. The bike lurched forward. Lights swept around them, slicing through the darkness. They were riding past the outhouse.

An amplified voice barked, "Stop! Stop there or we shoot!"

The shed splintered as they barreled past it and down a slope into an empty irrigation ditch. Walls of earth were on both sides of them as the spotlight and needle rifle fire swept the night above their heads.

"Linus, stop! Where's Eve?"

"They got her."

Dawn nearly lost her seat as they hit a slope. The bike shot up a concrete gutter and jumped a low fence. Landed with a jarring shudder. But Linus kept the bike under control as they found the road.

She looked behind them. The armored car was just off the road, but it was moving. "They'll hit us with more rockets."

"Yeah. Better hope they're out."

Her sense of direction was momentarily lost before she realized Linus was driving them back towards the old service station. They raced past the back gate to the farm. The flames still burned but Dawn couldn't make out if Captain Fields had gotten his crew together to join the pursuit.

"How are you even here?" Dawn asked.

"Eve had me trail you both in case you tried something." When Dawn muttered a curse, he added, "Bet you're glad I did."

"We have to go back for her."

"I know. But that can't happen right now. We're all burned. If they weren't trying hard to get us before, they are now. What are you holding?"

She adjusted the duffel bag. "I need to go through this. They destroyed the outpost's car and all the belongings of the station workers."

Linus shook his head in disgust or disappointment. "Eve's lost and you stole laundry. I'd tell you I've worked worse missions than this, but I'd be lying."

Linus took them through a Salina Crossroads residential area with single homes on small properties. Dawn's head pounded. Her hands nearly slipped from around his shoulders a few times. The ringing in her ears had only gotten worse.

He pulled into a driveway past a dark house. A cottage stood in back, set among a small grove of fruit trees. An illuminated stone pathway led to a front door with a heart wreath. She needed Linus' help to stand. He led her to the door and found a key under the mat. Inside, the cozy abode smelled of baked bread. A loaf of bread and a bottle of wine with two glasses sat on a table, and the bedroom had a four-post bed with a canopy, frilly comforter, and too many pillows.

Dawn resisted the urge to collapse. "What is this place?"

"A family's trying to run a bed-and-breakfast. Found it on the local net while you guys were doing your B and E. Told them there would be three of us. The love seat in the living room is a futon." He guided her to the bed. "This is you."

He turned on a table lamp before helping Dawn with her boots. He gave her a quick inspection.

She bent her arms and rolled her shoulders. "Nothing broken."

"Lucky. Bathroom's yours. I'll wait my turn, but don't use all the hot water. The place also has a cat, FYI. Scones and tea at nine, if we're sticking around for it."

A sign at the door read, "Checkout at Eleven. Enjoy Your Stay."

He vanished into the next room and closed the door.

She peeled off her jacket and tottered to the bathroom. Studied her face in the mirror. Blood crusted her nose and a corner of her mouth. Abrasions and some dirt on her cheeks, but otherwise undamaged. Her jaw clicked as she moved it.

She washed her hands before sniffing the water. It had a sulfur smell. Had worse. She drank, not realizing how parched she was until the cool water ran down her throat. She splashed some on her face and used one of the tiny pink towels to dab herself dry. Then she returned to the bedroom and ate some of the bread. Tiny chocolates on a saucer. Devoured them, and opened the wine bottle and didn't bother with the glass.

The duffel bag waited. She dumped the contents out onto the bed.

While the bag had no name, each item of underwear or t-shirt were initialed V.C.

Verna Cho. The outpost's supervisor and Pascal's boss. But besides t-shirts, bras, and underwear, there was only a pair of cargo pants and five bundles of gray socks. None of Verna's toiletries or anything else personal remained in the bag.

Dawn's chest felt tight as she looked at the clothing. This couldn't be it. Eve lost, their one chance at learning something a bust. The sip of wine in her stomach burned sourly.

The floor creaked opposite the door. "If you're not going to use the bathroom, I'm coming through. You decent?"

"Give me a minute."

She went through each article of clothing before turning the duffel bag inside out. Something white stuck to a seam. She took it. A magnetic keycard with Verna's initials. It bore no other marks. A common design, easily spoofed, not for anything high security.

Dawn used her implant to play back what she had seen inside the outpost. The place had actual key locks on the doors, including the front. The card didn't appear to go to a vehicle. So what was it for?

Linus barged in. He had stripped down to his skivvies. "Snooze, you lose."

He went into the bathroom and grabbed a towel and threw it over the shower curtain rod. Then he started the shower.

Dawn continued to examine the card. Sipped wine. "Close the door."

He obliged. Soon, wisps of steam wafted from under the door, along with the sounds of splashing water.

With the right reader, the card's information could be gleaned. But it might be nothing more than a magnetic code to pop a lock. She tucked the card away before going out into the living room. Linus had brought his belongings inside. She found the key to his motorcycle. Considered the door.

What chance was there that Pascal lived? Low to none. There was nothing else keeping her. No upside to getting caught or killed by a well-armed gang of Reilly-Bigg thugs. A successful investigation would yield little more than a corpse. Or ashes.

Eve could take care of herself.

Dawn flopped on one of two plush chairs against the far wall. Stared at the door. Listened to the sounds of the shower, took a swig, and allowed herself to nod off.

The toilet flushing woke her. She bolted upright from the chair. Morning light pushed in through the dropped blinds. She rose, ignoring the countless aches, and glanced outside. The sun was just coming up. No one in sight, but there was smoke trickling from the main house's chimney. The bottle of wine stood empty next to the futon. The cutting board that had held the bread was also on the floor, the bread gone.

She put the motorcycle key back with Linus' kit.

The bed in the second room appeared slept in.

Linus emerged from the bathroom with his pants on. "You're still here."

"You sound disappointed."

He shrugged. "If you had taken off, I could go find Eve and tell her whatever I want about her brother. He's gone, you know. Those guys weren't messing around."

"You left your key for me to find."

"I guess we're both fools. We need to go rescue her. Most of the equipment is stashed back with the quad bike at the reservoir, so there's that."

"I'm not arguing. If you're done babysitting me and are willing to help, we stand a chance of finding her."

He grinned. "Excellent. Now let's go see what kind of early breakfast we can coax out of our innkeepers. Hate to clock in to work on an empty stomach."

Chapter Eighteen

They traded the bike for the bed-and-breakfast owner's electric car. Linus sealed the deal with a credit chip that covered their night's stay and more, judging by the old man's poorly concealed grin as he accepted the chip.

Rust stains marked the wheels. The vinyl roof had a long gash and the seats smelled of mold.

Dawn wiped the seat before getting in. "You were holding out on me."

"Emergency stash. Never leave base without one."

Something in the engine whirred any time Linus sped up too quickly. It shuddered over every bump and felt like it was going to come apart as they crossed hard ground approaching the old service station. Beyond stood the fence to the farm, a haze hanging in the air where the outpost vehicle had been burned.

"How much did you spend on this thing?" Dawn asked.

"Enough left for a vending machine lunch. At least the air works, right?"

Dawn tried the dash controls for the environment controls but none responded. She felt the tickle of a draft from below the center console.

He slowed to a crawl. "How close do you want to get? They were ready for you last night."

"Up ahead, near those trees."

She found a pair of binoculars in Linus' things. She also found her dart gun and clipped it to her belt.

The high ground was barely a hill, but it provided a vantage point. From there, she could make out the gate and a corner of the storehouse where the outpost vehicle had been hidden. The storehouse had a collection of antennae on the roof, as expected. A runner was parked just inside the compound.

Whether this was the one that had attacked them with rockets, she didn't know.

Two soldiers guarded the road and were stopping traffic. They were checking each vehicle before waving it along.

What she couldn't see was the door to the storehouse or the caretaker's trailer.

"I need to go in."

"Risky. Didn't work out for you last time. If Fields is in there, he's probably sent his report. Is it worth it?"

"I thought you wanted to help Eve."

He showed his palms. "I'm not going to stop you. If those boys are home, we're not going to escape on this rig. But I don't have a better plan."

"Your weapon loaded?"

He tapped a pistol he now wore in a shoulder holster. "And waiting to please."

"A simple yes would be fine."

They got out of the car. He adjusted an earpiece and climbed to the roof of the car with the binoculars. A mic check confirmed their coms worked.

She headed down the slope, pushing through the Scotch broom that choked the ground between their position and the road.

Keeping low meant going slowly, but it was the only way forward. She crawled through the grass, emerging roadside where a dip in the shoulder afforded her a place to surveil.

Like the night before, she detected no security—scratch that. Motion tracker from the top of the Reilly-Bigg runner was active. Her eye provided a topographical map of sensor shadows. Her jacket would help; the sensors would miss her if she didn't move too quickly.

The caretaker's trailer was the best cover. The last of the traffic passed and the soldiers on the road got close to one another to talk.

She strolled across the road and eased herself over the fence. While her landing produced only the slightest crunch, the metal mesh jingled. Listened. Voices from inside the storehouse. Too soft to overhear, but calm.

Captain Fields and his white-haired goon.

No alarms yet.

From inside the caretaker's trailer came the muffled sounds of music. Her implant tuned it out and muted the ambient sounds of the breeze, the grass, and the noise from a car passing on the road. She put her ear to the aluminum wall. Breathing. He was home.

The dog appeared around the corner. It had two milky eyes. It raised its head and its cheeks puffed.

"Good boy."

Its bark was a feeble cough. It whooped a few times before pausing. Dawn remained frozen.

When it whooped again, the caretaker shouted from inside, "Jasper, shut it!"

The dog smacked its lips before turning and plodding off towards the front of the trailer where an oversized stuffed pillow waited. Dawn fell in behind it. The motion sensor had the dog locked in. Dawn guessed she could move in its shadow, at least for the moment.

The flaw in her plan became apparent when the hound continued to totter past its doggy bed towards the armored runner parked in front of the storehouse.

"Hey!" she hissed. Made a kissy sound. "Dog! Jasper!"

When it ignored her, she reached for it and tapped on its backside. The dog spun, nearly fell, and blinked as it once again considered her. Its sharp yowl made her flinch. But she kept still as the dog finally wound down and stared dully at her.

Time to hurry it up.

She sent a bug to scurry past the animal. The motion tracker was accounting for the dog and everyone marked by its AI as a friendly. The drone leaped to a tire, up a fender, and made it to the top of the vehicle. Pulsed a copycat signal. The motion tracker would continue to see everyone it was reading, but the dog and the corporate goons would remain locked in place. It would also ignore anyone new.

She zoomed in on the burned wreckage. No way to know what evidence had gone up in smoke the previous night. Were there bones among the ashes? Doubtlessly. Why else reduce the outpost's car to slag? But there was no time to take samples. She hid in the shadows along the side of the trailer.

Her second and last drone went into the storehouse.

Find Eve. Get out. Mourn their brother later.

Captain Fields and the white-haired soldier were packing up gear and appeared to be preparing to leave. The captain was on his com. "Don't worry; they'll let you through." A pause. The captain paced. "If you had better policing in this town, I wouldn't have to be doing your job. I keep the road by our facility safe. No private property was destroyed. Your citizens should thank us."

He tapped his earpiece. "Idiot." To his grunt, he said, "Henderson, go to the gate. Sheriff's coming."

"Sir, you're scowling."

The captain forced a smile. It looked like he was about to sneeze.

Corporal Henderson hurried out of the storehouse, where he hit a remote and opened the rolling gate. A moment later, a cruiser with a light rack, big tires, and a raised suspension appeared. The doors bore the Salina Crossroads Sheriff Department logo. Chrome rims. Tinted windows. It was the first car Dawn had seen since coming north that didn't have a spot of dirt on it.

The drone in the storehouse explored the far end. A large cage served as a cell. Eve lay within, unconscious on the floor with her wrists zip-tied behind her back. She had abrasions on her cheeks, a split lip, and a swollen face and eye.

The sheriff climbed out of his vehicle, along with the deputy they had encountered at the bar. The sheriff was stocky and might have been muscular in his youth. But now a paunch hung over his belt. His black hair was slicked back and glistened. He wore a weapon belt and a pair of burners.

In the trailer next to her, the caretaker stirred. He grunted, farted, and stepped outside.

Too many targets.

Dawn kept her breathing calm as she imagined every potential outcome. She might hit two or even three of them with her dart gun, but she was outnumbered. Linus remained too far back to offer support with nothing but a handgun. She didn't dare call him closer. While the motion tracker might be fooled, the runner could have a defense system. A flick of a switch by any of the soldiers, and she might be facing more sentry dogs, auto turrets, or more rockets.

The sheriff and deputy went with the captain into the storehouse. Both men strained to haul Eve out of the cage and bring her outside. They shoved her into the back seat of the cruiser.

"You seeing this?" Linus called.

She ignored him. Blinked to engage the drone. The tiny machine scurried to the deputy. It fixed itself on his pant cuff as he slammed the door to the back of the cruiser and got in.

The captain jabbed a finger at the sheriff. "You don't talk to her. No one talks to her. And any word you hear about her accomplices, you find me."

"Captain Fields, you may be the man with the credits. But don't ever tell me my job."

"I wouldn't dream of it. But if you think I can't have you replaced within the week, think again. Any of your deputies will fill your shoes just fine. Is there anything else?"

The sheriff glared for a moment before climbing into the cruiser. He revved the engine a few times before making a multi-point turn and hitting a deep rut near the fence on his way out.

"They're getting away," Linus said. "I'm going to follow."

"Wait," Dawn whispered. "I have a bug on them."

"And what's the range? You're going to lose them."

"No, I'm not. Hang tight."

She couldn't make out his grumbling over the com. If he abandoned her now, she'd be forced to steal a vehicle and risk capture.

The two soldiers on the road returned and gathered bundles of gear. Personal packs, mostly. Both were armed with needle rifles. They placed their gear into the armored runner. Captain Fields approached the caretaker.

"Clean up the mess," Fields said.

The caretaker grunted. "There going to be more nights like last night? Didn't sign up for this."

"You want me to conduct a contract review? Your stock supplies are light, there's missing machinery with no service tags, and judging by the rubbish heap out back, you've had unauthorized guests at a Reilly-Bigg-owned facility. You like your posting out here?"

With eyes downcast, the caretaker shrugged.

"That's what I thought. We'll be out of radio range again, but if you hear or see anything, flag it on our network. I'll be checking back in soon."

"She looked like a soldier. Who were they?"

"No one we need to worry about. And if they are soldiers, you'll want me to find them first."

Captain Fields joined his troopers as they boarded the runner. The motion tracker switched off. Dawn recalled her bug. As it returned to her, the caretaker went to the gate. The runner rolled out onto the road and the caretaker watched them leave. As the gate rolled closed, he was returning to the trailer when Dawn stepped out of the shadows and shot him with a tranq round.

He grabbed the dart and scowled before pitching over. The dog continued to snore.

"Linus? Bring the bike."

"Heading your way."

She went inside the storehouse. A quick search found little of interest. Eve's bike and gear were gone. The trailer next. She breathed shallow as the palpable stench of body odor and spoiled food struck her like a wet glove.

A pot of noodles cooked to a hard glue soaked in the sink. A stack of soiled dishes waited on the counter, along with dirty glasses and mugs with remnants of tea, beer, and what Dawn guessed might be soup. Laundry lay piled in a basket.

She went through the drawers and shelves of a wall cabinet. Junk, mostly. Expired foodstuffs, personal effects, a collection of wood etchings and watercolors, and boxes of old batteries and silicon parts with circuitry.

From outside came the whine of the electric car.

"This guy's still alive," Linus said over the com.

"Don't kill him."

A pocket door slid aside to reveal a toilet, shower, and mirror.

"Dawn, time's wasting."

"Be right out."

She was about to leave when she opened the mirror. Inside the medicine cabinet was a soap dish with the remnants of a soap bar, pill bottles, and a lidless jar filled with trinkets. She rifled through the jar.

Gold or gold-plated rings, chains, bracelets, with a few gemstones set in the various baubles. The rings were likely too small for the man lying in the dirt outside and were in several sizes. Wife, perhaps? She examined one under the light spilling through a ceiling vent. Felt her heart squeeze.

For my true love Race. Always with you.

Not a common enough name to be a coincidence, she was certain. The ring had belonged to Race Saputo, one of the outpost employees.

She exited the trailer and went to the caretaker.

"I need a minute."

Linus was on his haunches, petting the dog with the car parked next to him. "Need a hand?"

"I got this."

She shook the caretaker before cuffing him. He blinked and his lips moved.

"Wake up. The people who died in the truck you burned—you had time to loot the bodies?"

"Wh-what?"

With her device, she brought up a picture of Pascal. "Was he with them? Was he?"

"No bodies. Just belongings."

Linus was up and leaning over her shoulder. "Hey, Dawn? They sent the remains back to the city."

Next, she produced the ring. The caretaker focused on it before his eyes rolled back.

"Did you burn the dead here? Like the man who wore this ring? Answer me!"

"What dose tranq did you hit him with?" Linus asked. "You know that stuff takes hours to wear off. Meanwhile, Eve gets further away."

She dropped the unconscious man and inspected the ring before sliding it into a pocket. "I said I had a drone on the deputy."

"And what range does your tracker have? A klick, maybe two on a good day? They've been gone long enough. They're past that range."

"We know where they're going."

He climbed into the car. "And what if you're wrong? If they're dragging Eve to some shack in the hills to question her about why she's here, we've lost her. Now leave him and get your butt over here."

She hadn't closed the door before they were rolling. If the property had any more clues or evidence, the caretaker would surely destroy it.

Chapter Nineteen

"If you crash, we don't do Eve any favors."

Dawn didn't think Linus had heard her. After a minute, he eased off the accelerator.

He had passed a string of robot trucks, even taking a blind corner around two and needing to swerve onto the gravelly soft shoulder to avoid an oncoming tractor.

They were nearing the Salina Crossroads downtown.

Linus studied the street ahead. "Sheriff station is on the next block. Tell me you have a signal."

She blinked to refresh up the app. If the sheriff or the corporate thugs were being careful, her drone's transmitter would be detected. They'd be walking into a trap. But no signal would mean Linus was right. Dawn had wasted too much time and Eve was gone.

Nothing yet.

Linus slowed the car. "Talk to me. We heading the right direction?"

Dawn raised her device. It synched with her implants and boosted the range.

Not a blip.

"Tell me you have *something*."

They coasted past the sheriff's station. A department motorbike stood out front, but no cruisers.

Dawn turned in her seat and tried to will the sensor to find the signal. "Pull around back."

"That won't make a difference. We need to widen our search if she's not here."

"Do what I tell you, Linus. Go around back or I'm jumping out."

The back of the station had a small lot and a lower level. *Ping.* Faint signal. Did the building have a basement? Enough earth and enough steel could obscure the drone's transmission.

The police cruiser with the raised suspension was parked at a fire exit behind a utility box.

"Probably at least two cops in there," Dawn said. "Three, if their receptionist is in. Let me prep an ID. I can send a drone in upstairs and get a layout. Then we—wait!"

Linus stopped the car behind the cruiser and got out. A camera stared directly at them. He produced an electric lock pick and popped the door open in seconds. Dawn hurried to follow.

No alarm sounded. That didn't mean their presence wasn't flagged by the security system or anyone monitoring the station.

The signal was just up ahead. Deputy Sanjay was halfway in a closet. Brooms, mops, an assortment of boxes, and more junk lay spread out around him. He wrangled with a collapsed wheelchair, trying to stuff it in amongst the clutter inside.

Linus pulled his weapon. Dawn patted his arm and slipped past him. When the deputy turned, she pointed her dart gun at his face. He instantly shrank. "Don't! Whatever you want...just don't!"

A quick search found no weapon on him.

"You're looking for your partner! She's in a cell down in the basement!"

Dawn relieved him of his keys. "Who else is here?"

"No one. Receptionist is sick today."

"Where's the sheriff?"

"On patrol. Looking for you guys."

Linus pulled him from the closet and slammed him against a wall. "And who does the sheriff think we are?"

"Corporate mercenaries. Aren't you?"

"Bring him," Dawn said. "Let's get Eve. We'll continue this discussion downstairs."

Eve was catatonic.

Linus kept tapping her cheeks and sprinkling her with water. She was flat on her back in the center of a cell. The other two cells were un-occupied. The jail had a fresh coat of paint, no scrawl on the walls, intact cots, and functioning sinks and toilets with no sewer aroma.

After patting him down and relieving him of a phone, Dawn placed the deputy in the neighboring cell. "What did you do to her?"

"Hit her with a sedative. That's why I needed the wheelchair. Look, who are you with? We can work something out. We're reasonable and don't want trouble."

"Looking for another payday? Let's talk about what Reilly-Bigg wants first."

"I can't disclose our arrangement. I signed their NDA. Surely you understand; I'm a responsible partner with our corporate allies."

"Surely. But you're a Commonwealth citizen and, I assume, a sworn peace officer. Does the Reilly-Bigg corporation run this town?"

"No. We have a mayor and city council."

"And I assume you actually enforce the law. What do you know about the outpost up on Road 442?"

Deputy Sanjay's jaw tightened. "I can't discuss it."

"No calls up there? Is it even in your patrol area?"

He said nothing.

"Is that where Captain Fields was heading again? Back north? Is he sharing any information about what they're looking for?"

"I can't tell you."

"Then what about the accident with one of their vehicles? That's your business. Multiple fatalities, from our findings. This was reported to the Commonwealth. It's not confidential. What happened?"

"It's in the report."

"I want to hear it from you."

Linus had gotten Eve sitting up near the sink. "Rise and shine, sarge." She remained slumped over with her eyes closed. "I'm going to find a med kit." He vanished up the steps.

They couldn't waste too much time inside the jail. Dawn tried to sound calm.

"You get a lot of traffic accidents like that?"

"Some."

"You can understand why it would be the subject of interest. Lots of expansion, and every corp has a board of directors wanting to know if a community is a safe bet. If this is just a case of a local with connections having one too many and causing a wreck, that's different from a gang of raiders murdering six Commonwealth employees."

"Five," Sanjay corrected.

So he knew the details about the accident.

"Five. Excuse me. You must have seen the vehicle. Your office handled the bodies and sent them back to New Pacific?"

"I told you I can't tell you—"

"Look, we're close to being done here, Deputy Sanjay. You give me enough to put on our report, we ride out of town and you never see us again. What can you tell me about the bodies and the accident scene?"

"That's part of what I signed. The sheriff told me that if anyone comes asking, to remind you of the Commonwealth's fair competition regulations. Reilly-Bigg and whoever you represent are free to do your business within the respected shared boundaries of New Pacific law."

"I've heard enough." Eve said.

She wobbled from her cell. It took a moment as she steadied herself on the bars as she closed in on Dawn and Deputy Sanjay.

"Move, Dawn."

"I've got this. We're talking."

She shoved Dawn hard enough to almost send her sprawling before charging into Sanjay's cell. He scrambled back, but there was nowhere to go. Eve seized him by the uniform shirt and thrust him against the bars. Grabbed his hair and spoke into his ear.

"Five bodies made it back to New Pacific. What happened to the sixth one?"

When he hesitated to answer, she slammed his head.

"There weren't five, only four!"

She leaned on him. His sweating face pressed into the metal bars. "What do you mean, four?"

"It's how many there were! I don't know!"

Dawn attempted to pull her arm back but it was like trying to bend steel. "Eve, stop. This is no good."

The pressure increased. A line of dribble ran from his mouth.

Dawn pressed the dart gun into her ribs. "Don't make me."

From the vents came a series of electric snaps. Burner fire? A sharp *krak-krak* followed. Small arm, not a burner. Then a dull *whump* that shook the ceiling and caused the lights to flicker.

Eve let go of the deputy as she looked up. "He brought the grenades?"

With no one holding him, Sanjay sank and crawled to the corner of the cell.

Linus came charging down the steps and appeared in the doorway with his pistol in his hands. "Sheriff's here!"

Dawn crouched before the deputy. "Hold him off. Eve, get to the stairs."

Her sister didn't argue. She used the cells to support herself as she limped away. Linus fired his weapon two more times, the report echoing throughout the jail.

"Deputy Sanjay, I have one last question before I leave."

He was shaking. His eyes darted between Dawn and Eve.

She showed him the white magnetic key card recovered from Verna Cho's duffel bag. "Do you recognize this?"

Sanjay shook his head. He had barely glanced at it.

"If you can tell me anything, it will make us go away. If not...." Dawn let the sentence dangle as she nodded towards Eve. Eve was holding the door open.

"It could be to anything," he said.

"It belongs to something in the Commonwealth base."

He wiped snot from his nose. "I doubt that. Everything belonging to the Commonwealth has a mark on it. I don't know what it unlocks, but it's probably not New Pacific property."

More muffled burner fire, and Linus shooting back.

She recovered her drone from the deputy and slammed the cell door on her way out.

Chapter Twenty

Eve needed Dawn's help to get to the electric car. She was heavy and slow and threatened to cause them both to fall as they piled in.

Linus sprinted to the vehicle and tossed his pistol into the cup holder. His left hand was curled up against his chest. A raw burner wound, the skin singed. He was missing two fingers.

"Can you drive?" Dawn asked.

He got the car in gear and they were rolling. He spoke through clenched teeth. "Don't suppose there's a first aid kit in here?"

Nothing in the glove box or under or between the seats. "Maybe in back."

"Suck it up," Eve said as she looked through the rear window at the jail. "They'll be on us soon."

"Maybe not so fast. That explosion was his personal car going boom. Get your last look at Salina Crossroads, ladies, because we are out of here!"

Dawn checked the load on her dart gun. "Only four bodies."

Linus swallowed hard and was blinking sweat as he focused on the road. "Yeah, what a twist. So your brother and one of the team are in a hole somewhere. Or there wasn't enough to bag. My condolences. We did our due diligence to family. But they're gone and sticking around is only going to get us all killed. We're outgunned here, sarge. Now we've upset the locals and that sheriff doesn't believe in chitchat."

"That deputy didn't act like there were bodies to be found."

Eve was massaging her legs and flexing her hands. "Just means he's a good liar or the local cops weren't involved in the wet work. But they were being paid off for a reason. So we go back and run at the sheriff."

"We don't have the manpower or ordnance," Linus said. "You can barely walk and my hand needs some attention."

Dawn checked the maps on the town network for alternate routes. Once she cleared a few ads, she found it. "He's right."

"You're willing to throw in the towel?" Eve said.

"No. I want answers just like you. But it's too hot here, and this car isn't going to get us where we need to go. The Reilly-Bigg troopers know the truth about what happened. But first we need to get him to a doctor."

Linus nodded encouragingly. "Your sister makes a lot of sense."

"Your pain implant should have you comfortable," Eve said. "Eyes on the road."

Still, no one followed. Dawn used one of her own breathing exercises to calm her heart. "The sheriff may know something; he may not. The whole town's going to be stirred up now. And Captain Fields and his men will get a warning well before we can catch up with him. We're burned."

"I'm thinking about something less sneaky. Not your forte."

"You think they killed him?"

Eve didn't answer her.

They fell in behind a robot truck, trundling along the eastbound lane. A delivery dog sprinted past. One of the sleeker models that rode on two wheels. Essentially, a motorbike with a cargo box in the center and a whip antenna on its hindquarters. Something about the machine caught Dawn's attention.

They were still in range of the Salina Crossroads network. She blinked and logged on. The town map, the directory, a list of essential and emergency services. Nothing different from before.

The nuisance ad in the center of her vision was for Secure and Fast Data and Shipping. Storage, Encryption, Notary. Best Rates in Salina Crossroads! The center image showed a delivery dog with rocket packs sending it on an arcing trajectory off-planet.

Dawn pulled out the white key card. Marked V.C. for Verna Cho. "Take the next right, and the right turn after that."

"That takes us back towards town," Linus said.

Eve studied her sister. "Do as she says."

The lot to the delivery and storage service was a few blocks down next door to a yard where workers were loading a septic tank onto the back of a truck. A few other businesses occupied the commercial block. No visible police or surveillance.

Linus got them parked in a cul-de-sac beneath the shadow of an elm tree. "How about that first aid kit?"

While Eve rummaged in the back of the car, Dawn headed for the office. An attendant worked behind a desk collating several stacks of multicolored papers. Even with so much in electric form, people needed their hard copies of contracts, wills, trusts, licenses, and financials. One wing of the office was dedicated to private mailboxes. A blue terminal allowed for the sending of voice and data through whatever network the place subscribed to.

Dawn flashed Verna's white card.

The attendant wore a mullet neatly trimmed around his ear, with a long drooping front lock curled down to his eyebrows. "ID?"

"Not on me. Remind me of my box number. Last name Cho."

"Show me identification and you get the box number. House rules, hon."

Dawn maintained a pleasant smile. Flashed her Jill Foster, Commonwealth accountant ID. "I'm investigating Verna and some of the facility staff who died in that horrible accident. You heard about it?"

"Yes. Sounded awful. Sheriff hasn't been big on sharing details."

"He's been cooperating with us and getting help from Reilly-Bigg security. But no one's come for Verna's mail locker?"

"You're the first."

Dawn showed the key again. "Okay, that's a surprise. If you can tell me which box number...."

"You made it clear you're not Verna. I'll need a power of attorney and death certificate, or a warrant. Come back with the sheriff if you need to. I don't know you."

"I'm afraid my investigation doesn't involve the sheriff's department. A conflict of interest. A warrant from a New Pacific judge will take too much time. If you could just open the locker and let me catalogue the contents, that would help me. If it's empty, I save a lot of time and inconvenience. If there's data waiting to be transferred, I'll get that warrant."

The attendant stiffened. Dawn knew what he was going to say before he said it. "I'm sorry. Store policy."

Dawn shot him. The dart stuck in his left pectoral and he collapsed, vanishing behind the counter. She wasted no time in going from box to box, swiping the magnetic card. There were a couple of hundred boxes. Box seventy-three clicked and the LED went green.

"Let me see your hands!" a woman shouted.

With the card still between her fingers, Dawn raised her arms. "He's only asleep. I'm here for what's in this box, and then you don't see me."

When Dawn slowly turned, she saw the woman was holding a shotgun.

"Don't move a muscle or I shoot!"

"There's no need for that." Dawn activated a drone. It ran down her sleeve and dropped to the floor before heading for the woman.

"You don't tell me what I need." The woman tapped an earpiece. "Sheriff. Emergency. Hannah Mizuki at Secure and Fast Delivery."

The drone couldn't block a signal. It was racing up Hannah's legs and crawling to her shoulder. No way to know if the weapon was loaded or not. Hannah appeared to know how to hold the shotgun, and even a novice could murder someone at such a short range with the weapon.

How long before the emergency service system forwarded the woman to the sheriff who was already hunting them?

Dawn fought to sound calm. "I'm going to ask one more time. Let me have what's in this box. The owner's missing or dead. This might be the only clue to what happened to them. Reilly-Bigg is covering up a crime, and I—"

"Stop talking. The sheriff's coming. You can tell him whatever you want."

Dawn clenched her jaw. Nodded. Sent the drone scurrying up Hanna's face. She flinched and swatted at the thing. When the shotgun barrel dipped, Dawn drew her dart gun and fired. Hannah went down with a dart in her thigh.

"What's going on in there?" Eve called.

"It's under control. Bring the car."

Dawn grabbed the contents of the locker. A thumb drive. That was it. No papers, and a small screen inside the box's door read "Information Cache Empty."

Either Verna Cho had sent out whatever she had saved and stored, or there was nothing else besides the tiny drive. She collected the drone on the way out. Jumped into the back of the car. Linus lay unconscious in the front passenger seat.

Eve barely fit behind the steering wheel. She spun tires as she drove over a flower bed on the way out of the cul-de-sac.

"Did you get it?"

Dawn showed Eve the flash drive. "Yeah. Trouble with the owners. The sheriff knows where we are, so we need to get out of town."

"What's on that thing?"

"That's what I'm going to find out."

Chapter Twenty-One

You're not supposed to be reading this.

Dr. Zel said I could write whatever I want, and no one would see it. So if you're reading this, you've stolen it.

Plagues be upon you.

Dawn looked out the window. She hated reading while driving, and the road had gotten bumpy. They were once again heading for the reservoir. Their car's engine was working overtime and was growing louder. But finally it made the top of the grade and the way ahead was smooth enough that she could keep reading.

I named him Eric. The brown rat with the pink nose likes sweet potato. His friends don't come out, but I hear them behind the walls at night.

Eric makes a mess. I tidy up after him. I don't mind.

Verna said not to feed it. It will mean more rats. Saputo said he'd kill it. I told him not to.

"Pascal was keeping a journal," Dawn said. "It's a transcript."

Eve glanced at her in the rearview mirror. "I didn't know he wrote. What was it doing at the delivery dog place in Verna Cho's name?"

"Safe keeping. Or slated for delivery. But according to the memory chip's history, Verna didn't upload it to the service. She was sitting on it for some reason. Looks like three weeks of entries."

"Go to the last one."

Dawn scrolled to the bottom. "'5:45 am. I'm going out to meet Quint. Verna told me not to. Said she didn't think it was safe. But she's asleep, and McGuinn has early watch and never notices when the front door is opened. I'm bringing a present.'"

"Who's Quint?"

"Not anyone at the outpost. Someone who lives nearby, maybe, but we didn't see any settlements."

Eve's fingers drummed on the steering wheel. "Pascal went from not talking at all to talking to everybody."

Linus had his eyes shut and leaned against the passenger side window with his bandaged hand cradled against his chest. "Do you mind?"

He had taken something for the pain they had scrounged from the first aid kit. Eve's drumming stopped.

"The date of the last entry is September 15," Dawn said.

"Same day as the crash."

"Same day everyone got murdered."

"It doesn't mean anything. Could be the Reilly-Bigg goons attacked the place and Pascal and Verna just didn't get collected."

"Yeah."

Dawn's heart was going like a jackrabbit. The journal wasn't the tidy bow on their investigation that would allow them to part ways. It was another loose thread. And what she didn't want to share was what Eve no doubt was already thinking.

He might still be alive.

"I need to read the rest of this. We have to learn who this Quint is. Then we go back to the outpost."

Eve looked at Linus. "Say the word and I give you the quad bike. Shoot you up with the rest of our painkillers. You've ridden with worse. According to the map, there's a village east of Salina. You make it there and find a doctor."

He kept his eyes shut. "Hate to miss out if you decide these guys did your brother. I'm sticking with you."

She nodded and returned her focus to the trail ahead.

Dawn kept reading. She paged backwards at first.

The person named Quint, who Pascal was meeting, lived some place north of the outpost. Pascal shared few details, but a couple of passages caught Dawn's attention.

The solar panels were hard to reach. I had to scramble down through the manzanita. Some of it was poison oak and blackberry bushes. The panels were in perfect condition, and there were more of them than I imagined. The power conduits run to a shack hidden by more bushes. The panels appeared clean of dust and there are signs of recent repairs.

When I went towards the shack, I spotted the roving spider bot. I kept down and watched. Didn't want to be seen or heard. It went to a neighboring meadow where it moved about near some junk and an old foundation. But I saw pipes venting steam and smelled sulfur. Waste heat from what? Sulfur smell might be sewage treatment. All the warning signs of toxic waste and here I was like a stupid person.

But that's where Quint went. I watched for a while before it was time to leave.

I didn't want Verna to be mad.

Quint seems scared. Nerves, Dr. Zel would call it. He looks over his shoulder a lot. There's never anyone there. We met again at the palm trees. He's very interested in my jacket and the silver buttons. He still has the little metal car I gave him and shows it to me as if it was made of gold.

We laughed.

Dawn took in the landscape to let her stomach settle.

Reading about Pascal perceiving things like Quint being scared was something new.

Her brother had never understood it when Dawn had confronted him about going into her room and dismantling her toy spaceship model she had spent two weeks building from scrap printer plastics. Had just stared when she had found her favorite print book, The Velveteen Rabbit, and had scribbled his nonsense in black marker all over its pages. Didn't get it when their mom left the house crying after he had busted every plate in the kitchen cupboard in a full-throat rage fit. Eve had calmed him down during that episode.

Eve's head bobbed and she inhaled sharply, reaffirming her grip on the steering wheel.

"Pull over," Linus said.

"I'm fine. I'll get us there."

"You're juiced out. Either let me or your sister drive. We crash, and we'll be up the creek without a snowball's chance of catching a ride. And if *we* found this road, it's a safe bet the sheriff or Captain Fields will suspect we might have come this way. Can't assume they're not looking."

Eve had Dawn take over driving. Dawn fought her own fatigue as the rough trail ground on across the hills. Finally, the reservoir came into view, and beyond it, the stream with the yellowing willows.

The quad bike and their gear appeared untouched.

While Dawn pulled a tarp over their car, Eve walked shakily to a soft patch of ground, glanced about as if making a decision, and plopped down onto the dirt. In moments, she was breathing heavily.

Linus raised his wounded hand a few centimeters. "I'd help you, but...."

She finished covering their vehicle. "I've got it. Is it bad?"

"Had worse. But then we usually have a medic on hand. All Eve can do is to tell me to pop a pill. You don't have battlefield surgeon on your resume, do you? For real-sie?"

"Not even as an alias. Tell me about what Eve's doing. I've heard about engineered soldiers having modded hormone dumps. Is that what's happening?"

"Every rise has its descent. She's been running hard for days and not eating enough. She'll be fine."

He went to the quad bike trailer. He brought a blanket to Eve and placed it over her before finding his own spot nearby.

Dawn took in their surroundings. No signs of anyone. Their location was as good as any, and she, too, felt ready to collapse.

"How long will she be down?"

"Is this where you make your escape?"

"Cut the crap. I'm not abandoning you. But if she's going to sleep through the evening and into the night, I need to know. And you're in no shape to help."

He winced. "Your sister called me useless even before I lost two fingers."

Taking a break was the last thing she wanted to do. But she forced herself to eat one of the food bars and have some water as she went through their gear. Besides her dart gun, Linus had also kept her fanny pack. She pulled out her carefully stowed goggles. With them on, night became day. She took the rest of the darts and topped off her gun. Then she located a grassy patch beneath a broad willow. Good vantage point. Thought she might doze.

Instead, she opened Pascal's journal.

Everyone looks south. Why did they take the job? I've logged weather data and Verna has taught me how to calibrate the sensors placed in the field data readers.

She says she hates it here. She goes to town to her bar whenever she can. Calls home, even though there's no direct lines up most of the time. The others sometimes go with her. I don't.

I observed a ladybug with broken wings get eaten by ants. When I watched the grass roll as a storm front blew in while we were out by one of the weather boxes, Verna told me to snap out of it.

Mud and weeds, she says. Uses bad language. She complains more than Dawn.

Back at the outpost, Saputo has set out spring-loaded traps. Eric has avoided them so far and even got the peanut butter off one of them. He's smarter than Saputo.

Verna won't let me take a runner out on my own. Says I don't have a license. Took it anyway. She got mad, but that's okay, because I won't tell her what I found. What would she care, anyway?

A grove of palms grew past the base of the last ridge near Data Reader Eight. Hooded Orioles swooped in and out of the fronds and clung to the bark. I watched them for an hour before exploring a massive thicket down in a gulley. Spotted rabbits.

I found solar panels. I thought they were old, but it turns out they're being maintained. If someone lives out here, they don't leave much, because there's no track or trail.

I made a friend. He doesn't like to talk much. Named Quint. I told him I'd be back tomorrow to bring him a present.

On the rise near the reservoir, a vehicle appeared and pulled to a stop.

Dawn zoomed in. Barely enough light to see clearly, but the vehicles had distinct profiles. Salina Crossroads Sheriff Department. A second vehicle pulled up behind it. One of the Reilly-Bigg armored runners.

"Guys?"

Linus grunted and raised his head. Eve remained asleep. Dawn moved to her and forced her to sit up, but she was dead weight.

"Wake up!"

Even with Linus' help, she wasn't responsive and her eyes rolled as they dragged her towards their tarped-over electric car.

"This is no good," Linus said.

"Talk less, move more."

They shoved Eve into the back seat. On the ridge, both vehicles remained in place. The gully campsite was well hidden, but wouldn't be for long. Eve's feet wouldn't stay inside the cab. Linus was trying to pull her in from the opposite door.

Dawn stopped pushing. The route from the reservoir towards the outpost was rough when she and Eve had taken motorcycles. The tiny electric car had a low suspension and had barely managed the drive to the gully. They'd never bring Eve along on the quad bike.

"We have to leave her," she said.

"We didn't bring her this far just to let her be captured again. Get her feet into the car."

"She's not the mission. She'd tell you that."

"And you're not my boss to give me any orders," Linus snapped.

"We can't blow past them to get back to the road. The quad bike's the only way out of here."

"They'll hear it once the engine starts."

"I'm counting on it. They haven't seen us yet. You and I ride off, and they'll chase us and maybe miss her."

"That's a big if." He went to the trailer and produced Eve's rifle case. "We give them something to think about and they might run."

Her implant had an ordnance wiki. It took a half second to know the rifle wouldn't penetrate the Reilly-Bigg vehicle's plating. The two vehicles might carry eight or more deputies and corporate grunts. Once they engaged, they'd soon be surrounded by an enemy holding an elevated position.

Dawn fought to keep her voice calm. "Whatever they're doing, they're motivated to keep us from finding out what happened to the outpost. My brother and Verna Cho found something to the north. It could be nothing. Maybe they got gunned down with the rest of them. But I need to know what happened before Reilly-Bigg finishes their coverup."

"So you do care," Eve said. She coughed as she struggled to sit up.

Linus hurried to help her. "Trouble, boss."

"I heard enough. Dawn's right: this car won't make it out of here off-road. Give me my gun. I'll keep them busy as you guys get away."

"You can barely raise your arms, your pupils are dilated, and I doubt you can see straight."

He helped her up and brought her to the quad bike. When she tried to get up to take the rifle case, he snatched it off the ground and stowed it in the bike trailer.

Eve's eyes hardened. "What are you doing?"

"It'll be cozy, but you two have the best chance of finding your brother. I'm going to take the car and take those boys up there on a tour around our lovely lake."

"Out of the question."

But Eve could do little but watch as Linus headed for the car.

"What's your plan?" Dawn asked him.

"Drive straight at them and make sure I have their attention before running. If they get too close, I'll surrender. Tell them I'm a spy and tell them everything which, to be honest, isn't much. They'll get out of me enough to know you're still out here, but they only saw the one car and might not know we had a backup. Don't crash. And for all that's holy, if you find what you're looking for, pay my bail, assuming they don't, you know...."

Dawn leaned into the car and confirmed his pistol remained in the cupholder. Still loaded.

"They see this, they won't hesitate to gun you down. Not after what you did at the jail."

He got in the car. "Can't make it too easy for them. Besides, if they take me, maybe they'll give me something better than the expired pain-killers your sister hit me with. Hey, sarge?" He shot Eve the middle finger with his good hand before slamming the door.

Dawn climbed on the quad bike. "Eve, can you hang on?"

Her sister nodded stiffly as Dawn started it up. The engine wasn't loud, but if the vehicles on the ridge had audio sensors, they would hear them.

Linus revved his car's electric engine. After a tight U-turn, he raced up the slope.

Dawn put the quad bike in gear and drove off in the opposite direction, sticking to the cover of trees. After twenty seconds, the staccato cracks of echoing rifle fire split the air.

Chapter Twenty-Two

Eve wouldn't stop wriggling on the seat behind her. "Stop this thing now!"

Dawn nearly lost control of the quad bike as they careened through the trees. She didn't dare let go of the handlebars as she squeezed the accelerator as hard as she could.

"We can't."

"He's...they're going to kill him. I need my rifle."

"This isn't the mission."

The admonishment had little effect. Eve kept turning as if to see, but with the branches and gloom, there was no way to know what was happening back at the reservoir.

All too quickly, the sounds of gunfire faded. If the soldiers and police were pursuing them, their vehicles were silent. If they had flying drones, they had a good chance of spotting their infrared signature. Dawn and Eve needed more distance. More trees. More rocks and hills.

But when they hit a hard embankment and nearly went over, Dawn slowed down. Even with her eye implant and goggles, she could barely see the ground well enough to navigate safely.

"We need rest. I'm going to find us a place so we can catch our breath.

Eve was still leaning heavily on her and didn't respond.

They had come that way during their first drive to the outpost, but at night, everything was different. Trees she didn't recognize. A cluster of rocks that hadn't been there before, had it? And past it, a sudden drop-off.

A large group of oak trees appeared promising. She eased the bike into the center of the grove and killed the engine. Eve needed help to make it to the base of the nearest tree. Dawn sagged to the ground next to her and they leaned on each other.

Her sister's breath hitched. Was she sobbing?

Dawn rubbed Eve's hand. "We don't know what happened. Linus will be fine. They won't kill him if they think he knows something."

"It's not that," Eve said. "I'm coming down from a second round of adrenaline. The gunshots trigger it. My doctor never quite got it zeroed in. When I'm tapped out like this, it takes a few hours to get everything balanced."

"Will food help?"

"What do we still have?"

Dawn got up and rummaged through the trailer. Linus' bag had a couple of food bars left. "Chickpea and pine nuts or mango with citrus peel."

"God, neither. But give me both. Water, too."

A quick search confirmed they had no more water. Had she set the bottle down on top of the trailer before their flight? Didn't matter; it was gone.

Eve devoured the first bar, not taking the time to see which one it was. Halfway through the second, she offered Dawn a bite.

Dawn took a few nibbles before giving the rest back. "He's been with your unit for a while."

"Yeah. We all got processed together. Always had my back."

She waited for more but Eve began to breathe deeply and put her head back against the bark. Dawn tried to get comfortable next to her. A bird somewhere in the branches was peeping, a rapid set of irritable trills. After a moment, it was once again silent.

Dawn spent the next few hours straining her ears for signs of anything else heading their way.

***

Smoke rose above the canyon ahead of them. The sun peered above the eastern hills, the sky cloudless. The plume to the north dissipated into a violet haze.

They had been driving for almost two hours, Eve up and alert and impatient as she urged Dawn to go faster. But the terrain hadn't been easy with a motorcycle and the old quad bike wasn't nimble or fast. Detaching the trailer would help, but it would mean leaving behind the rest of the equipment.

The outpost lay shattered. Only one section of the western wall still stood. Where the dorms had been, she recalled numbly. The rest was rubble. Soot drifted through the air. The ruin continued to smolder.

Dawn studied the scene from the ridge. "No drones, no spiders. It's safe if you want to get closer."

"What's the point? It's gone. You already went through everything they left behind. Them coming back to blow the place up tells us enough. They're covering over a crime scene."

Eve was right. Why else level a place after scrubbing it down? Dawn did a quick review of what she had seen inside. A nagging suspicion lingered, like something lodged in her teeth. If the Reilly-Bigg troops had executed the staff, it hadn't happened here. So there was another motive for the destruction.

She put her goggles away. "It can't just be to discourage the Commonwealth from keeping a base. They can throw up another outpost. I think they believe they missed something. Seems risky to do all this because of Pascal's journal."

"Hmm. Means they know Pascal *had* a journal. Means they got someone talking."

Too much speculation, but Dawn kept her doubts to herself. "Pascal found something north of here. That's where I want to go next."

Eve had the rifle case out and had assembled her weapon. She inspected the long arm and sighted down its scope before slinging it across her back.

"No argument?" Dawn prompted.

"If you're asking me what I want, it's to head for their barn while they're out looking for us. Means their forces are split. Then I thin their ranks."

"I'm glad I didn't ask. You're keeping that thing out while we drive?"

"I'm not getting caught flatfooted again."

The fuel gauge on the quad bike didn't work. Dawn checked the tank. The opaque plastic showed a hair under 50% gas left.

She had grit in her mouth and desperately wanted to clean the dust and grime from her face. No water, and no streams or polluted reservoirs in sight. She applied lip balm and found some relief.

Another check of the trailer confirmed what she knew. No more meal bars.

She shut the lid. "We don't know where we're going. North, roughly, but if there were any maps of the data readers and outpost sensors, they didn't survive."

"Daylight's wasting."

"We give it until noon."

They rode.

Her sister didn't speak as they bypassed the canyon and explored the rolling hill country beyond. She'd give out again, Dawn feared. She knew enough about the genetically enhanced super agents to know they ran on calories. No gas meant no energy. Dawn felt her own concentration flag.

Fought to keep her eyes moving. The grass was thin across the smoothest sections of ground and there were tire tracks. Outpost staff traveled this often enough that it was almost a trail.

A small box lay ahead near a lichen-covered rock. The plastic case appeared the size of a beekeeper's hive popular among the settlers around Seraph and New Pacific. But on the opposite side of the rock stood a plastic pole with attached sensors. One of the outpost's data collectors.

She searched it for a plaque or identifier. A faded "2" was stenciled on one side. She opened the lid. The box collected the information wirelessly. No transmitter. A small panel revealed memory chip ports, but no chips.

"Sensor memory has either been removed, or the outpost staff hadn't gotten around to replacing them."

Eve climbed the rock and used the rifle scope to scan the horizon. "Figures. Theft or incompetence."

"Anything?"

"I'd tell you if there was."

Too much grass to see footprints. But a nearby patch of mud had a wide tire mark that might belong to one of the heavy armored runners. Crushed anise and thistles nearby confirmed the vehicle's recent passing. At least within twenty-four hours, Dawn reasoned. But she couldn't tell whether they had been coming or going.

They continued to ride north.

The older tracks split at the base of a wooded hillside, leading roughly northwest and northeast. No sign of the larger vehicle having come this way.

Near noon, and they had found three more of the data readers. All had their memory chips removed. None were number eight.

The rugged hills around them had no signs of human habitation save for a row of old concrete driveways and the remnants of foundations of homes long swept away by disaster, weather, or time. Had they missed a trail? Quite possible. Weeds and grass grew high everywhere.

Dawn's stomach rumbled.

"We're not giving up," Eve said.

"I'm not saying we do. But we're run down and ragged and are only going to make a mistake and get caught if we keep pushing."

Eve didn't reply. She used her scope on the scenery before lowering her rifle. "Greener grass near those trees down there."

They rode down an embankment, half-braking, half-sliding before reaching a sandy stretch that brought them to a running stream. They spoke no words as Dawn brought them to a stop. Eve went into Linus' things and brought out a hand-operated filtration pump. Soon, they were drawing water from the ankle-deep brook. They drank. Dawn spent some time washing her face and neck, luxuriating in the cold.

Eve filled two bottles and stood ready to leave.

Dawn tried her best to dry her face with her undershirt. "Don't think we're going to find food out here." When Eve didn't reply, she spoke louder. "Don't ignore me. You want to help Linus or find Pascal? It means we get out of here and regroup."

After a moment, Eve nodded.

"There are secondary roads to the west. We have enough fuel to make them and head south. Once we get to a place to recharge, we buy rations, camping supplies, trade this bike in for something better."

"No. Pas is gone. So is Linus. And we don't have credits. We get to a place with a signal. I send a message and they'll come and collect me. Maybe you can use one of your fancy IDs to lie and tell them you caught me. Maybe there's a reward out. Then you can go back to your life."

Dawn wasn't sure what to do. Eve had her head down and stared blankly at the ground. What did normal families do? Hug? Promise things that weren't true?

"We should go."

She followed an easy grade up a hill. From there, she hoped they could find a vantage point and choose a path heading west and eventually south to avoid any patrols searching for them.

Near the crest she stopped to take in the view. Featureless hills in the direction she wanted to take them. A glance northward gave her pause. She zoomed in but didn't get a clear enough view of what she was seeing, so she asked for Eve's rifle scope.

A cluster of palm trees sprung from the ground in a small vale two kilometers away.

She gave the scope back, made a turn, and was taking them downhill again.

"Where are we going?"

"Pascal's journal mentioned trees like those. It could be nothing."

Probably was. But she didn't want to say more. Grasping at straws, probably, but the glimmer of hope she felt in her chest was impossible to ignore.

As they drove beneath the palms, Dawn coasted to a stop and looked up. A bird swooped down from the high fronds, followed by another. Bright orange yellow markings, with black faces and wings. They weren't the only bird, but the most striking.

Hooded orioles, her implant's wiki identified.

"He was here."

"What?" Eve asked.

"The last place Pascal went in his journal. He came here before he vanished. The birds, the trees."

Eve was off the seat and scanning the hedges and grasses before crouching. "Tire treads. Narrow wheelbase. Might be to one of the outpost's cars."

"Maybe. The truck they shot up and burned was bigger, but it wasn't the outpost's only vehicle. Locals, maybe?"

Dawn made her own inspection. A few dry tracks vanished into a broad mud puddle. Nothing recent had passed through it. She headed towards something past the last tree that caught her eye.

An antenna. It had been broken and appeared to belong to one of the data collectors. It was stuck in the dirt and leaning on an oak shrub. Tied to a branch was a flattened piece of aluminum on a string and cut into a crude circle. The circle was dimpled with tiny holes forming a spiral.

A religious symbol? A dreamcatcher? It could be anything—a child's bauble or junk from someone bored playing around with scrap metal and tools. But what was it doing there?

She took it from the branch and tucked it away. Further ahead she spotted something made from dark metal or plastic in the grass. Part of a data recorder? If so, if this was the spot where Pascal had met his friend, the recorder had been moved. She headed for it.

When she was a meter away, it moved.

Her breath caught. It was a spider drone. It rose on its legs, its lens eyes catching the sun as it took her in. Then it started shrieking.

Chapter Twenty-Three

The ear-splitting screech was an alarm. It deafened Dawn as she reeled back, trying to get away from the drone. It sidled from side to side like an excited puppy, bouncing and weaving as it continued to stare.

The machine had no weapons.

She fumbled for her dart gun as the sound needled her ears. But even as she aimed, a boom erupted behind her and the bot exploded into shards of plastic.

Eve lowered her rifle and adjusted a setting on the scope.

"You...could have hit me."

"Could have. Didn't. We just made a lot of noise."

Dawn's hands trembled as she crouched to inspect the shattered robot. Same model as what the soldiers were using. They could be close, at least close enough to send the drones scouting. And the machine would have sent an alert to the operator, if one was in signal range.

"They'll be coming," Eve said casually. "What did you find?"

Dawn showed her the bauble. "Did I miss Pascal going through a jewelry-making phase?"

"No. He'd make nothing this crude."

Blackberries grew beyond the grass where the drone lay scattered. Past them stood a row of solar panels. Too thick to drive, so Dawn went on foot.

Older design, but her implant didn't have current uploaded specs on panels. They were clean. With the incessant weather, panels needed maintenance. Dirt, weeds, wear and tear. Someone cared for them.

Exactly as Pascal had described.

The power collected from the array had to go somewhere. A walk through the collectors found a central hub, but from there no conduits ran off to any power lines.

Strange.

Could all this be for some future project? It didn't make sense. No roads, all the weeds. Who did it belong to? She hurried back to Eve and drove them up the hill so she could get a better look. While there was another rise at the far side of the vale, she saw no signs of any other structures. From up high, the solar panels were hidden, as if perfectly place in the recesses of the ground below.

Eve was more interested in watching the way they came with her rifle. "Maybe they're running the power in buried lines."

"But why? Any slope would be better for panel placement. And I don't see signs of digging or any equipment. We must have missed a track or trail for whoever is maintaining the site."

They stood in the shade of a tall poplar tree. Eve leaned her rifle and resumed scanning with the detached scope. "Someone might come for that drone. Maybe all of them. Might be time for us to go."

"This is the closest thing to a lead on where Pascal went. I want to go back down there for a second look."

"Take the quad bike. If you hear shooting, run."

Dawn didn't argue. They couldn't spend too much time on the search, but the place felt somehow special. Pascal had made a friend here. Was Quint part of a local farm? Here were enough cells to power twenty homes. Residences, even the most hermetic communes, needed roads.

She drove to the northern edge of the solar collectors. Too rocky to park close. As she scrambled down, she realized her route was a mistake. The thorns and brambles were too thick to get through. But they had been pruned away from the solar panels.

She began a circuit along the edge of the briars. Several branches hung heavy with green, under-ripe blackberries. Had the ripe ones been picked? She blinked away her apps' suggested further reading on the topic.

A collapsed shed stood dead center of the thicket. The roof sagged with an open hole in its center. Dawn was about to continue when she saw the berry bushes ran along the entire northern edge of the collector field.

Taking too long. Eve no longer had a com unit, so Dawn had no way of letting her know her search had been fruitless. She climbed the nearest rocks. The shed looked as if it were being held up by the gnarled bushes. But there, leaning at the side of the shed, was a bicycle.

She felt it in her stomach. Pascal had been here. Had made it here before the soldiers had come to the outpost. Wanted to believe it, even as she feared what fate he might have met in this place.

Her remaining two bugs scurried forward, easily navigating the thorny branches, jumping from limb to limb before making it to the shed.

The bicycle was unremarkable, an inexpensive and common manufacturing design. But stenciled into the frame was the New Pacific Commonwealth logo and it was painted in the sickly green-blue of most Commonwealth vehicles.

Her bugs went inside the shack.

A warped wooden floor, no furnishings, with sunlight shining through the gaps in the ceiling. She breathed a sigh of relief upon finding no bodies. Had the bike been stolen from the outpost, or had Pascal given it to someone?

She recalled the drones.

The echoing thunder of Eve's rifle exploded from the top of the hill. A second shot boomed, and a third. Before Dawn could move to return to her sister, an off-road runner appeared on the crest of the hill above her, racing towards Eve's last position. Dawn ducked. The runner skidded to a halt. A cloud of dust rose. She couldn't see. One of her drones went up an anise stalk.

A second vehicle was above her location. Two armored figures were coming her way with needle rifles in hand.

The drone caught up with her as she crawled. No choice. She pulled her hood closed and headed straight into the tangle of blackberries. Thorns clawed at her jacket.

Another report from Eve's rifle gave her the impetus to scramble as fast as she could. The dry growth crunched beneath her as she found a way forward beneath the thickest section of brambles.

She froze when she heard the high-pitch hum of needle rifle fire. Not shooting at her, she realized. She elbow crawled through the last of the berry bush, dragging branches along with her. It took a moment to disentangle from the worst of it. Even with her tough jacket, she felt a thorny prickling along her arms, belly, and legs.

One of the approaching troopers was taking cover at a rock opposite her, but she couldn't see the other one. Armor was too heavy to chance a shot with the dart gun. The trooper's attention was fixed on the heights above.

The second soldier appeared to Dawn's right. He moved along the far side of the brambles. He was approaching a shorter section of berry bushes and if he turned, he would spot her.

She crawled into the collapsed shed. Caught her breath and listened. The shooting had stopped. The last echo died away. Had they killed Eve? Had she evaded them? Either way, the soldiers would begin sweeping the area.

The interior of the shed was strangely neat. Very little debris, few weeds, no sign of any nests or animal droppings. Why her tired brain was focusing in on this, she didn't know.

She crept along the floor to peer out the back. As she moved past a wall, she noticed a bundle or bag on the floor in the shadows. It moved. A young boy or girl scrambled away from her towards a gap in the debris. She dove and clamped her hand on an ankle.

The child let out a wordless protest, soft yet panicked.

"Easy! Easy!" Dawn whispered. "I'm not going to hurt you." They continued to struggle. "You can't go out there. It's dangerous. Do you understand me?"

The child, a boy, she guessed, punted at her, but Dawn yanked him closer and wrangled him under her control. She clamped a gloved hand on his mouth.

"Just stop! Once they leave, you can go."

He fought for a moment before going limp. She maintained her grasp, fearful he'd bolt once she relaxed.

She sent a drone to the roof of the shed. The soldiers were standing together and no longer taking cover. One nodded, as if receiving instructions over his helmet. He pointed to the north side of the vale and they walked with their weapons raised, sweeping left and right as they went.

Her heart squeezed at the thought of what must have happened to Eve.

The boy mewled. Tried to bite her. Kick. His heel caught her in the knee and pain exploded. Then the back of his head connected with her face. The hard knock jarred her enough to cause her grip to relax. He slipped from her and scrambled away towards a corner of the shack.

"I won't hurt you!"

He glanced at her before dropping away into a previously unseen gap in the floor. She dove forward and got her hand in a trap door before he could close it.

She proved stronger. But as he let go, he resumed his flight, worming downward through a tunnel.

Was she really going to chase him? She took a breath and wriggled through the trapdoor. The sloped tunnel was larger than she had thought, but still cramped. The earthen walls were smooth. It ended at a metal grate. He was on the opposite side, trying to place the grate into its grooves. She kicked it. It sent him tumbling.

She pushed the metal aside and grabbed him. He wailed.

"Stop it. Do you want them to hear you? Do you? They're looking to hurt anyone they find. Stop!"

He stiffened. She fixed her grip on him. Caught a whiff of vinegar off his skin and hair. The tunnel had very little light trickling in from above, and she was amazed he had navigated the tunnel so quickly. Beyond the grate was a concrete landing and a ladder going down. Not child sized.

Where were they?

The air carried the soft hum of machinery.

"Do you live here?"

The boy didn't answer. Started wriggling.

"The bicycle upstairs? Is that yours?"

It got his attention for a moment before more struggling.

"Is your name Quint?"

He relaxed and looked up at her with confusion.

"You're Quint. You met Pascal. Pascal is my brother."

"You talk too loud." His voice sounded hoarse, a practiced whisper.

"Then I'll speak softly. My name's Dawn. Can I call you Quint?"

Quint nodded. "You shouldn't have destroyed the drone. It called them."

"You knew about the spider outside?"

He nodded again.

"All those panels—you take care of them and keep them running?"

"That's the custodian's job."

"Does the custodian live down here too? Is this your bunker?" He didn't answer. "How many of you are down here?"

"I'm not supposed to talk to anyone. I'm not supposed to be up here at all."

"You don't want anyone to know you're here. It's your family's rule, isn't it? I understand that. It's how I live my life, too. But Pascal is important to me. He's part of *my* family. What happened to him?"

He mumbled his answer.

"Quint, it's important that you tell me. What happened to Pascal?"

His eyes were wide. "The custodian found him. And he took him."

Chapter Twenty-Four

Alive.

Pascal was alive, or at least he had been before his captured by the custodian.

What was this place and who were these people?

Dawn held the boy at arm's length to get a better look at him. While he was dirty, his hair was closely cropped and his shirt and pants were in good condition. A key dangled on a chain around his neck.

"Is Pascal hurt?"

"I don't know. No. Let me go."

"I can't. Not until you take me to him."

"They won't let you down there. I'll get in trouble."

"Is Pascal your friend?"

"Yes."

"That means he's important to you. I'll do what I can to keep you from getting in trouble, but Pascal doesn't belong here. I'm taking him home. Will you help me do that?"

He nodded. "But no one is supposed to go inside our home. It's the rule."

"Some rules have to be broken, don't they?"

The key belonged to a steel door at the base of the steps. It swung open quietly. It was painted and free of rust. The corridor beyond was clean, appearing to have been painted, swept, and perhaps even mopped in the past few days.

Quint led her to an alcove with a shower and a drain. "Wash up."

"Yeah, we don't have time for that. Take me to Pascal."

He tugged on her arm. Again with the mewling. She allowed herself to be led under the showerhead. The pulsing jet of water washed the soil from her but she got out from under it before her clothes became sodden. Quint waited until she finished before allowing himself to be soaked through by the water. He wiped his face, spat, and stripped to his underwear.

He collected his dirty clothes before trying to march off ahead of her. She stopped him and took the lead. They came to a second door. He used the key again and they emerged into a room with yellow lights.

Uniforms of gray hung on a rack. A line of booties waited beneath. Like spacer wear. There was a sink with soap and a first aid kit mounted on the wall. A doorway with a red button had a plastic curtain drawn across it. It led to a chamber with a grating on the floor and ceiling.

She pressed the red button. A giant set of fans above and below drew air downward through the chamber for several seconds. Quint was using a brush to scrub his fingernails. He had placed the wet clothes in a bin. After finishing with his hands, he pulled on a jumpsuit that fit him perfectly.

"Should I put one of those on?" Dawn asked.

"It won't matter. You're still dirty. They'll know you don't belong."

"Look, is there someone we can call to let them know we're coming? I'm not here to hurt anyone. I want to see my brother. Take him home. That's all."

Quint was about to say something. Stopped.

"What is it?"

"They won't let him leave."

"Why not?"

"Because he knows about home. You do too. They won't let you go either. And then they might do to you what they did to the other lady."

Dawn felt ice down her spine. "What's her name?"

"I don't know."

Pascal had two women working with him. Rebecca Wong and Verna Cho. Rebecca was white. "Tall woman? White, with freckles and long hair?"

"No."

"About my height, then. Asian."

He shrugged.

"Was this woman named Verna? Verna Cho?"

"I guess. I wasn't allowed to see her."

"What happened to her?"

"She was hurt."

"Okay, Quint. Listen to me. You said Pascal was your friend. You want to help your friend, right? How do I get to where he's being held?"

"Down two levels at the custodian's office."

"Does this custodian have weapons?"

He nodded.

"How many of them are there?"

Before he could answer, a small light fixture high on a wall began to strobe.

"That's the alarm," he said. "They're coming."

The room had no visible cameras. "Did we trigger a sensor? Can they see in here?"

"No, the cameras down here broke and no one's fixed them. This way."

He waited at the plastic curtain. It meant going further into the redoubt. When she hesitated, he said, "If they catch you, I'll be in trouble too."

They ran past the chamber with the fan and came out to a balcony above an open flight of stairs. Several doors to their immediate left or right. Below were multiple passages. Yellow lights cast the space in an amber glow.

The shuffle of approaching footsteps.

Quint tugged at her and pointed to a door. It was a closet full of pipes and gauges. He crawled beneath an oversized round valve and motioned for her to join him. She closed the door softly before wedging herself into the cramped space. He hugged his knees to give her room.

The door had a ventilation grate.

Dawn sent a drone through it. Three men hurried up the steps. All wore jumpsuits and had weapon belts and sidearms. They didn't speak. They walked softly and paused only once to confer via quick sign language before vanishing into the fan room. If they were mounting a search, the utility closet would be a terrible hiding spot.

She recovered the drone and led the boy out into the corridor. He resisted her leading him to the stairs.

"Which way?"

He pointed and they hurried together down a wide hallway. An open wall had three turbines that vibrated. More passageways led left, right, and straight ahead. They took a couple of turns before coming to a dead end with a sealed door and a camera.

"That one works."

Too late. If the camera had an operator or an active security system, they'd be seen. The door had no sign and a mechanical deadbolt.

"Unlock it," she said.

"My key doesn't work."

She clenched her jaw. Produced her snap key and made quick work of the bolt. It clicked as it unlocked and she pushed the door open.

A man at a terminal was rising from a chair. He fumbled with a pistol when Dawn shot him with a dart. He collapsed to the floor. She scooped up the pistol and slid it into her belt.

Quint trembled. Dawn seized his wrist and pulled him inside the room. She patted the man down and took a set of keys.

"You said Pascal was here?"

He nodded. Pointed to a door.

Six cells made of crudely welded bars stood in the dim light. Each space had its own cot and toilet. Pascal sat in one of them and squinted at her. His black hair was trimmed to Commonwealth recruit spec maximum length, he wore a week's worth of face scruff, and he had a gray jumpsuit zipped up to his chin.

"Hi, Dawn. If you're here, that means you went home to the apartment. Did you touch my cars?"

Chapter Twenty-Five

The keys opened the cell. Dawn went to Pascal and hugged him. He stiffened and endured it.

"Are you hurt?"

He shook his head. His face brightened when Quint entered the jail. "The bike I brought you was too tall."

"It's perfect," Quint said. "I just haven't had a chance to ride it."

Pascal bringing Quint a gift and then being concerned it wasn't perfect was something new to Dawn. But this wasn't the time to explore her brother's new behavior. She checked the pistol she had taken from the jailer. A six-shot revolver, small caliber. Unlike so much of what she had seen in the redoubt, it was not only old but speckled with spots of rust.

Four bullets, all of them seeping green. She snapped the cylinder shut and put the weapon back in her belt.

"Quint, what's another way out of here?"

"Through the cisterns. But we won't get far. Only the custodian and the water keeper has the keys."

"Are they locks like these?"

He nodded.

"Then take us there. Let's go."

Out in the corridors, they descended more steps. The surrounding plumbing shuddered. Fluid bubbled through the pipes and one of them vented steam. Something churned in a chamber as they hurried past, reminding Dawn of a giant washing machine.

So many questions, but she didn't want to stop. Verna Cho alive?

What trick had been pulled to make the families believe they were receiving their loved ones' remains?

Pascal kept looking and listen. She took him by the hand and led him along. Quint wasn't slowing down. Wasn't running away from them, either.

Voices ahead. Quint paused at a side corridor before ducking down it. "Wait!" she hissed.

He led them into a repair shop. Machine parts, silicon chips, computer peripherals, jars of screws, nuts, and bolts, an anvil near a bin of scrap metal waiting to be shaped. Tools, too. In better condition than the revolver. Another light on the ceiling winked a silent alert.

They waited beneath a workbench as another group of armed people hurried past down the corridor. Only a couple of firearms. The rest carried knives and spears. She tensed up, preparing herself for the inevitable assault. But they weren't stopping to search.

"Is all of this because I came down here?"

"Breach alarm is two flashes, then one," Pascal said. "General alarm is three flashes. See? It's blinking three times."

"How do you know that?"

"Breach alarm sounded when I came here. Only the custodian came to get me, along with one of the security guards. After they put me in a cell, I listened to them talk."

"What does a general alarm mean?"

Quint chewed his lower lip. "It means we're being attacked."

Another shudder ran along one pipe. Not normal sounds, but the reverberations of what she guessed were above-ground explosions. Had she led the Reilly-Bigg soldiers to the redoubt entrance?

The corridor was clear. She got Pascal and Quint out from under the workbench.

"Take us to the cisterns."

But Pascal dragged his feet as she tried to lead him from the workshop. He was staring at shelves full of bins holding electronic and computer scrap.

"Wait," he said.

He grabbed a flexible tablet with a cracked screen. It bore the Commonwealth seal on the back.

"We don't have time for this. Put it down."

"This was Verna's."

"Okay, take it. Come on."

Verna was there somewhere. She wasn't the mission. Any more delays and they'd be stopped or caught. It already felt wrong trusting Quint, but she had no choice.

From down the corridor, Quint snapped his fingers. "Psst." He waved them on.

They descended yet another set of stairs to a landing with an arched doorway. Quint waited at a wide door with a metal bar and lock. Two locks, she saw as they got closer. Too big for her snap key. As she plied one and then the next with her manual lock picks, the tumblers refuse to budge. Each keyhole appeared different. It required two keys, she suspected, and both needed to be turned simultaneously.

Clang-Clang!

A man stood at the guardrail at the top of the steps. He wrapped a wrench over and over, but ducked out of sight when Dawn drew her dart gun. The noise continued as he struck a pipe over and over while remaining out of view. Seconds later, a response echoed around them.

So not all the redoubt security was heading upstairs.

"Does your key work on either of these?" Dawn asked Quint.

He shook his head.

She tried the first lock again with her picks. It resisted. Pascal tried to grab the picks from her hand.

"Let go," she said. But the tug of war continued.

"Let me try."

She was stronger and wrenched the picks away. "This isn't a game, Pas." Then she thought about it and handed him the kit after withdrawing two picks she knew would fit. "We both try at the same time. Put the tension tool in first—"

"I know how to do it."

She had her doubts until she saw how he lined up the tools and worked the first lock. She started on the second one when she caught movement above them.

The security guard peered down. Snapped his fingers. Quint snapped back and signed a response that Dawn couldn't follow.

Pascal paused his work on the lock. "Don't leave, Quint."

But the boy ran. There wasn't time to stop him. More people were coming. While the guard above them didn't appear to be armed with anything besides his wrench, the others might carry firearms.

Dawn worked her picks. "We need to get this open."

Pascal copied her movements, then withdrew his tools from the lock. "I can't go."

"What do you mean? Get that lock open. I can't do this myself."

He held up the tablet. "Not without Verna."

"We can't save her. We escape, we get help."

A group of guards stormed down the stairs. The first in line held a plastic riot shield. Pascal looked up at the railing where Quint hid behind one of the security guards. Then he set the tablets and lock picks down and raised his arms in surrender.

Dawn sprinted for the nearest passageway. The narrow space required her to duck beneath a series of pipes. She spun and raised her dart gun in search of a target, but the security force had stopped at the corner. Behind them, a guard wrestled Pascal to the floor. Someone aimed a sidearm with a targeting laser down the hall.

She shot out the overhead light. Smashed another as she ran. She slipped on her goggles, turning the sparse lighting into day. The passage narrowed further, forcing her to duck and squeeze and finally climb. It was as if whoever planned the redoubt hadn't bothered replacing old plumbing and ductwork, but continued to add to it, layer upon layer.

None of the gaps and crawlways led in any direction that made sense. Surely some of the pipes fed or drew from the cisterns. She climbed up. Her arms and legs ached and she blinked sweat from her eyes.

Who were these people? A reclusive family squatting in an abandoned waste facility? Had the redoubt once been part of some greater municipality swept away by one of the many catastrophes to have struck the planet?

Didn't matter.

They knew the place better than she did, so she needed to keep moving and get Pascal back while they still were dealing with the above-ground intruders. Because once that crisis was handled, there'd be twice as many people hunting her.

She squeezed herself into a cramped sublevel with enough space to crawl.

Judging by the size of the plumbing, she guessed she had found a sewer line running down from above. Near it was a ladder leading up a chute with a plate or trapdoor at the top. A spring latch without a lock held it closed.

She listened but heard nothing besides the sigh of gas and liquid traveling the pipes. The trapdoor moved without a sound as she pressed upward and found herself in a round chamber. Rays of white shone from the ceiling. Not fixtures, but sunlight reflected down metal conduits.

A circular platform occupied the room's center. A dozen long boxes stood in a row. Each held something obscured by plastic sheets.

A greenhouse? Or were those coffins?

The air tasted humid. An astringent chemical smell stung her nose. Reminded her of a hospital.

The sunlight meant she had made it to an upper level. Amber lights burned from beneath several sconces around the chamber. The winking alarm was absent here.

A double door stood closed. Dawn emerged silently from the hatch and pressed her head to the door. Heard nothing. She was about to open it. Paused. Green LEDs glowed faintly from beneath the plastic.

She approached the platform. Condensation clung to the sheets. She pushed through a gap. Gasped.

An interconnected series of beds housed in a hard shell ringed the platform. Each had a port window that revealed the hazy face of a person lying inside.

The closest shell felt warm to the touch. A control panel had a series of buttons and a display. A container of what she guessed was urine hung beneath the foot of the bed.

She had seen this before.

Adapted from deep space hibernation, a process that had never measured up to its promise of keeping men and women safe during decades-long travel. She had helped end the ambitions of a maniac named The Host operating in the desert beyond Seraph. He had been kidnapping people and placing them into sleep chambers in the belief he could exploit their skills and memories.

Were these victims of a similar plan?

As much as the sight filled her with horror, she knew there was nothing she could do about it. She didn't dare touch the controls. They were alive.

On the nearest wall, a terminal hummed. A server stack. Hard drives. A row of ancient monitors lined the center shelf. She tried the power on a few, but they wouldn't turn on.

So there was a computerized control system, just no obvious means to know what was happening. A central workstation must exist somewhere where the redoubt dwellers could monitor their wards.

Victims, she thought coldly.

The wall had an intercom box with a port for what might be headphones or a mike. More old tech.

The way the security teams had whispered, the sign language, the lack of an audible alarm. The place ran silent. Even the boy Quint had barely spoken above a whisper.

A click at the doors as someone unlocked them. As one shushed open, Dawn ducked into the shadows of the cubby with the trapdoor. A woman walked past wearing a jumpsuit and soft slippers, her footsteps silent. She carried a case around her shoulder and produced a tablet. This she plugged into a panel at the base of the platform.

Using a stylus, she scrolled and tapped the screen. Wired network? Didn't matter. Dawn couldn't wait any longer and the device might help her learn where Pascal had been taken.

A dart and a soft thud. Dawn locked the unconscious woman in a closet.

The dropped tablet was old, like every other piece of tech inside the place. Once unplugged, a power indicator flashed on the screen. Dawn plugged it back in.

The battery was dead. For it to be useful, Dawn needed to keep it connected. If it powered down, it might need a moment to reboot. Then it could lock her out and ask for a passcode or thumb or face image. She tapped the screen. Time to learn what she could about the place.

The minimal interface had a barebone operating system. While the tablet remained plugged into the port by the platform, it displayed a single page of data.

Creche 4/61. Beds 1-12 active. A list followed, with names in alphabetical order followed by their temperature, heart rate, breaths per minute, and blood pressure.

TWO FEEDINGS REMAINING. REFILL NOW.

Bed Eight TEMPERATURE ALERT.

Twelve people's lives held in the balance by a system with dead batteries, defunct monitors, and software unfit to alphabetize a phone directory.

A whirring began. She hadn't touched anything. All twenty beds inclined several degrees. A new readout updated the blood pressure data. The feeding and temperature alert appeared a second time.

If there were sixty-one creches, they had a lot of people in storage. It was the Host all over again.

She scrolled. The names weren't always alphabetical once she sorted through the other creches. Some had vacancies. No doubt if they were all full and someone new was plugged in, they wouldn't bother moving everyone around like they were dominoes or playing cards.

But what were the criteria for the people here?

She couldn't find ages, but judging by the shapes she saw in the beds inside the room, they were of all heights and shapes. Could this many people have been abducted from the surrounding communities?

Doubtful.

She searched by name, scrolling and scanning rapidly. Didn't think she'd find what she was looking for until she made it to V. The list had a Verna. No last name listed. Creche Twelve. While there might be another Verna, Dawn had the queasy suspicion the Commonwealth outpost's supervisor was a guest of the redoubt.

A schematic revealed Creche Twelve was down a hallway.

After she unplugged the antique tablet and tucked it away, she headed out the doors. The corridor outside went in every direction, with more hallways crisscrossing every ten meters. No one in sight.

Another rumble reverberated through the ducts.

Signs labeled the doors. One creche each. Creche twelve was a larger room with no access to the sublevel. Twenty beds, eighteen people in wrappers. Bed three was open. Bed four, according to the schematic, was Verna.

Through the coffin's window, it was impossible to tell if it was her.

Do the job, get paid, get out.

Verna wasn't the mission. Even if it was her and Dawn could figure out how to extract her, would she be mobile? Or, like most of the poor victims of the Host, would she be blind, crippled, or barely alive?

She appeared to be the same size as her bio. Unlike the Host's antique metal sleep chambers, the plastic boxes didn't appear to be filled with fluid.

The tablet powered up once plugged in and didn't require a passcode. It revealed Verna's life signs were normal.

No obvious options for patient retrieval in the tablet menu.

A quick inspection revealed a series of covered power switches in the center of Verna's bed, along with a release lever.

Too risky.

Between the switches, she discovered an input jack identical to the one for the tablet. Not power, but data. A hardline connected to the box where Verna slumbered. A quick check confirmed the neighboring patient likewise was plugged in.

A feed to a central terminal.

The redoubt schematic on the tablet felt incomplete, centered on the creches, a clinic, and an operating room. But despite the sun beaming through the overhead cylinders, this wasn't the top level.

The top level, after an unintuitive flip through the interface, was labeled Control Room.

Perhaps something up there would help her understand the place. Next, locate and extract Pascal, and get them out alive.

Chapter Twenty-Six

A snap of fingers out in the corridor.

Dawn emerged from the room and caught motion to her right. A teenage girl in a jumpsuit ducked behind a corner. The sound was answered by a tap on a wall in the opposite direction. A tongue click and a hiss from down the hallway ahead. The shuffle of soft footsteps coming closer.

The route to the control room meant getting past them, but now her way was blocked. Dart gun out, she retreated towards the creche with the trapdoor that had brought her to the upper level. She was about to open it when from below came the scrapping of hurried climbing.

She ran back into the hallway. No one in sight. Only whispers.

She chose a direction. The creche numbers next to the doors were going up. She took a turn, then another, but the limited schematic she had scanned from the tablet showed only a series of dead ends ahead of her. She picked a creche door, number 37, and was about to open it when someone hissed at her.

Quint.

He crouched at a corner and beckoned her towards him.

She aimed her dart gun as she strode forward. A quick check confirmed his hallway was empty, but they were coming.

"Ssst," he whispered and hurried to a closet off the corridor.

It held a floor sink, mops, brooms, and a few cleaning supplies. He opened a metal door to one of several large breaker boxes. Instead of a panel, there was a narrow wall space.

His clipped, soft words tumbled out. "This way. And close the door behind you. Don't breathe too loud."

She closed the closet door behind them. "I'll try not to."

He squeezed into the space and shimmied downward.

"Wait. You need to take me to Pascal. I have to get him out."

"He's back at the jail. I'm bringing you to the exit so you can go."

"I'm not leaving without him."

The shaft ran up and down.

A man's voice called. "Intruder? Come out peacefully. We don't want to hurt you, but we will."

She strained her ears. More shuffling. Did they know where they were? Could she even fit in the wall space? There were enough hand and footholds. Her sister would never have managed. Dawn eased herself in and pulled the breaker box door closed.

Quint turned on a flashlight clipped to his waist. "Latches."

Two hooks locked the breaker door. Hardly solid, but it might throw off anyone searching for her momentarily if they hadn't seen her vanish into the closet. Time later to know if the crawlspace was Quint's alone or if anyone else within the redoubt knew about them.

When she began the slow climb upward, Quint hissed for her. "This way. Down."

She ignored him. He changed direction to follow, moving quickly and remaining directly beneath her.

"Is there a way out near the control room?"

"Yes. But there was an explosion."

Another few meters of climbing and she smelled smoke. A panel like the one in the janitor's closet let out into a hallway. A thick cloud choked her breathing and nearly obscured the floor lights. A silent alarm pulsed on the ceiling. Several locked doors before she came to one with a keypad. Easy to bypass under normal circumstances. She slipped a spoof card from her belt. It would usually work on simple electronic locks. She swiped. The red LED blinked once, stayed red. She tried a couple more times before putting it away.

"You know of a way in?"

Quint shook his head.

She pulled at the doors. No latch. Solid. Smoke poured from a vent at the top of the wall. She sent in her drones.

The bugs skittered into a hazy room wall to wall with old computer equipment. Most of the monitors were cracked. A body lay on the floor, a rolling chair tipped over next to him. He had a keycard clipped to the belt of his jumpsuit. It took both bugs to move it.

The smoke tasted foul. Quint struggled to contain a cough.

She pulled her shirt over her mouth even as her eyes watered. She strained her ears for any incoming footsteps. Her heart raced and her gloves grew clammy.

The bugs dropped the card twice while trying to climb to the vent. Finally, she directed them to shove it beneath the door. The frayed laminate caught as the corner of the card appeared. She snagged it with the tips of her fingers and tapped it against the card reader. The door clicked. She opened it, conducting Quint inside before closing them inside.

She checked the pulse of the man sprawled on the floor. Dead. His soot-coated face stared blankly into nothing.

The room was in shambles. A pair of cracked sun tubes in the ceiling drizzled dust. A faint breeze swirled the smoke. A table served as a workbench for the computers, with a soldering iron and silicone components awaiting repair. Wires dangled from peripherals tucked into every inch of shelf space.

She stepped past the body to examine the controls. Door lock sensors. Power levels. Air temperature. A few other gauges she didn't understand, but this place was the nexus of the redoubt's many systems.

With the shake of a mouse, two monitors came alive. Camera view outside the redoubt. One looked south, capturing a portion of the panels and a grassy plain beyond the trees and berry vines. The other was directed towards the shack and the rocks above.

Two of the redoubt defenders lay sprawled in the dirt. Two more took cover behind a boulder. One was bleeding with his arm tucked against his side. The other defender had his weapon out but was doing his best at keeping low.

The console had a joystick but it didn't move the camera. At the edge of the screen, a sheriff department buggy stood parked at the top of the slope. The sheriff and two of the Reilly-Bigg soldiers were using the vehicle for protection. One soldier was plinking with his needle rifle. The sheriff busied himself with a tablet.

Past them, one of the Reilly-Bigg off-road runners burned.

But the sheriff and soldiers didn't appear to be too worried about anyone not down in the vale below.

Dawn refused to believe they had killed her sister. But the evidence was clear. The bad guys controlled the area. Eve was no longer a threat.

Now, the remaining visible redoubt defenders were outgunned. They would soon be flanked and murdered.

No wonder the defenders had only a few people searching for her.

But what had happened to the control room? She scanned the wreckage and let her implant analyze what she was seeing. Too much smoke and debris for a definitive answer. Her software flagged a sliver of black metal. A drone leg segment. About the same size as the one patrolling the barn where the soldiers had set up base camp.

With the solar tubes providing light, along with whatever ventilation system the place had running, the redoubt was hardly secure. The soldier's killer machine had found a way in and blew up their nerve center.

The cameras had a channel toggle switch. A click up or down, and the footage vanished. The corner of each image had a numbering system but most of the screens were blank.

Quint was trembling as he stared at the body at Dawn's feet. No doubt the boy knew the man.

She tabbed through the dead camera views. "Look away from him. We'll leave soon."

He nodded stiffly as he watched her work. It took only a moment to find the camera above the jail door. As Quint had said, it worked. A redoubt defender was crouched at a corner with his weapon drawn. One of the men who had taken Pascal.

If Quint was right, Pascal was once again inside the jail. But his safety would last only as long as the defenders held out.

When the two men burst into the room, she barely had time to duck as bullets struck the wall of dead monitors. She grabbed Quint and pulled him to the floor as plastic shrapnel, silicon, and glass rained around them. She had a corner of the desk as cover. As they spread out, they'd have a clear shot in moments.

A guard aimed at her. "Let the boy go."

"He's not my prisoner. I was protecting him from you. Lower your gun. You have bigger problems."

"Hands where I can see them!"

She let Quint go. He ran off and slipped out the door. Fingers splayed, she raised her hands and kept her head bowed. One guard threw her down and pinned her to the floor.

"I'm not your problem! Look at the monitor."

The guard took her dart gun, the keycard, and the stolen revolver. Zip ties went around her wrists. Her hood was torn back and the guard searched her as the other checked the fallen man.

It was hard to speak with a knee on her back. "That wasn't me. You had a breach. Drone with a bomb or grenade. My sister's up there fighting those guys."

The larger of the two hauled her out into the corridor while the other tapped at the console controls. He snapped his fingers, getting the large guard's attention. A moment passed where they exchanged hand signals, their signing emphatic, their faces intense.

When both looked at her with grim resolve, her heart sank. The large guard raised his pistol. She met his gaze. "I'm not with them. I'm here to bring my brother home."

He thumbed back the revolver's hammer. Licked his lips.

"You see my dart gun? It's non-lethal. Those guys up top are here to kill you."

The smaller guard gave the other a signal. Dawn didn't need to understand their silent language to know the meaning. *Hurry up and get it over with.*

"Let me help you."

The weapon lowered a few centimeters. The larger guard's voice was oddly tender. "You brought them here."

"They were looking for this place. Or at least they were really interested in who lives here and keeping it a secret, judging by what they did to the research station. You want to argue about this? Looks like they're going to be in here soon, if they're not already."

"How can you help?"

"I can fight. And unlike you people, I know how to fight dirty."

Chapter Twenty-Seven

At least she had her dart gun back.

She crept forward up the redoubt hallway towards the ladder that would take her up into the collapsed shed. The redoubt defenders no doubt had their weapons aimed at her. Would shoot if she turned back.

Pascal remained their prisoner.

She gleaned from the sign language conversation between the small group of defenders that they'd let her go. Only the large guard spoke with her.

"Do as you said you could. If you run, your brother dies."

If the sheriff and his corporate thug allies won, they'd *all* be dead. She kept the thought to herself.

A spider drone lay twitching in the corridor. She disabled it, smashing its eye with the blade of a tiny screwdriver she kept on her belt. It might still have a microphone and power, but she didn't want to waste time to demolish the thing.

Needle gun fire from above. She climbed to the top of the ladder and deployed her two bugs. They hopped through the shed's interior and climbed up the doorframe to the roof.

The two pinned-down defenders were dead. An armored soldier crouched and examined the bodies.

The sheriff stood over them, one of his gleaming silver burners pointing at the sky. A spider drone like the one in the hallway stood obediently at his heels. The cat-sized machine moved every time he shifted, like a dutiful pet.

He pointed at the shed. "That's the only way in I've found, boys. I'll leave you to it."

The soldier murmured in his helmet. Two more armored troopers hacked their way forward through a section of thorny vines. They were going to assault the place, send in more exploding drones, or drop grenades. Maybe all three.

The first soldier joined the sheriff. "Captain wants us to wait. Possible resistance after you lost your spider."

"It was one dirt grubber with a pistol. Lucky shot. You won't have a problem with all that fancy gear."

"We can make a batch of gas and pump it inside. Otherwise, we're looking at a lot of corners and rooms."

The sheriff grew loud. "Captain told *me* he doesn't want to wait that long, corporal. He put me in charge while he's dealing with...that other piece of trouble you boys brought down on us. It's easy pickings down there. Now do as you're told."

Dawn moved her bugs. They tumbled to the dirt and raced beneath the worst of the thorny bushes towards the sheriff.

The other two goons were through the thickest part of the bushes. One called, "I don't see a ladder."

The sheriff was once again on his tablet. The spider at his feet perked up. "It's in that wreck. Just kick down a wall and you'll see it."

She only had a moment before they broke in and spotted her. Her bugs scurried to the spider. The sheriff and the soldier next to him didn't react as they broke cover and climbed the larger drone's metal legs. One dumped its entire battery charge, deactivating the spider's receiver.

"What the—"

Her second bug found the small housing with the processor, neutralized the pin switch disabling the override, and plugged itself into the motherboard.

The drone, to Dawn's relief, wasn't military, but a consumer-level construct. It had all the components of the automated bots used by both sides during the Caretaker War, except for the advanced encryption software. Armor configuration, weapons, terrain navigation, servos, and actuators awaited instruction. Dawn uploaded her own tiny program via her little bug. It fed the script into the drone's brain. And the spider was hers.

It leaned back and its forward two legs raised. Each snapped open a curved blade.

The sheriff kept jabbing his tablet before shaking it. Dawn sent the spider running at the two troopers closing in on her. The disadvantage to having cut it off from its user was she'd need to rely on its inboard programming.

Good enough because the soldiers didn't see it coming.

It sprang onto the first one, delivering a series of punching stabs with both blades to the man's helmet and chest. One strike caught the neck joint as the trooper tumbled forward. He rolled about, dropping his rifle, but couldn't dislodge the machine. The flurry of blows continued.

The second soldier had his weapon up and stepped back. "Recall your drone!"

He wasn't shooting, no doubt fearful of hitting his companion.

"What's happening?" the sheriff shouted. "It's not me. It's gone haywire!"

Dawn switched targets to the second soldier. The spider didn't hesitate; it withdrew both blades and sprang. The trooper fired a quick burst that mostly tore up dirt, vines, and a portion of the shed wall. He hit the drone too, severing one blade. But the machine was fast, slamming into his rifle and puncturing his arm. The trooper went down as he pulled and punched at the thing.

With her own bugs deployed and occupied, she had no view of the sheriff or the third soldier. She crept to the doorway and pulled her dart gun. She'd need a lucky shot to take down an armored target. Exposing herself to needle rifle fire was an invitation to a messy death.

What choice did she have?

The soldier was wading through the bushes to help his comrades. Dawn aimed and shot him in the face. The dart bounced off the helmet. He snapped up his weapon, but the strap caught. She fired again, a third time, and a fourth as he freed his weapon. One dart found its mark on the man's neck. He staggered and fell.

A section of wall burst and burned. The sharp sizzle-pop of a plasma weapon. The sheriff was backing up and firing his silver burners. She ducked, had a target, squeezed the trigger.

Click.

Her dart gun was empty. She sent the spider after him. It took a moment to dislodge itself from its second victim, and had somehow lost a back leg. It hobbled through the scrub and towards the sheriff.

A series of blasts took it down. It twitched on the ground.

The sheriff slapped fresh batteries into one of his polished weapons. He had holstered his second burner. Only one spare battery? Her implant referenced his weapons. Eight shots at the highest power level, barring any mods.

He delivered a coup de grâce that also fried both of Dawn's bugs

She had no more darts. She glanced around the corner. A blast sizzled the air near her face, forcing her down.

Seven shots.

She spotted him through a gap in the wall boards. "Sheriff? Drop your weapons and leave. I have no fight with you."

He made it to the top of the slope and had fallen prone. "You broke into the station, didn't you?"

"Yeah. And you were helping Reilly-Bigg cover up a murder. Is my sister still alive?"

"If you're asking about the big gal with the sniper rifle, Captain Fields has her. Now you come forward with your hands up, and we can keep talking."

Motion to her left. A scraping sound. Several meters away at a bare concrete block where a lamp post might have once stood, a hatch opened, concealed by a false section of ground covered in grass. Another exit. Could the sheriff see them once they emerged? If so, they'd be an easy target.

Dawn pulled her dart gun and let it dangle on a forefinger before stepping out from the shed.

"Toss that weapon, girl."

She did as he asked, flinging the gun into the bushes.

The sheriff stood, his burner pointing. Not the steadiest hand, but his burner had aim compensators even if the man didn't have any mods.

"I'm here. I'm surrendering. I don't have any other weapons. There's a bounty on me, if that helps."

"Maybe it does; maybe it doesn't. How many more of you down there? And don't lie."

She couldn't see the redoubt defenders to know whether they had emerged from their hole. "I don't know anything about the folks who live here. Why does Reilly-Bigg want to kill them?"

He licked his lips and stiffened his arm as if the burner had grown heavy. "Their business, isn't it? Why don't you come forward?"

He was going to shoot her. She felt a pit grow in her stomach. "You know there's evidence about what they did? The coverup hasn't worked. That's why they have you searching for us."

"There were just the three of you. Town surveillance system. We're not all dumb hicks out here."

"You think we're the only ones trying to find out what happened to the outpost?"

"Don't really matter. More show up, we'll take care of 'em. A bonus check makes the missus happy."

"And the people who live here? You're going to just kill them because Reilly-Bigg tells you to?"

"Look, Missy, I'm not going to do anything of the kind. I keep the peace. I prevent people from making too big of a wave in my community. My mouth stays shut. Reilly-Bigg, Evergreen, and whoever else wants to put their foot down on a bunch of hole squatters, that's their business. Now, my throat's dry and the sight of all this blood is making me queasy. So you come up here. No more jawboning."

She felt dizzy. Her legs felt stiff as she waded through the cut in the bushes. Thorns pricked and clung to her.

Ka-KRACK!

The loud report startled her but she didn't hesitate to dive into the briars. The gunshot echoed around for a moment before silence.

"Come out," a voice called from behind her. "It's safe for now."

The pale man wore wrappings around his arms and neck, and a broad-brimmed hat. He glassed the hilltop with a scoped rifle. The large guard appeared next. Revolver in hand, he hurried past her and up the hill to the fallen sheriff.

A gunshot, and he waved.

Dawn extracted herself. Raised her hands but lowered them when she realized no one was aiming a weapon at her.

"We could have asked him questions."

The man with the rifle added a bullet to his weapon. "He had no answers I wished to know."

Dawn had seen him with the other guards before they agreed to allow her to help. "It could mean more trouble for your people."

"Perhaps. You fulfilled your promise."

"You're the custodian. Quint mentioned you."

He didn't answer. Kept studying the surrounding hillsides.

The large guard descended to the first fallen trooper. He stooped to collect a dropped needle rifle. He had the sheriff's silver burners in his belt.

"Those weapons may not work for anyone but them," she said.

The caretaker's voice rose barely above a whisper. "Then we'll scrap them for parts."

The large guard stripped the other soldiers of their weapon belts. "One of their vehicles left recently. One remains."

"Check it for anything useful. Find the keys. We will use it in our defense."

Dawn approached the caretaker. "More soldiers will come. A lot more."

He inspected one of the fallen trooper's armor.

"Are you listening to me? They said something about gassing your facility."

"Not your concern. You did as you said. I'll have your brother brought up. Then you leave."

"What about you? You need to evacuate."

"We can't leave. There are too many of us. Most cannot travel. And go where?"

"I saw what you did to all those people in your hibernation chambers."

"They are volunteers. We do that to preserve resources."

Dawn fought to keep her voice even. With a word, he could have her executed. "And what about Verna Cho from the outpost? She's no volunteer."

"We found her mortally wounded after the soldiers ambushed their vehicle. Shrapnel in her heart, in her head, and more in her legs. We performed surgery and saved her life. But our dream chamber was the only way we could stabilize her."

"How about take her to a hospital?"

"We don't leave. For anyone."

She waited for more, but the custodian added nothing to his statement. "It looks like you don't have a choice. When Reilly-Bigg returns, you can't outfight them. They have at least a few more armored vehicles. Some have rockets and mini-guns."

"Then we will do what we always have. We hide. We endure. We survive. Your brother will be brought to you. Go in peace."

Chapter Twenty-Eight

Pascal wouldn't budge from the bottom of the ladder.

The custodian had done as he said and brought Dawn's brother from the jail.

Dawn crouched at the trapdoor inside the ruined shed and beckoned Pascal towards her as if he were a stubborn cat beneath a bed. "Come on. We talk about this later. This isn't a discussion we have time for."

"I'm not going."

"Yes, you are. Eve's in trouble and I can't leave you here. There's more men coming. They'll hurt you and everyone else down there."

"Then I'll help stop them."

With that, he turned and brushed past the custodian. She slid down the ladder. Almost hoped the custodian or one of the other redoubt defenders might put a hand up to stop her, but they stepped aside as she caught up with her brother.

"You can't help anything. This isn't a game. This isn't a sim. There are real soldiers coming with actual weapons who don't care how many people they've killed."

"I'm not twelve anymore. I'm thirty."

Then act like it, she almost said. "I know. I know you're thirty. My implant doesn't let me forget birthdays, just like you don't forget anything because you're you. But sometimes, Pascal, it feels like you *do* forget, and you do it on purpose. Eve and I came here to find you. We thought you were dead."

He considered her for a moment before throwing his arms around her. It was an aggressive hug that took her off her feet. He had always hated hugs.

"Okay, okay. Let go. You don't have to do that."

He released her. "I wanted to. I wanted to do a lot of things and I did them. Like joining Commonwealth Services. And then bringing Verna here."

"What happened to her?"

"The soldiers tried to kill everyone but they missed her. I was coming back from a visit with Quint. She had run and was wounded. Quint told me a little about his tribe. They could help her. And they did, didn't they?"

"You saved her?"

The slightest smile. "So I have to stay. CS guidelines say that we need to 'consider the welfare of our fellow team members in everything we do and say.' Saputo wasn't good at doing that. He killed Eric with one of his traps."

"The rat you were feeding at the outpost? I'm sorry about that. Your log. I found it."

"You weren't supposed to read that. But I'm not Saputo. I won't trap a rat. But I will help Verna. And Quint."

She'd need to physically remove him if she wanted him to go. "What if *I* need you?"

"You don't need anyone, Dawn. Mom says so."

"Is that what you believe? Don't answer. But I need you. I always have. It's just been hard to come back."

"Hurricane Mom."

She chuckled. "Yeah. I left you with her. You had to be alone and care for her. I'm sorry. Eve or I should have worked something out. But right now, it's Eve who needs me. I can't help her if I'm here caring for you."

"I don't need to be cared for," he said flatly.

"You don't. If we were back in New Pacific, it would mean leaving you alone in the apartment. But out here, you know it's different. There's nothing normal about this."

"I'm not stupid."

"You're anything but. You might be the smartest person I know."

His face looked like he was working out a math problem. Finally, "How can I help?"

"You know how to drive a drone?"

The redoubt dwellers were busy removing the dead. Dawn had time to take the sheriff's tablet before Quint and another boy struggled to carry the body down towards the solar panels. She had lifted the vehicle key card from the large guard and had slipped it into her pocket.

Pascal had the presence to catch up to Quint before the body was carried away. He unlocked the tablet using the sheriff's thumb. A few swipes and taps of the screen later, and he had reset the passcode.

He showed it to her. She nodded and they hurried up the hill.

The ruined armored runner continued to smolder. Nearby, the sheriff's buggy was intact. It had a tailgate rack where a civilian might stow a bicycle. A second folded drone hung there. Fully charged. All it needed was to be turned on.

The buggy was intact and had three-quarters of its battery charge. No weapons. Unlike the deputy's runner, the vehicle had plush faux leather seats, an autodrive system, a fancy stereo, and a cooler loaded with sandwiches, cookies, and bottles of beer.

A suite of cutting-edge electronic gear was a testament to either Salina Crossroads having an oversized law enforcement budget or the sheriff receiving payouts from Reilly-Bigg.

Pascal was busy with the tablet as he followed along behind her. The caretaker appeared at the bottom of the hill. He and the large guard were coming. They'd want the vehicle.

"Get in," she said.

Her brother paused, as if considering the request.

"If we're going to save Eve, we need the car. The caretaker won't let us leave with it."

He got in. The engine purred when she started it, smooth as can be. She punched it as the guard waved for them. He shouted for them to stop.

The vehicle wasn't one of the armored runners with a heavy weapon. It would do little to help with their last stand. So why did she feel guilty?

"Put on your seatbelt," she said.

"Where's Eve?"

"That's what we're going to find out. Keep your eyes peeled."

Pascal found a spare pistol clipped beneath the seat. "There's also a shortwave jammer. You want it left on?"

"Give me that." She stowed the weapon behind her. "Interesting. Either the sheriff thought it would keep the redoubt from calling out or he wanted to control Captain Field's ability to communicate with his men. Leave it on."

She drove a quick circuit of the ground around the trees where Eve had taken cover. The quad bike remained where she had parked it. Near an oak tree, a few branches had fallen. The soil and bark were torn up by either an explosion or bursts of small arms fire.

A quick scan of the ground revealed little. No easy way to know what had happened.

The radio blathered.

"You have a signal? Isn't the jammer working?"

Pascal fiddled with the controls to a black box beneath the radio. "It's a digital recorder. The sheriff was eavesdropping on Captain Fields. Parabolic microphone on the light rack. Looks like the captain wasn't using encryption either and the sheriff recorded more if you want to hear it."

"Later. We need to leave."

"Okay. But here's the last message."

He hit play.

Fields' voice was crisp. "Get here quick and clean this place out. I'm leaving a lance behind to get the job started. I've got another asset to ask a few questions to before we pack up."

Asset? He must have been talking about Eve. His call also meant there might be someone in radio range coming, unless the jammer was running and Fields hadn't waited for a reply.

Dawn considered her brother. "She's alive."

"Then we help her."

"We do. And if Fields has her, I know where he's going."

She focused on the terrain ahead. A rough drive, but the buggy's suspension handled the deep ruts and rocks with deftness.

Her stomach grumbled. She tried a sandwich from the cooler. Egg salad, heavy mayo, with chunks of celery. It would normally make her gag, but on that day, it was the best thing she had tasted in months. She ate a second one and washed it down with a lager.

With her implant, she reviewed the specs of the spider attached to the back of the vehicle.

Smaller than the first of the sheriff's drones, it had no armor and no blades. It was a machine a first responder could send into a collapsed building or fire. Also a scout, although it lacked the hacking abilities of Dawn's destroyed bugs. While it might be quiet, it would easily be spotted by the Reilly-Bigg military-grade sentry dog.

Going up against more soldiers alone, without equipment save for a spider bot and a handgun. Would she place Pascal in the line of fire?

In her head, she plotted the best route to a road that would lead them south. For the next hour, they'd be crossing the same ground the runner with Eve might have gone.

No Reilly-Bigg vehicles charging her way.

It meant she and Pascal could slip south. Perhaps the redoubt defenders would have time to prepare for what was to come.

Do the job, get paid, get out.

The residue of beer became bitter in her mouth. "Things just got complicated. I have you. I need to take you home."

"What about Evie? We're going to save her."

"We might not be able to. You heard the captain. He has more soldiers. And if the message was jammed, more might be where we're going."

"If you want to leave, then go. Drop me off. I'm going to find her."

"You would do it alone, wouldn't you?"

She put the buggy in low gear and raced up the next slope.

***

The sheriff's scout drone relayed the view of the barn from the top of a tree.

The captain's armored runner was parked behind the farmhouse. A second and third car with Reilly-Bigg logos had arrived in the past twenty minutes. While none of them were combat vehicles, it was the extra soldiers Dawn had feared.

There had been an argument, with Fields chewing out the gang of soldiers. Four of them piled back into one of the smaller cars and headed out. Still, too many remained, but she couldn't get a count.

The robot sentry dog actively patrolled the perimeter of the barn. She set a targeting square on it and confirmed a second one was likewise moving about in the weeds and sunflowers along the side of the farmhouse.

Pascal got comfortable with the tablet on his lap, his feet on the dash, his concentration complete.

She applied lip balm. "Can you get an angle inside the barn?"

"Not from here."

He had likewise marked the two sentry dogs. The spider went forward, using the farmhouse as cover as the closest sentry made a circuit. They were six hundred meters out. If he triggered an alert, she would get them out of there.

It's what Eve would have wanted.

She leaned closer to look at the tablet he was using. "You rearranged the icons, didn't you?"

"...no."

They were color coded like a rainbow along the task bar. Just like his model cars.

He maneuvered the bot past a line of trees. There was little but the rise and fall of the ground and thick grass between them and the farmhouse.

"Good job. Just go slow."

"I know."

"There. Stop. Any closer, and that dog will ping you."

"*I know!*"

On the control panel, he selected LIDAR. A cone map of the farm appeared, including the interior of the barn. Three people moved about inside. All three were armed. One was Captain Fields. As the image improved, a fourth figure became visible. Eve. She lay secured to a cot or bed in a horse stall. Her feet hung over the end of the cot and she was hooked up to an IV.

The soldiers had the rest of their gear collected at the door to the barn. Packed and ready to go. Fields wasn't going to bother bringing Eve along once he got what he needed from her.

"Recall the drone," she said. "It's still three too many."

"We're saving her."

She knew the tone. End of discussion. While she believed he had his tantrums under control, he might physically try to stop her from driving them away.

She checked the automatic pistol they had found in the buggy. No advanced safety. It would have to do. If it came to gunplay, she'd be dead.

"Then we have one chance at this. I'm going in. Stay put. It's not optional."

She left Pascal and the buggy behind her and descended the hill, careful not to fall or make any sounds. Hiding and a stealthy approach would take too long. She turned on her jacket's suite of electronic countermeasures. Hoped they worked after everything she'd been through.

If the sentry dog was advanced enough, it would note an anomaly heading towards it. The only thing that couldn't be spoofed was sound, so she needed to be quiet.

Breathe steady, walk smoothly, stay calm.

The trite reminders had never worked. Her heart hammered and her mouth grew dry.

She kept her head down and her eyes on the ground, as if she were approaching a human target. Bots didn't have a sixth sense of someone watching, but the habit was impossible to break.

Pascal's drone wasn't sharing what it saw; they hadn't taken the time to synch it with her implant. But the bot was there right by the farmhouse. She could overlay the ground image with what she had seen during their first reconnoiter. But she kept it simple. Soon enough, she saw the sentry dog's outline.

It sat stone still, its head erect, with no lights to indicate it was even on. Only the cheap ones gave away their position.

She had double checked the load on the pistol, hadn't she? A quick replay with her app confirmed it, but the tide of doubt continued to rise. Each step forward was a possible sound. Her jacket wouldn't cut it with a military-grade motion tracker fine-tuned to watch for someone like her.

This was a mistake.

The sheriff's drone under Pascal's control remained somewhere behind her.

Her brother could undo her progress with a twitch of his finger.

She crossed the last stretch of dead grass towards her target. Soft crunches beneath her feet.

Deactivating it would surely trigger an alarm. Couldn't be helped. She held her breath as she reached for the drone. Her jacket would give her one chance. A single jolt spending all the jacket's battery charge should send the dog into shutdown mode. She had never tried it against so large a machine.

The drone's head twitched, a doglike sideways tilt as if raising an ear to the sky.

She froze. Didn't dare exhale.

"You must be Dawn," Captain Fields' voice said over the sentry's speaker. "We've been looking for you."

The whine of a motorcycle engine rose from behind her. A bike appeared at the top of the hill and raced towards the buggy. She zoomed in with her eye.

A flash, then an explosion as the buggy went up in flames.

Chapter Twenty-Nine

A light blazed from the sentry dog's eyes, blinding her.

"Don't move," Captain Fields said from the sentry bot. "The bounty on you is diminished if you're brought in dead."

The motorcycle was coming.

Dawn leaped for the sentry. Her hand touched the dog. Her jacket delivered an electric jolt, and with a sharp *snap*, the machine's eye winked off. It lit up again in moments, in the throes of its reboot cycle. It would be down for a minute, maybe two.

She ran for the farmhouse. The smell of burned insulation rose from her jacket. Countermeasure system offline. At least she wasn't on fire.

The second bot galloped around the corner towards her. It trampled the sunflowers and crashed through the undergrowth as it charged.

The motorcycle gained speed as it made it to level ground. Its headlight lanced across the grass and caught her.

Voices from the barn. The runner's spotlight was a sun peeling the night back from the farmhouse.

Only seconds before they surrounded her.

She ran for a shuttered window and tore it open. No time to see what lay inside the dark home as she dove inside.

Her jacket wasn't responding to her implant. There would be no second charge to disable the dogs.

The bot clamped onto the window frame and peered inside. Its bright headlight illuminated the interior. She scrambled across the rotted wooden floor into a hallway. Deteriorating carpet squished with moisture. The crumbling roof let in enough illumination from the spotlight that she could make out the interior of a kitchen. An old refrigerator stood empty, with its door missing. A sink sagged on exposed plumbing. The stench of rot filled her nose. The motorbike pulled around near the front of the home.

"She's inside!" the rider barked.

She aimed her pistol in anticipation of the sentry dog following her, but it didn't come.

Dizzy. Breathing too fast. She allowed her implant to trigger her neurotransmitters to throttle back her adrenaline response. Blinked sweat from her eyes.

If the runner had its rocket launcher loaded, they were holding back on using it. And the soldier on the bike? Most likely, he had lobbed a grenade that had killed Pascal.

The rest of the farmhouse was a burned-out frame with no cover. The only option was back through the side window where the sentry dog was waiting.

Seconds left before they started chucking frags.

A square section of old flooring stood raised. A cellar? She found a pull ring and opened a trapdoor. A wooden stepladder led down into the dark.

Footsteps on the dilapidated porch outside.

Nowhere to go but down.

A rung beneath her foot gave way, snapping and sending her falling. She struck the cellar floor with a jarring impact that send a wave of pain through her tailbone and spine.

She tried to clear her head. Where was the pistol?

Dropped it.

She slipped her goggles on. Too much clutter. As the light amplification adjusted to the hot light spilling down from above, she could see rows of collapsed shelves, smashed jars, and spilled containers around her. Spoiled fruits and vegetables were everywhere. The floor was sticky. While the home above was a shamble, the cellar had recently been in use, judging by the preserved food.

She crawled forward towards a shelf. Beneath it, she found the dropped weapon.

Boots clomped from above and approached the trapdoor.

Taking a moment to aim, she fired several rounds into the cellar ceiling.

A man screamed. A body thumped above and the cries continued. She was about to climb up the ladder when the house floor over her creaked.

"Making this harder than it needs to be. Don't be like your sister."

Something hard like a rock clacked, bounced, and rolled on the floor above. A grenade dropped into the cellar. She dove for cover around a corner.

A flash of lightning and a *WHUMP* blasted her senses.

Her night vision was overwhelmed. Her ears rang. She tore the goggles off her face. Blinked. Phantom images clung to her retinas. Thunder echoed in her head.

She felt her way forward and plowed through shattered jars and other debris. Found a pillar. Not a pillar, another corner. The cellar was large, perhaps larger than the footprint of the house.

Too dark to see what lay in the alcove, but at least it would be better cover.

Something big thumped onto the floor behind her.

She resisted the urge to fire. How many bullets had she used? Three, maybe four? Her implant told her ten. She had panicked.

Sloppy.

A quick glance confirmed an armored figure at the bottom of the ladder. A shoulder light flared and blinded her.

"I see you there," Captain Fields said.

She hit the ground. A burst of needle fire tore the wall to shreds. Crawling again, but there was nowhere to go as splinters of wood from the disintegrating wall sprayed everywhere.

The crunch of glass behind her. She spun onto her back and aimed the pistol between her knees. The armored soldier appeared, leading with his rifle. She popped off three rounds.

He tumbled backwards out of sight, his shoulder light wild across the cellar's ceiling. He groaned.

Got him.

But before she could rise, another explosion of rifle fire ripped across the cellar.

"She's still alive!"

Not the captain's voice. The captain must have been talking via a speaker on the soldier's armor.

She shoved a crate aside to reveal a crawlspace. Furnace vent? No choice. She squirmed into the opening. The horizontal shaft led straight. Keeping the pistol in hand slowed her down, but there was nowhere to put it and she didn't want to surrender the weapon while it still had a few rounds left.

At any second, the soldier would find the tunnel. Dead end up ahead. She hesitated before finishing the crawl. No room to turn around. Her breathing came quick and she was hyperventilating. Her implant wasn't keeping up. The ground pressed around her as if the Earth itself was breathing, and with each swell of the walls and ceiling, it threatened to smother her.

She swiped sweat and grime from her eyes. She had come all this way to die in a hole. A photo and scan of her corpse would be a small payday for Captain Fields. Killing Pascal was a final detail Reilly-Bigg could cross off the list in their effort to wipe the outpost away from memory.

Eve might stand a chance in some corporate black site until they realized she was too much trouble to keep alive.

And their mother?

Stuck in jail. Her daughters disappeared, her son still lost. Dawn was about to die without even the hollow satisfaction of leaving behind enough credits for a decent memorial, not that there was anyone left who would truly grieve for her loss.

Muffled chatter behind her. In front of her, too. A faint breeze tickled her face.

She pulled the goggles back on. Her fingers were slick and she realized her gloves were gone. Grit rubbed her face where the device touched the skin. Finally, she got the clasps to seal and her night vision returned. One eye, at least. The other was blank, the lens cracked.

A few feet ahead of her, a second tunnel led off to her left.

She clawed at the dirt to pull herself along. Wood slats braced the tunnel. Who had built the place? How had it lasted so long? While the house was a ruin, the cellar had been in use and the barn out back was intact.

Her answers waited less than ten meters ahead.

The tunnel led to the bottom of a stone well. Three bodies moldered in a heap. Two women, one child. The gray skin was sunken around their faces, the eyes wasted away. Their clothes were torn and the bodies riven with wounds. A small cloud of flies buzzed about.

Dead for at least a few weeks, Dawn guessed.

Light spilled in from above. The well had a cover, or at least a few boards placed across the top.

While the farmhouse was a ruin for many years, these people had no doubt lived there. More blood spilled by Captain Fields and his crew.

It would be mere moments before her pursuer found the tunnel, if he hadn't already. They'd send in the robot dogs or use grenades.

The sides of the well were slick with slime. Far enough apart that her legs alone couldn't brace her body to keep her from falling. About halfway up, she found no more handholds. She leaned forward, catching herself on the opposite side of the well's shaft. Took a moment to breathe before continuing the laborious ascent. Centimeter by centimeter, she finished her climb as her arms and legs burned for relief. A final leap to the edge and she caught a lip of stone mercifully free of moss. She knocked a board aside to fix her grip. It clattered. Couldn't be helped.

She pulled herself up and over the side of the well.

The captain's runner was parked nearby. The barn stood behind it. Head down, she sprinted for the vehicle. The back gate stood ajar. A pile of gear sat in a heap. Eve's assembled rifle leaned on top of it all.

A 13mm Bryer-Actual Type One. Eve didn't believe in plasma or lasers.

Dawn's heart dropped as she realized the weapon wouldn't fire for anyone but Eve.

A click-click-click of metal feet tapping across the gravel. The second sentry dog appeared at the corner of the vehicle. Dawn raised her pistol and shot it. The stark report was a thunderclap. The bot careened to one side before collapsing.

Captain Fields appeared in the door to the barn. He was fast as he went for his weapon. She was faster. She squeezed the trigger. The gun clicked. Empty.

Fields peppered the back of the runner as Dawn dove for cover. Fire tore across her thigh. An explosion of pain. Her legs gave out from under her and she tumbled forward.

The captain rounded the corner of the barn as she scrambled through the weeds in the barn's direction. Tall grass and thistles scratched her face. She elbow crawled away even as the captain closed in on her.

"You're far more trouble than you're worth."

A low, dark shape in the grass scurried towards her. A third drone. Trapped. She tossed the pistol aside. Turned to face Fields.

He was grinning ear to ear as he raised the needle rifle. The smile vanished as the spider drone scampered past Dawn and sprang at him. It was the sheriff's machine, the one Pascal had been operating. It struck the captain's rifle and sent him tumbling. The bot kept running, snagging the weapon and dragging it along like a monkey stealing a prize.

He snap-drew his sidearm and unloaded in the drone's direction. Dawn didn't hesitate as she pushed herself to her good leg and hobbled along into the shadows along the side of the barn.

Fields was reloading. "Don't you ever quit?"

A bullet smacked the wood wall next to her. She hit the dirt and crawled.

"Running is stupid," Fields shouted.

A burned out camper or recreational vehicle lay ahead. Long as a bus, its scorched sides partially melted. A firepit stood before it and scattered trash lay everywhere. A flashlight beam caught her square in its center. Dawn had nowhere to go as Fields caught up with her.

She sat herself up against the tire. "Who were these people?"

Gun and flashlight pointing, he strode to the edge of the firepit. "Doesn't matter, does it? Squatters. Remnants. Caretaker loyalists unwilling to play by a new set of rules."

"Didn't know Reilly-Bigg had a death squad."

"Says the mercenary spy taking credits from at least three different corporations. Tell me the name of your last employer, and I'll point out your own hypocrisy. Your sister is a soldier in a unit with quite the reputation. Have you asked her about her last op down south? Made a few headlines in our cozy community. Reason why Evergreen wants her back."

"I can't speak for her. I never murdered a family scraping by like you did with those poor souls down in that well. And what about the Commonwealth outpost? And the people inside the redoubt?"

"Recording our chat with your implant? That'll need to be wiped. But I was hoping you could enlighten me as to what happened back there and how you made it out. Are my men still alive?"

She didn't answer.

"No matter. I'll have more there soon. With you under wraps, they're the only loose end left."

"Loose end for what?"

He shrugged. The grin was back. In that moment, she knew he would kill her. Motion at the barn. The spider emerged from the back door. Right behind it limped Eve. She had a walking stick. Not a stick. Her rifle. Had the bot brought it to her?

Captain Fields turned in time to see her raise her weapon. The ear-shattering report and the bullet arrived simultaneously as his head exploded. She fired two more times towards the farmhouse before scanning. Finally, she lowered the weapon and almost fell.

Leg throbbing and wet with blood, Dawn used the camper to stand. "Eve?"

Her sister staggered to the corner of the barn. She set her rifle down and appeared winded.

The drone scurried over as if sniffing at the fallen captain. It then vanished around the camper, appearing a minute later and pacing before Dawn.

"All clear," Pascal announced through the drone's speaker.

Her breath caught in her throat. "Pas? Where are you?"

He appeared from the darkness. His face was swollen and covered with abrasions. One eye wept blood. His nose leaked twin rivulets of red. In one hand, he clutched the sheriff's tablet. But his smile? She had never seen him looking so pleased.

Eve whistled and motioned for him. He vanished into the barn.

Dawn's torn up leg kept her from moving. "A little help here."

"Keep your shirt on," Eve called. "Pas, make sure that's tight."

What was he doing? Then she remembered there had been another soldier inside the barn.

Pascal appeared a minute later. He plonked down a large first aid kit at Dawn's feet, pulled out the medical foam, and started reading the label.

Dawn held out a shaking hand. "Give it here."

"I can do it. Sit down."

She sat. He had to use scissors to slice off her pant leg. A wave of dizziness rolled through her as she saw the blood. He deftly applied a line of the foam. Instant numbness, and she felt the world slipping away.

Chapter Thirty

Their soldier captive was a medic. He wore clip-on AR spectacles with one lens broken and was zip tied and seated on a cot inside the barn. He kept his head bowed but couldn't take his eyes off Eve.

She sat across from him on another cot, the rifle in her lap. Bandages covered her neck and left arm. She casually stroked the wooden rifle stock as she glared.

Dawn emerged from the stall the soldiers had been using as a washroom and lavatory. They had two chemical toilets, a sink, and a shower.

Her jacket was ruined. Enough of the electronics had been destroyed she wouldn't feel comfortable attempting a repair. An unreliable tool was a useless tool. But its cut, fit, and color would be hard to replace. She had her balance back, but her leg remained swollen and painful. Didn't want to sit.

She tried to put on lip balm, but her applicator was gummed up with dirt. With a sigh, she tossed it away. "We need to leave."

Pascal was operating the drone via the sheriff's tablet. The machine was outside somewhere, monitoring things.

"Pas?" Eve said. "Step outside and close the door."

He didn't argue as he hurried to leave the barn.

Dawn joined her sister. "I don't want him out of our sight. Why are we still here?"

"Because I have questions for this scumbag and he's not coming with us."

The medic's eyes widened. He looked beseechingly at Dawn. "I…was just doing my job."

"You talk to *me*," Eve said. "One thing left for you to do, soldier boy. Ready to die for your corporation?"

"I patched you up. You and the other soldier we captured at the reservoir. I told you he's alive!"

"Yes, you did. Linus. He's at the infirmary at your southern field property, right?"

"Yeah. Captain Fields wasn't supposed to kill any of you."

She brought the rifle upright. Checked the load. "Only because we have a price tag. Not the case with the poor saps of the outpost. Explain."

"That was all the captain. He ordered the troopers to do what they did. They ambushed the car but missed one. The outpost supervisor was hurt but slipped away, from what Henderson told me. I wasn't even with them. He divided up the remains after they got burned so it looked like there were five bodies. Then we learned there was a sixth we had missed. Please!"

"You haven't answered why."

"I don't know why."

Eve made a face as she looked at Dawn. As if to say, "See? That's what I'm dealing with."

"Let me try," Dawn said. "You said the troopers were ordered. How many are in your detail?"

"Twelve. Three are with the other prisoner."

"His name's Linus," Eve growled.

"Linus. The others were left behind at the squatter's tunnel to mop up."

Dawn clenched her jaw. "Your unit is all dead."

"Oh, god."

"Why do you call them squatters? What about the people who lived here? I saw their bodies down in the well." He didn't answer. "You killed them too."

"It wasn't me."

"Someone patched up the outpost supervisor. You're the one with the first aid kit. You were there, weren't you? What were you asking her?"

"Captain Fields wanted to know about any other locations like the tunnels."

"Why?"

"Reilly-Bigg wants them gone. That's all I know. She escaped before telling him anything."

To Eve, Dawn said, "Verna Cho would have died but for making it to the redoubt. She and Pascal got lucky."

"We know where Linus is. We don't need him anymore."

The medic sat up straight. Tears budded in his eyes. "You need my help to rescue the other...to get Linus!"

Eve rose and tapped a finger on the trigger guard. "All right. Shut up. Hmm. It's the first thing he's said that makes sense. Still be easier to drop him here with the others."

Was Eve asking her opinion? "Getting Linus shouldn't be an option. We're in no shape to get into a fight. At least three guards, plus whatever other soldiers are circulating around the area."

"That's why I brought you along. To figure stuff like that out."

Eve napped in the back seat of the Reilly-Bigg runner with one arm around the shoulders of the captured medic.

Dawn's eyelids drooped as she navigated the winding road leading downhill towards the region near Salina Crossroads.

"Let me drive," Pascal asked for the ninth time.

"Keep an ear on the radio. No more surprises. Ronald, are you sure there's no radio code before we arrive at the gate?"

The medic, Ronald Ashraf, according to his corporate ID, shook his head. They had his credentials, along with one they had retrieved from Captain Fields' body. "They'll let you in. At this hour, the other three soldiers are off-shift and might be in town."

Eve gave his neck a playful tug with the crook of her elbow. "Remember what I told you about lying?"

"They're guarding Linus. It's probably one soldier, though. They monitor all staff interactions and are keeping him isolated, as per our orders."

Dawn caught his eye in the rearview mirror. "Do you have access?"

"Yes. But they'll want to know what's going on. We've been trying to root out the sources of the radio jammers and who's been sabotaging the signal towers. It drove the captain nuts. We'd locate a jammer, tear it down. It would be up again in a few days."

"So Reilly-Bigg thinks it's the Remnants doing it."

"Them, bandits, separatist farmers—he blamed everybody. Even suspected the sheriff."

"Who does the captain report to?"

"Vice President of Ops. But Captain Fields operated outside of the typical command structure."

She recalled her brief and final encounter with the captain before Eve shot him. His heavy armor had a full suite of electronics, including surveillance. The runner they were driving would coordinate the unit's voice coms and video.

"Pascal, get the memory unit out of the computer in case we need to switch vehicles."

It took her brother only a moment to pop the card from the back of the command CPU. An array of warning lights blossomed on the dash.

He examined the card before slipping it into a shirt pocket. "There goes the warranty."

"Was that a joke?"

"No, I'm serious. The runner is produced by Transom Mechanical. It's a JD-486 and only five years out of production. While this particular car is modified, only a certified Transom-trained mechanic may make any repairs or perform a service, and never while the runner is in operation."

She was about to tell him to relax, no one cared about the warranty, and that the car police weren't going to bust them but said, "I'm glad you're safe."

"Did I make you mad?"

"No, I'm fine."

"Then why are you crying?"

"Because just maybe we're going to be okay."

No one stopped them at the farm gate.

The metal mesh barrier rolled open automatically with a flash of the captain's card to a scanner.

A stiff breeze buffeted the door as Dawn slid out of the driver's seat. No time to prepare a proper fake ID, or even tidy up. She hobbled, her leg stiff and no doubt in need of fresh dressings. The first aid foam had its limits. The ache and itchiness that had plagued her during the drive was now a flurry of prickling bug bites. She gritted her teeth as she headed inside the clinic.

Had the three soldiers seen her before? Had the captain had time to share her picture with the rest of the security personnel?

She was about to find out.

She felt Eve's eyes upon her as she headed through the automatic entrance.

The cozy lobby had no receptionist. A chime sounded.

A woman in scrubs appeared through a door. "Can I help you?"

"Captain Fields sent me to collect the prisoner. Doctor..."

"Silva. And who are you?"

Dawn thought of all her IDs. Could pretend to be one of Captain Fields' soldiers. But Dr. Silva had a visible sheen on her right eye. An implant, and even now she might be calling security.

"I'm Dawn Moriti. Reilly-Bigg has a warrant out for my arrest, or at least has forwarded a bounty to your security team. You have three soldiers here watching the man you have in your clinic. My team has killed Captain Fields, along with most of his command except for a Specialist Ashraf, who we're releasing once we take that man off your hands."

"You're serious."

"Like a heart attack. If the rest of my team has to step foot out of the runner outside, it's going to be a bloodbath."

The doctor stepped aside. "I'm not armed and not resisting. He's right in here."

"What about the security team?"

"They went into town for drinks."

So Ronald had told the truth. She gave the doctor a quick once over. Didn't appear armed.

Linus lay in the next room with oxygen on his nose and a hydration supply on his arm. A display at the foot of the bed relayed his vitals. Both wrists and his head were bandaged, and he had a hard cast over the hand with the missing fingers. His eyes fluttered. An attempt at a laugh turned into a cough. He winced.

"Ow."

"I need you to move."

He pressed a fob. A second feeder dripped medicine into his line. "Give it a sec. Yeah. There we go. I'm ready. Where's the sarge?"

"Waiting outside for my signal to unload on this place if I don't bring you with me."

"Sounds about right. Tell her to go easy. The doc here—she's one of the good ones."

Linus needed a wheelchair. The doctor assisted Dawn in getting him to the runner. Pascal helped to pull him up into the back as their captured medic spilled out past them and sprinted off down the dirt road between rows of greenhouses.

Eve brought out the rifle.

"Let him go," Dawn said. "Linus is going to live. The other soldiers are gone. We're leaving and there doesn't need to be any more killing."

Her sister glared before stowing the rifle and slamming the door. "He was as much a part of the captain's team as the rest of them."

"I don't doubt it. We've got enough to shine a light on what they were doing here. It's enough for now."

"You really believe that?"

Dawn let the question hang as she made a U-turn and got them out the gate and on the road.

Chapter Thirty-One

She could have slept for days, but five hours was all Dawn allowed herself before her implant woke her up in the small hours of the morning. They needed to put more klicks between themselves and any Reilly-Bigg response that might be in pursuit.

Her head buzzed. Pascal alive. Here with her. Eve had survived as well. The redoubt, Verna Cho, Quint and his family—she couldn't save them all.

Had Captain Fields sent for reinforcements? Would the custodian button down the redoubt sufficiently to hold off the inevitable assault?

No way to know. The pang inside her heart wouldn't be ignored.

They continued east along a rough track that finally wound up at a town in the foothills. No cops, no cameras, no corporate presence. A bar had an attached deli with a sign boasting "Fresh Eats".

They purchased hot sandwiches, bottled water, beer, and a few bags of freshly made kettle corn. Dawn asked about any trails heading north into the mountains. The helpful counterperson had suggestions, but didn't recommend traveling that way without a guide.

Pascal had accompanied her inside and was distracted by the handful of diners eating breakfast. A rough-hewn bunch who eyed them suspiciously.

As they emerged from the bar, he asked, "Why did you ask about going north?"

"Because not everything I say is truthful."

He nodded as if he understood. "In case anyone asks."

"Exactly. We're going to need to talk about that before we get back.

There's things you won't be able to tell people about, at least not yet. It wasn't just Reilly-Bigg. Commonwealth Services is involved and maybe complicit. You might be in trouble for knowing about what happened."

"But I didn't do anything."

"No, you didn't. Sometimes, even when we do the right thing, certain people take offense."

"Okay."

"Just okay?"

"It's like Saputo and the rat. The rat was chewing up power cables and pooping in the food supply. Plus, she was going to have babies. So Saputo was doing the right thing in setting a trap and killing it."

"I didn't know Saputo. He knew you liked that rat. Sounds to me like he was being a jerk. But it's like that."

"The right thing for me would be to go back to Quint and help him."

"It might be. We need to learn if they were attacked. Hopefully with what happened, Reilly-Bigg will pull back and reassess. Maybe later, after we see what we can do to make sure Reilly-Bigg doesn't send any more of their killers out, you can return."

"You'd let me?"

"Pascal, I love you. You're all grown up now and can do whatever you want with your life."

"I thought you'd be mad. You and Eve got hurt."

"And you realize that. What we do—what either of us do—and the choices we make affect others. From what I've learned, it's a lesson we sometimes have to learn over and over. Eve and I helped you because it's what family does. If you want to help Quint once we settle in, that's a decision you'll make."

"Okay."

Linus stuck his head out of the runner's back window. "ETA on breakfast?"

She gave Pascal a half hug. He bunched up and endured it before she let him go. Then she shoved the bag of groceries into the runner before getting them rolling.

***

Pascal drove.

It was a straight enough road. Eve snored steadily in the back and Dawn couldn't keep her eyes open. But once her brother took the wheel of the Reilly-Bigg armored runner, she was wide awake and fighting down the urge to grab the steering wheel as he slowly veered from left to right.

"Verna gave me a driving lesson a few times with the outpost's truck. No one else would let me touch the wheel."

"She was your friend. Did you give her your journal?"

His brow creased as he kept his eyes on the road. "No one gets to see that. Doctor's orders."

The flash drive with his diary felt hot in her pocket.

She got comfortable and watched the scrub. They followed along the shore of a murky section of the inland sea. A giant alkali puddle of sea foam water. Formations of algae clung to the rocks. Half-submerged dead trees thrust from the murk. Not all dead. A few sprouted green. Birds pecked along a sandy stretch of ground, scattering to the sky as they rumbled past.

Linus clicked his tongue. He had propped himself up against the back door, with his feet on the seat between him and Eve. The sheriff's tablet screen lit his face as he scrolled. "Sheriff was doing plenty of eaves-dropping and took notes. Captain Fields had an entire strategy laid out. He has the location of a Caretaker-sympathetic gang—bunch of crack-pots with motorcycles and a few pop guns. Near as I can tell, Fields was planning a strike to take them down. Convenient. Blame them for any collateral damage, including the burning of the outpost."

"What about the redoubt land?" Dawn asked.

"Near as I can tell, it's close enough to a few other pins near the reservoir where Reilly-Bigg wants to expand. Captain and sheriff knew they were out there. They just couldn't find them. There's a log of word-of-mouth interviews with a few squatters up that way. They were chasing down rumors while rousting anyone they could find."

She couldn't forget the image of the dead family in the well. "Not everyone wanted to leave. So were they squatters or just people living far enough from town they didn't warrant legal protection?"

"Hey, don't get me involved in a semantic argument. Wait for your sister to wake up for that."

It wouldn't be the first time pre-returnee locals were moved, especially ones who didn't want to be folded into a growing municipality. Some people didn't want to play with others. Some didn't like the new neighbors. The fighting to the south where Eve's unit served was mostly the latter, once the layers of rhetoric were peeled away.

They stopped in a larger town. Sandy Shores, population 1,200. Eve was awake and directed Pascal to a radio tower. It had a small building and a few cars parked along the side. She got out without explanation and hobbled towards the door.

"What is this place?" Dawn asked.

Pascal was still on the tablet. "Radio station. Plays sports broadcasts, news, and talk."

Dawn realized she could have looked the information up. Sandy Shores had its own network. She stifled a yawn as she considered the few options there for food and a place to stay. Even Pascal was flagging. He hadn't spoken for the last two hours, even as he appeared intent on not relinquishing the driver's seat.

A group emerged from the radio station office. Two men, two women, dressed in work pants and long-sleeved shirts. One woman had AR lenses and stared at them for a moment before they piled into a truck and drove off.

Dawn watched them leave in the side mirror. "We need to get off the road and get rid of this car."

Linus grunted. "And I'd like a kitten but Eve says no."

"Reilly-Bigg isn't going to wait for us to go to ground. We have to assume they're putting the word out. There's probably a price on all of us. Going back to New Pacific is a mistake. We change vehicles, we resupply, stay on the back roads, make it for Seraph."

"Take it easy, baby sister. Eve's got it under control."

"How can you be so calm?" she shouted.

Pascal stared at her wide-eyed. "Mom says no yelling in the car."

She raised a hand and nodded. "I'm sorry. You're right; I was yelling."

"That's okay. I yelled sometimes. You just weren't around to hear it."

Linus perked up. "See? Eve's back."

Eve slammed the door after getting in. "Get us driving."

"No 'Here's the sit report,' boss?"

"The sit report is you shut up and we get on the road."

"Trouble?" Dawn asked.

"Maybe. Maybe not."

Linus nodded sagely. "Told you she'd take care of us. Everything's under control."

Eve directed Pascal to a grain and produce depot. They parked behind a metal warehouse marked D-17. A soft drizzle blanketed the orchards nearby as workers tended the trees and went about their business.

Rifle on her lap, Eve remained alert. Pascal had found a pistol from somewhere in back but was content to sleep. Dawn tried to fight the nods, but likewise napped as the hours passed.

Late afternoon, and a robot truck pulled up beside the warehouse. The back gate dropped and three soldiers with black tactical gear walked out towards them.

Dawn got Pascal down and wriggled over behind the driver's seat. She spammed the start button too many times. The engine whirred without starting.

"Take it easy," Eve said. "These are the people I called."

"Who are they?"

Eve got out of the runner. "Acquaintances."

Dawn kept a hand on Pascal as he cowered in the passenger side foot well.

None of the three had insignias of rank or any clue to which corporation they worked for. Mercenaries.

She only caught part of the conversation, and it was brief. Whatever details needed to be hammered out didn't require a discussion.

Eve tapped the window and waved for them to come out of the

runner. A merc with a braided black beard took the key card and drove the vehicle into the back of the robot truck. Eve and the lead merc, a man with big eyebrows and white sideburns connecting a round beard and a curly mullet, led them to a front compartment. The robot truck sections were now detached, forming two separate vehicles. They weren't heading in the same direction as their stolen Reilly-Bigg ride.

A gate dropped and formed a set of stairs into the truck's interior.

Dawn stepped inside to discover a studio with couches, a television, a bar, and a toilet stall. A poster of an anime woman with goggles firing a pair of pistols decorated the back wall. On another wall, someone had spray painted a hand giving a double raised finger in runny black lines. Beer bottles lay scattered about, as did dirty dishes, food wrappers, and soiled clothing.

The merc directed them inside. "This is your home for the next few hours. Get comfortable."

Pascal's mouth curled down as he inspected the place.

When Dawn tried to move past the merc, he stopped her. "You're the sister."

"Who hasn't she told about me?"

He gave her an appraising look, as if he were sizing up a livestock purchase.

"Is there a problem?"

Eve inserted herself between them. "No problem at all. Mike here is in awe that there's two of us."

He laughed before shutting the gate, sealing them inside.

Dawn squared off with Eve. "What was that about?"

"Mike and his crew are okay. Just relax. They're going to get us into New Pacific. Once we get there, you're free to do whatever it is you do."

"My bounty, Kaja Stepnova. You're going to release her to me?"

"A promise is a promise."

Dawn mulled over the words as the truck got underway.

Chapter Thirty-Two

The ride in the back of the robot truck was surprisingly smooth.

Dawn had a hard time keeping her eyes open even as Linus put on the replay of a cricket match on the big screen. They were in signal range, and several nets were accessible.

Pascal had his ear to the wall of the truck and appeared endlessly pleased with the sounds of the road and the whoosh of wind pushing against the side of the vehicle.

When Linus came around with bottles of lemonade and a platter of flatbreads and hummus, Dawn declined. "Pascal won't be eating that either."

Eve was up from her couch. "What's the matter, Dawn? Think I was going to slip something into your food? Hand you over for the prize, even though I told you we'd be square once we got Pascal home?"

"It crossed my mind."

Her sister grabbed a piece of bread, swiped a glop of hummus, and ate it. "See? Nothing. I can hear your stomach grumbling. You're not the only one with good ears. Starve if you want, but don't tell Pascal what to do."

Pascal kept his attention on the wall. "I don't like the hummus with garlic. That has garlic; I can smell it."

Dawn waved Linus off. "This has nothing to do with Pascal. I know he's his own person. Did you forget you ambushed me? Now you've made plans with your mercenary friends to get us back to New Pacific without telling me what's going on. So excuse me if I'm a little leery."

"Mike's not exactly a friend," Eve said.

"That doesn't make me feel better about this. Calling in a favor?"

"That runner is payment enough. He keeps it. We get our ride. Will you please eat something?"

"I'm not hungry."

The rest of the drive was quiet.

Dawn finally dug in. Her stomach *was* grumbling.

When the truck pulled to a stop, it only took her a moment to ping her location on the local splinternet. Commonwealth zone. They were in a dirt lot between two small apartment buildings. A few vehicles were parked nearby.

Mercenary Mike waited for them to disembark before sealing up the truck and firing off a mock salute to Eve before climbing into the cab.

Dawn's motorcycle waited between two compact electric cars. She confirmed it was hers before following Eve, Pascal, and Linus into a side entrance to one building.

"What is this place?"

Eve led them through a center atrium. "This is where we part ways."

One of Eve's soldiers appeared at an apartment door. A gaunt man with orange, white, and black splotches on his skin like a calico cat. Not makeup, but a skin mod. He wore a turquoise polo shirt and baggy slacks and packed a pistol in a shoulder holster.

A second soldier stretched out on a couch while watching a vid screen. Big guy. They, along with Linus, were the ones who had captured Dawn and taken her to the safe house.

Kaja Stepnova emerged from the kitchen with two cups of tea. "You're back."

She set the cups on the coffee table by the couch. She had changed clothes since Dawn had last seen her, now wearing shorts and a tank top. Her hair looked wet and tied back in a ponytail.

"You okay?" Dawn asked.

"Once they left with you, they brought me here. I'm fine. Can I go home now?"

The soldier by the door chuckled. "Sarge's sister is going to cash you in for a payday."

Eve was in the doorway. "Webb? Schooner? Out."

Both men left the apartment.

Once they were gone, Eve faced Dawn. "As promised. Your gear's here and packed up. Your bounty is waiting."

"Wait, what?" Kaja asked.

"You think you've been on holiday here? My sister is going to take you and cash you in before riding off with her spoils. Isn't that right?"

"Sit down," Dawn said to Kaja. "We need to talk."

Kaja's lip trembled as she took a place on the couch.

Dawn found the remote and switched off the TV before joining her. "I told you about my friend. The detective. I turn you in to him, he keeps you off the books until he gets you sorted. Evergreen won't lay a finger on you."

"You don't know that."

"It's how these things work. If you don't come clean now, someone else is going to scoop you up and hand you over to Evergreen. It won't go so well for you there. How high up was your husband?"

"High enough."

"Right. You can take your chances by leaving New Pacific, but I'm guessing you stuck around here because it's what you know. Family? Friends?"

"All in the city."

"You want a chance of ever reentering your life? It's with me."

Kaja sipped at a teacup. Nodded. "And you get paid."

"I do. It's what I'm good at."

"It's a terrible job. You do terrible things. But I'll go with you."

"I'll wait outside and give you a few minutes to get yourself together. And if you decide to slip out the back window, I won't stop you."

Eve spoke in a huddle with her two men outside.

Dawn heard Pascal's voice in a neighboring apartment. She found him with Linus. The apartment's interior looked familiar. She didn't need her implant to inform her that every stick of furniture and piece of decoration had been taken from her mother's place.

Pascal was in the bedroom inspecting a line of model cars arranged on a shelf.

His car collection. Here. His bedspread, his poster of a cartoon chicken in racing goggles on a rocket-powered pogo stick, his blue ceramic juice cup.

She inspected the empty cup before offering it to Pascal.

He wiped dust from a model cobalt roadster with exaggerated fins and white tires. "I don't drink juice anymore."

Linus stepped in and tossed him a set of keys. "Evie wanted me to tell you the rest of this is yours. At least until things calm down."

"What's going on?" Dawn asked.

"I have my own place now."

"Says who?" she said too quickly.

"Eve. I have the key. My stuff's here, at least the stuff that I didn't take with me when I went to work."

"It's not that simple. She can't just give you an apartment."

"Why not?" Eve stepped in through the front door. "I own this building. At least half of it. The boys and Linus own the other half. This is the real safe house. I arranged for Pas' belongings to be brought here and set up. In case we found him. And we did."

Dawn was about to say something. Stopped. It was all wrong, his being here, but she couldn't place a finger on why it bothered her.

"What's the matter? You have your bounty, you have your bike. Nothing's stopping you from cashing in and taking off."

"What's the conditions on his staying?"

"None. His place. He'll be safe here, safer than at mom's."

"You and your grunts hardly make a place safe. I have people after me. How many are after you? Because we can both add Reilly-Bigg to the list."

"This zone is so beige it's almost translucent. And while the dust settles, Pas gets a fresh ID and a couple of skin mods to spoof the cameras. Once he gets those, he can go wherever he wants."

It was as much as Dawn had promised him. She looked at her brother.

"Is this what you want? Mom's apartment is what you know. But Eve's right; it might be dangerous for you there."

"Is there a swimming pool?"

Linus guffawed but slunk out between the sisters when Eve shot him a withering glare.

"No pool," Eve said. "An arcade and theater nearby, and a couple of parks in walking distance."

"What about my job?"

Dawn shook her head. "You can't go back to that. You need to stay in until we know no one's looking to flag you."

"And Quint and his family? And Verna?"

"I'll do what I can to learn who in Commonwealth Services I can trust. They'll investigate. It'll be messy and slow, but it'll happen. Once we spread the word about what Reilly-Bigg was doing up there, CS won't be able to hide anything. Verna and Quint will be safe."

"You said if I really wanted to, I could go back."

"I did. And you can. I'll advise against it. Eve will too. But neither of us will stop you."

He brushed past her and went into the kitchen. The clatter of dishes followed. He was removing plates and bowls and glasses from a cupboard before moving on to the utensil drawer.

"This could be a while," Eve said.

"You didn't have to do this for him."

"He's going to be okay. Looks like your girl is waiting for you."

Kaja stood just outside the apartment with a purse under an arm. "So, are you going to turn me in or what?"

Chapter Thirty-Three

The bounty office paid in credit chips, no questions asked.

Rumor had it on the dark web that this would change, but the tiny basement office near the Commonwealth central lockup remained a safe place for shady hunters to cash in their prey. Enough cops around that no one tried anything, but the unspoken rule was that no one doing business here would get harassed. Didn't mean other hunters might not be looking to follow Dawn once she was finished with Kaja.

Kaja went quietly.

Dawn's leg was in too much pain to ride her bike. Schooner, Eve's tank of a soldier, gave them a lift in his sedan and was waiting curbside.

A cop came out through a door and took Jaya away. She didn't look back.

Detective Satoko was a hunched, middle-aged cop with receding hair and a wispy beard. He wore a trench coat and a tattered felt trilby. Something about him always looked like he needed ironing.

He blew his nose with a cloth handkerchief before shoving it into a pocket. "You limped in here."

"And you have me profiled on your security feed."

"Huh. First time that worked. Countermeasures broken? They tagged you once you set foot on the sidewalk. Don't take it personal; I like to keep track of my CIs. Plus, you're hard to miss in that purple jacket. That thing's seen better days."

"You'll take care of Kaja?"

"Sure. I'll be on the other side of processing to get her statement. Seems her husband had her flagged, as we've already received a message to have her remanded to Evergreen security. What have you gotten me involved in?"

"You hand her over, she won't survive. Her husband beat her."

"Evergreen was offering a bigger payday than we were, but you brought her here. What happened to you?"

Dawn gave an exaggerated shrug. She must have been a sight. Wounded, scratched up, weary. She took out her lip balm and applied it. "I may have something bigger for you. Not an outstanding warrant. A major crime involving Reilly-Bigg and a farm community up north. Some people up the ladder in CS too. Can I call you tomorrow?"

"If it's that big, why not talk now?"

"Because I'm ready to drop."

She put the lip balm away and caressed the loaded credit chip in her pocket. Hardly a retirement windfall, but enough to pay her way out of the city.

Do the job, get paid...

He chewed his lip. "High crimes and misdemeanors. Figured I don't have enough on my plate. You know we have a major crimes division with ten times the resources of my midtown department."

"Yeah. I keep coming back to you because you're the only one who won't cuff me and ask questions later."

"Might be a day for that coming. You'll call tomorrow?"

Dawn nodded. "Satoko? Take care of Kaja. I mean it."

He stared at her as she turned to leave.

Schooner was still outside, occupying the sidewalk. Pedestrians gave him a wide berth. Even the cops passing along avoided eye contact. He was on the phone, but hung up once Dawn approached the car.

"That was your sister. Seems your brother stole your bike and took off."

***

Where? Where would Pascal go?

The obvious choice was he would return north. After everything they had done for him—nearly lost him—he was going back to where he would likely be murdered.

She leaned up from the back seat. "Can't this car go faster?"

Schooner kept both hands on the steering wheel. "This car is a city car and it goes precisely as fast as it can. It has all the latest safety features, including a speed regulator designed to obey the limit."

"I thought one of Eve's grunts would have disabled the thing."

"You'd be wrong. I drive my family in this car and safety can't be disregarded. As to going faster, you really want to risk getting flagged? I thought you wanted to make it home."

Home. Is that what he thought Eve's apartment complex was? Did he live there too?

"Just...do what you can."

Her leg still ached, but she knew she could take enough nummers, if she could score some. Stims, too. So groggy. Her equipment procurer hadn't been the fastest to respond to her texts of late. Next step: purchase or steal a ride.

Eve paced in the apartment courtyard, her phone to her ear.

Dawn let the gate slam behind her as she closed in on her sister. "He's gone."

"Yeah. I'm on it."

"What do you mean, you're on it?"

"What I said. Now shhhh."

Heat rose in Dawn's face. She felt the familiar tremble. Turned away and flexed her hands. While swiping a car and speeding north after Pascal would feel satisfying, it would also be a knee-jerk reaction to a situation she didn't understand. Which route would Pascal take? Could she head him off?

With her implant, she plotted likely routes north.

Eve, distracted, lowered the phone. "Sit down before you fall over."

The door to Pascal's apartment stood open. She went inside and inspected each item as if it might reveal a clue to what he had been thinking. Or what had triggered him. His cars? His poster? The few items of clothing he liked to wear? Nothing stood out.

The kitchen had a few groceries. Snacks, mostly, but also ramen, a few green apples, eggs, oat milk, a pack of spinach, some carrots, and Pascal's favorite condiments. Yellow mustard, low salt fish sauce, and an overly sweet Polynesian dressing he would glop onto everything.

A bowl sat freshly washed in the dish rack next to his favorite blue ceramic cup. The bowl was powder blue stoneware, with a noticeable chip in its lip. Pascal had refused to allow their mother to throw it out, despite her warning that the crack would permit bacteria to grow. For years, they had all treated the cup and bowl with care lest they break and trigger an outburst to end all outbursts.

Phone down, Eve stepped into the apartment. "You're back."

"Where is he?"

"That's what I'm working on. I had a bug on your bike. I sent Webb out to go looking. Figured you'd write the bike off when you left with Kaja. So why are you here?"

"Because we've returned to square one. What do you want me to say? He's going to get himself killed. Give me a car and I'll head out now."

"We're in no shape to do anything."

"Speak for yourself."

"I have my doctor coming. He's good. I'll cover your fees if you're being cheap."

"We can't just wait here."

"It's exactly what we're going to do. You're used to working alone; I have people I can trust. You turned in your bounty. There's nothing holding you to River City."

Dawn flopped down on the couch and tried to ignore how good it felt sitting on a soft, comfy cushion that wasn't moving. She set her injured leg on a hassock and felt instant relief. "Did Pascal say anything before he left?"

Eve sat heavily next to her. "No."

Dawn waited for more.

"Fine. He was pacing about in the apartment while I was sitting outside on the steps. He was getting spun up. I told him to eat something and take a nap, that he was exhausted."

"Like telling him to calm down ever helped."

"You weren't here. Can I finish? Once you left, he kept going on about getting *you* back. Didn't mention Verna or Quint. I went to the head and he was gone."

"I didn't think he noticed I left."

"Of course he noticed. He always notices."

Eve was up and speaking with Webb on her phone. Dawn listened in and caught most of it.

Webb's voice was matter-of-fact. "West side of New Pacific. Lost visual at a transit station. He parked the bike and I'm sweeping to locate. Best guess: if he's heading north, it's via bus. I'll check the terminals on foot next."

"Keep me posted," Eve said before ending the call.

Dawn had Eve copy the location and forward it.

Where could Pascal go from there? Points east and south were the most common destinations. But north was the only direction he'd choose. Several bus routes serviced the closer River City-adjacent communities. From there, he might pay for a private ride or hitchhike.

Pascal didn't have friends she knew of.

Too many possibilities.

It was late afternoon. She second-guessed everything she had said to her brother during their ride back to River City. Why couldn't he have waited? For now, all she could do was be patient. Let Eve's soldier do his work. Gather intel. Then she'd go find Pascal.

She browsed her familiar dark haunts on the splinternet. No one was offering anything for any of them. Didn't mean there weren't bounties, just none posted.

With a sigh, she closed the browser. "He's a grownup. You gave him a place to return to."

Eve grunted as she read on her phone.

Children played outside in the courtyard. Someone was grilling skewers in the courtyard.

"You said this building is yours?"

"There are a few tenants here not with my team. A few of my guys and their families own their units. The rest is mine. It's all on the books, nothing sketchy, but Linus and Webb made sure it remained off the tracking grids of everyone. We have a decent security suite, anti-camera infrared lights, motion trackers, and a garden and fruit tree orchard around back that Pascal will love."

"I'm sure he won't say it, so I will. Thank you."

Her sister went back to her phone. It pinged. "Doc's here. He just finished with Linus. You want your leg checked by someone who knows what they're doing?"

The doctor was younger than Dawn felt comfortable with, but he was all business. Eve had left the apartment. The doc applied topical painkiller and was removing miniscule bits of shrapnel embedded in Dawn's thigh. Once finished, he dabbed blood away from her skin and gave it a spray of something cold that further numbed her down. Then came the stitches.

He next produced a pill packet. "Two of these when the pain starts. I recommend two now to head it off, but if you're like Eve, you'll try to tough it out."

Dawn took two pills with water and got comfortable.

The doctor packed up and left, closing the door on the way out. Dark outside. No news from Eve's soldier. She considered getting up, but exhaustion and the narcotics slammed her hard.

3am, according to her implant.

Cotton-mouthed and stomach grumbling. Someone leaned on the counter in the kitchen as they ate a bowl of noodle salad. Only the stove hood light was on as she slurped down her late-night snack.

Dawn wiped the crust from her eyes. "Eve? I thought you had your own apartment."

Not Eve.

"Seems you girls let the lease slip," her mother Jenelle said. "So I guess I'm with you now."

"Mom? What are you doing here?"

"Pascal got me out. Said you and Evie had a place where I'd be safe. While I was reluctant to leave, he said he needed my help. And from the look of things, he's not wrong."

"Does Eve know you're here?"

"Where do you think I got the salad? But she was groggy. Looks like she took a tranquilizer and is likewise dealing with injuries. So, are you going to tell your mother what happened or not? Because Pascal says it's a secret."

"Where is he?"

Jenelle stabbed her fork in the air toward the closed bedroom door. Dawn opened it to find Pascal under the sheets in bed, asleep.

She closed the door and joined her mother in the kitchen. "What did you make him do?"

"Nothing. He showed up at the end of visiting hours and insisted I follow him. He had somehow managed to secure a keycard to the maintenance yard. From there, he led me outside. He said it was an emergency. Something about a friend in danger, and he insisted."

"They're going to be looking for you, mom. And him. You have to go back. Explain this was your idea."

"I won't do any such thing. I see you all got into trouble. Now, how about you let your mother help?"

Epilogue

Somehow, Pascal knew their mother had contacts with one of the transit companies. His solution, extracted after a thorough confrontation the next morning by Dawn and Eve, was to send a fleet of robot trucks to the redoubt, or close enough to it, and to help evacuate Quint and his community.

Never mind the fact that most of them were in stasis. And the trucks wouldn't be close enough to pick up anyone who wasn't able-bodied. And the custodian wouldn't allow anyone to go.

Who knew if they were even alive?

But Jenelle had promised to contact Transom to see what was needed to get the ball rolling. Meanwhile, Dawn collected what they had from Captain Fields and made her own phone calls.

Detective Satoko first. He had some names of midlevel Commonwealth services with good reputations. New Pacific also had a couple of news agencies who would bite at a story like this. Satoko advised against taking it to the media. It would cause more problems than you hope to solve, he had said.

Dawn sent out the data from the sheriff's tablet to both agencies, and a few of the smaller ones, for good measure.

A teaser article in a clickbait blog showed up that afternoon. Reilly-Bigg Military Overreach in Northern Farm Community. Massacre Rumors Denied by Senior Officials. Story to come.

It was a start as far as comforting Pascal. He had helped his friend. Quint and his community would be safe, Dawn assured him.

Pascal paced while chewing his thumbnails. "You want me to calm down?"

"We're all here and doing what we can," Dawn said. "What happened to my bike?"

He wouldn't make eye contact. "I parked it at the bus station. Then I traded it. A guard at mom's jail wanted it and let me copy her key card. I'm...sorry."

"I wasn't planning on doing much riding anytime soon." She produced the bauble she had taken from the grounds above the redoubt. The flattened aluminum circle was crude, yet somehow pleasing to the eye. She placed it on a bare shelf near the door. "Can I use this space, Pas?"

He nodded. "What's that?"

"Maybe Quint made it. Or one of his family. I forgot I had it."

"Now it's your first new button."

"I guess it is."

Their mom was putting lunch on the table. Marinated milkfish and garlic rice from a nearby deli. She had gone out without asking, and Dawn didn't know where she had gotten the credits to pay for it.

"Find your sister. Tell her lunch is ready."

Dawn found Eve upstairs in her apartment.

She imagined Eve Moriti living with spartan simplicity: plain walls, a bedroll on the floor, and maybe a vid screen and couch. Instead, the walls were adorned with metallic-print vinyl, bright landscapes, and colored lights. Three couches dominated the center of the room around a table with a large three-dimensional puzzle of a mountain. The kitchen was a mess, with pots and dishes soaking.

Eve and Linus occupied two of the couches. Both had fresh dressings on their wounds.

"Should I leave?" Linus asked. "Your little sister's got that look in her eyes, sarge. I think I should leave."

Dawn perched on the edge of a couch cushion across from them. "You're fine. Mom wants you downstairs for lunch."

Eve adjusted the pillow beneath her head. "Not going to happen. Pascal wanted her here; she's his responsibility."

"Have you even spoken with her?"

"No. And I'm not planning on it. Enjoy lunch."

"I'm in no hurry to be down there either."

"So you came up here?"

When a moment passed without Dawn answering, Linus grinned. "Aww, how sweet. You two going to kiss and make up?"

Eve scowled. "On second thought, get out."

Linus put a pair of ear buds in and rolled onto his side, away from them.

"Well, Dawn? There's a third couch if you need a place. Don't think I won't charge rent. Plus, I already paid for your checkup. The doc wasn't cheap."

"And mom stays free?"

"Pascal's place, his choice."

"I'm not sure any of us are ready for this. And you haven't exactly been clear on who might be after you and your merry troupe."

"We're safe as long as we stay in New Pacific. Once we leave, the gloves come off."

Dawn checked the couch. A spoon with dried on foodstuffs rested between the cushions. "I'll think about it."

She went out to the balcony and spent a moment watching the children play at a game of tag. A pair of girls shrieked as they evaded a boy who was "it".

A tired-looking woman carried a basket of folded clothes from the laundry room. Knick-knacks in windows. Potted tomato plants and roses. Frayed door mats. A red heart and hammer logo sticker on a door, the emblem for a Commonwealth cricket team. Another neighbor appeared, an older man carrying groceries. He had trouble with his lock, but got it open before Dawn could move to help.

Her implant flagged a message popping into an inbox. It was her Dawn Moriti folder and the text was from Detective Satoko. She called him.

He chuckled when he picked up. "I was curious if you even checked messages. How many IDs do you keep track of?"

"What do you want?"

"Hey, relax. Know this is a long shot. But seeing how you were in town and willing to show up with a bounty using your real name, I did some digging. You have no New Pacific warrants, so you can breathe easy."

"I know. If you're trolling for information, check for bounties. I'm not clean."

"Be glad that I'm not greedy, then. I had something else. Thought I'd float something past you. The lead on Reilly-Bigg got some attention. Seems an interested party was keen on hearing all about what they were up to."

"I gave you what you need to open a case."

"Let me finish. This party wanted to know who dug this up."

"When you talk like that, I get nervous. This isn't a Commonwealth exec you're talking about, but another corp, isn't it?"

"You should have come to work with us. But our pay is peanuts. This party...they've expressed interest in talking to you for some similar work. Said it will be worth your while."

"I'm listening."

Author Note

Dawn Moriti's journey started in *The Seraph Engine*, Book One of my Old Chrome series.

Old Chrome follows Miles Kim's adventure as he flees Meridian-controlled River City to rekindle his relationship with his son, Dillan, in Seraph. He's an ex-cop who finds trouble, and sometimes trouble finds him. Dawn Moriti is one flavor of trouble, an ally, foil, and occasionally an antagonist.

After seven novels, I decided she needed her own story, and I'm happy you found her tale.

There's more on the horizon for Dawn, Eve, Pascal, Jenelle, and Linus. I hope you tag along for their next adventure.

If you have time, please take a moment to leave a review. Even a brief comment or rating helps small press and independent authors find new readers.

Keep reading for a sample chapter of The Seraph Engine.

The Seraph Engine - Chapter One

There were three things Miles Kim didn't like about the bandits who had stopped the atomic grav train bound for Seraph.

First, one of the robbers, a rangy puke wearing a tattered duster and a paisley bandana around his mouth, had punched the porter, who had unlocked the passenger car to let the two men in. The porter's nose gushed blood as he cowered with the riders at the frontmost seats.

Second, both the little girls across from Miles who had been crying and fussing during the first half of their five-hour journey but had been finally distracted by their dad playing travel bingo and singing Tagalog lullabies were crying again. Their parents had them huddled and were attempting to calm them down.

And third, Miles was going to miss his appointment with the man who was scheduled to kill him.

The lanky bandit who had done the punching shoved his partner forward. The second robber was shorter, smaller, and, now that Miles glimpsed his face, looked about twelve years old. The kid held a burner in one hand and a pillowcase in the other.

"Give everything in your pockets to him," the lanky bandit shouted. There was an electronic buzz to his voice. An augmentation? "Anyone who hesitates gets a hole in the head."

Most of the passengers sat stunned, some gasped, and the man sitting next to Miles began to mewl softly. The family across from Miles shrank as if they hoped to disappear altogether. But not everyone was cowed, and this worried Miles.

On a seat right behind the family of four was a woman wearing a plum waistcoat and a matching petite riding hat. She had been staring at Miles throughout the ride, which wasn't unusual, but she hadn't looked away when he caught her. Instead she had given him a bemused smile. She spent most of the trip writing on her device, using a purple fingernail as a stylus.

And at the back of the passenger car was a marshal transporting a prisoner. Miles had spotted them instantly when boarding, the marshal trying to keep low key with his prisoner's manacles concealed beneath a coat. But there was no hiding the fist-sized weapon on the marshal's hip or the badge clipped to his belt. The prisoner got cuffed every time he tried to strike up a conversation with anyone.

As Miles glanced back between the seats, the marshal adjusted himself and his weapon rig.

Eyes forward again, Miles stifled a curse.

Of all the ways a bandit might relieve the travelers on board the Seraph Express of their pocket credits, jumping on board a train waving a burner about while shouting "this is a stickup" was easily the worst. And the last thing he needed was to be caught in a firefight with a trigger-happy hero.

The kid went from passenger to passenger with his gun pointing unsteadily. His voice held a prepubescent pitch when he screeched, "Hand it over!" He made it to the family across the aisle. The mother dropped in what they had without comment.

Miles scooched down in his chair, keeping his head bowed so his black round-rim hat would cover most of his face. The young bandit's feet were visible as he continued past, collecting devices, wallets, and jewelry. The kid had his back to Miles and was finishing with the opposite side of the car, robbing the woman with the purple hat and then a group of four older women who gave up their belongings with little more than reproachful glares.

Someone outside was shouting. Yellow sands swirled beyond the window, but whoever was out there wasn't visible. Because the track and train were elevated, Miles would have to crane his neck to see, and he wanted nothing upsetting the robbers.

Miles stole another glance back as the kid made it to the marshal. The kid was hurrying now. He barely paused as the marshal dropped a wallet and device into the proffered loot bag without comment. The kid skipped the prisoner and a few of the other passengers.

The marshal's steel-eyed glare followed, which the kid missed as he approached the seats directly behind Miles.

Meanwhile, the gangly robber at the front of the car had vanished outside.

Amateurs.

What did amaze Miles was the fact the robbers had stopped the train. The Insight module installed in his head gave the specifics of the train's nuclear engine, the weight of the cars, and how fast they had been going. A bullet train leaves River City via Devil's Bridge on its way to Seraph going 600 kph. How long will it take to reach your destination if a rangy puke and a boy not old enough to shave hit the brakes somewhere past the halfway point?

"Enough with the infodump, Insight," he muttered.

With a hard double blink, the barrage of data vanished. The train was big, had been cruising faster than anything most of these new generation planet-born kids had seen, and it wouldn't stop for anything. Passengers couldn't leave unless they busted out a tamper-proof window and jumped.

Yet here they were, going 0 kph at a few minutes to noon and over an hour from their destination.

The mewling man next to him surrendered his valuables.

"Let me see your hands, old timer," the kid said.

Miles raised them. Wouldn't look up.

"Device? Wallet? Come on, come on, come on!"

The kid sounded even younger than before. Was he reciting lines from a serial? Moving as slow as he could, Miles dipped a hand into his suit coat and removed a pocketbook which contained his credit chips. The bandit wiggled the pillowcase so Miles could drop it in.

"What about your mobile device?" the young bandit asked. *Come on!*"

"I don't carry one."

The kid reached over the mewling man, who let out a fresh squeak, and patted Miles down. He held the gun awkwardly and it would have been an easy grab. As advertised, the young bandit found nothing worth taking, and he left alone the paper card and envelope Miles kept in his inside suit pocket.

Miles caught a whiff of booze.

The bandit's hand gripping the burner looked soft and the finger-nails trimmed. But what Miles thought was a glove on the kid's bag hand turned out to be a synthetic limb. Graphene-steel composite, tough, high density, but without fake skin, so the implant wasn't high end.

With the gun, the kid tapped the lapel of Miles' black suit. "You look like you're dressed up for a funeral."

"Maybe I am."

It was the first good look Miles had of the kid's face. Barely a hint of stubble on his chin. Sunburned cheeks.

The kid flipped Miles' hat off and gasped.

Despite the burner pointing at him, Miles tried not to grin. It was a reaction he was used to. Was it the metal plates visible beneath the grafts of fake skin? The deactivated ports behind his jawline where an old school input cable could be plugged? Or the white right eye which contrasted with his hazel left eye? An experienced observer would know an ocular range finder and targeting system with no cosmetic pretensions when they saw one. Everything attached to his head was old, the type of thing the meat-and-metal hacks slapped on the soldiers to get them back into the thick of things. While Meridian had its share of cyborgs, there weren't many like Miles Kim walking around these days.

"They don't make 'em as pretty as me anymore," Miles said to the kid.

The burner kept waving near his face. The kid almost fumbled his weapon as he adjusted the bag and cinched it beneath an arm. Miles could have snatched it away, but the kid had a finger on the trigger. And the sooner the kid left, the sooner they could get underway.

The Insight module's facts began rolling in once more, with an uninvited feed in Miles' field of vision displaying the characteristics of the robber's burner: single or burst laser-plasma weapon, capable of ten shots at full power before a battery swap, ergonomic handle, possible encoding restriction feature, snap beam, with pricing options not available as his module wasn't connected to the net.

"You got my money. You're doing great. Now watch that laser," Miles said.

"You're...you're..."

"Nobody. And that hand doesn't look like it fits you. Are we done here, kid? You're ahead of the game with that sack of loot. Time for you to go."

"Don't call me kid."

"I don't want to call you anything. I want you to take your winnings and get off this train so we can get going. Sound good?"

The kid still stared.

The darker corners of Meridian had markets for old tech. Maybe the kid wasn't in shock but was sizing up a bigger score than a pillowcase full of credit chips and mobile phones. As the bandit's graphene hand was either a poor fit from a cut-rate surgeon or stolen off someone who no longer needed it, such a robbery might still be on the table.

Whoever was shouting outside shouted again, louder this time, and there were multiple voices. The young bandit glanced over his shoulder towards the door.

The lanky robber appeared at the front of the car. "Hurry up!"

The kid scurried up the aisle. Miles bent down to pick up his hat when the marshal sprang to his feet and produced his palm-sized hand cannon. As the marshal strode past, he raised the weapon.

Without thinking, Miles pushed past the mewling man and grabbed the marshal, turning the gun towards the ceiling. It fired. The shattering boom sent a shockwave through the train car and hurt Miles' ears and teeth. Plastic debris rained down on them.

"Get off me!" the marshal barked.

"They're not alone, you idiot."

As if punctuating the comment, a window exploded. Another popped, then a burning hole appeared in the ceiling. Anyone who hadn't ducked already hit the floor as more incoming burner fire battered the car. The marshal and Miles kept their heads down.

At the front of the car, the two bandits were gone.

"I had him," the marshal said.

"He was just the bag boy. And if you had blasted him, they might be doing more than just covering their getaway."

The incoming fire stopped. Miles crawled forward to the open door and peered out through an open hatch to the outside. The desert lay beyond. A curtain of dust rose, which didn't conceal some dozen riders on horseback and motorbike who raced away from the train.

They joined a second group, which appeared to be coming from the engine at the front. At least seventeen in the gang, by Miles' count.

The woman with the purple hat crouched next to him. "Is it safe?"

Miles got up and dusted off his hat. "They're leaving. No one lost anything they can't replace." He went to the porter with the bloody nose. "Check and see if anyone's hurt in the rest of the cars. And then find out how long it's going to take to get this train moving."

The porter nodded and went to a wall panel. "Power's out, and I can't open the doors to the other car."

"Then we go outside and head to the front."

The marshal pushed Miles against the bulkhead. "You're not going anywhere."

Miles tried to dislodge the man, but the marshal was larger and proved stronger.

He nudged Miles' ribs with the hand cannon. "You're with them, aren't you? That's why you stopped me."

"What are you talking about?"

The passenger car fell into a hush. They had everyone's undivided attention.

The marshal sneered. "Just pointing out the obvious. You're one of those good-for-nothing Metal Heads."